FALCO

The Dark Angel

by RANDALL MOORE

by Randall Moore

Falco the Dark Angel

Copyright 2013 by Randall Moore

All Rights Reserved

Cover Art Copyright 2013 by Randall Moore

To my lovely and loyal wife, Barbara,
who has stayed with me through
all manner of calamity, heartache and pain,
yet still brings a smile to my heart.

This book is a work of fiction. Names, characters, places, and incidents either are the products of the author's imagination or are used fictitiously, and any resemblance to actual events or persons, living or dead, is entirely coincidental.

by Randall Moore

Table of Contents

Part 1: Prologue: BLOOD MOON 7

Part 2: FALCO 49

Part 3: ABDUCTION 94

Part 4: A PROPOSAL 119

Part 5: THE GANG RESURGES 138

Part 6: ABANDONED DETROIT TOURS 145

Part 7: MOLOCH 151

Part 8: THE RECKONING 180

Part 9: EPILOGUE 205

by Randall Moore

Part 1

PROLOGUE

BLOOD MOON

1

I awoke in the first-floor hallway of an abandoned hotel in a dilapidated part of the city. This part of the city was the picture of urban blight. Storefront after storefront abandoned, windows smashed, burned out cars, filth and garbage covering every surface. It gave decay a good name. This was post-civilizational debris.

How did I get here? I asked myself while pain pounded my head, throbbing like a boom box bass. I started to lift myself up and suddenly lightning bolts of agony shot through my shoulder and chest. I looked down and saw an enormous splinter had nearly impaled me. It entered my back just below my armpit and was poking out through my left breast. The blood had nearly congealed. I reached behind my back and grasped the thicker end of the splinter and started to pull on it. Excruciating waves of pain shot through my shoulder as it started to move. Fresh blood started to gush from the front and back. With a sucking sound and a pop, it came out. I looked up at the shattered floorboards where I must have come through. Then I remembered. I'd been out on a date with Julie. We had gone out to dinner at a tapas place and then a nightclub in the fashionable part of town. Plenty of neon, beaucoup restaurants, bars, nightlife. It was the bang-up place to go for a good time.

"Where do you see yourself in ten years?" I asked her.

She paused pensively. "Married I hope. At least I was brought up with the expectation I'd marry. Maybe a couple of kids. Between diapers, cooking, and cleaning, I'd work on my blog. I'd have hundreds of advertisers and tens of thousands of followers posting and debating in the comments section. Then my husband would come home, sweep me off my feet after a long, hard day in the trenches earning his way, and make a romantic dinner with candles. After dinner, he'd always volunteer to do the dishes and I'd help. After the kids were put to bed and the dishes put away we'd retire to the bedroom and make mad, passionate love." She laughed a happy laugh. "How's that for a fabulous 50s fantasy?"

That made me smile and my heart warm. "What would you blog about?"

"The Arts. Art, literature, poetry, music, dance, theater, cinema, television, cooking, wine. Everything that enriches life and enobles our existence. This is what I'm really passionate about. I would like to create and manage a one-stop compendium for all the things I love."

"And the romantic dinners? Do you think you could help me wash the dishes?"

She opened her mouth in a half smile, lowered her eyelids, and dropped her head down toward her chest, her lovely blonde locks brushing over her breasts like wild grass blowing in the summer wind as she reached out and touched my wrist. Wave after wave of warmth rushed from my wrist through my body down to my toes.

"You know you're in the running, but you haven't asked me yet."

"Marriage? I'm not sure I'm ready. You do make it tempting."

"Well let me know when you're ready. I'll let you know whether or not I'll help you with the dishes."

We laughed, the spell broken.

I said, "You ready for some crazy, Euro techno time?"

"You bet. I'm ready to go completely crazy tonight! I've got something in me that wants to explode and do something completely dangerous and outrageous."

"Whoa, cowgirl! All in due time!"

We got up. She leaned into me and kissed my cheek, sliding to the corner of my mouth. I felt her breath and her scent. Her hair brushed on me. I wanted her so much. I felt the desire growing in my gut. We turned and walked out of the restaurant to head for the nightclub.

2

We walked down the street to this place called "Far Gone". They specialized in fusion jazz/rock/techno. Kind of a Euro-trash vibe, but great to dance to. Julie loved dancing like this. After sweating to this craziness for a couple of tunes, we looked for a table and someone to bring us drinks. A spiked-haired waitress wearing a sleeveless leather studded vest came up and asked us what we wanted to have. She had an amazing array of piercings. Eyebrows, earlobes, nose, lips, cheeks, all had a ring, ball, or a stick through it. I was kind of glad that it was extremely unlikely I'd see what other parts of her body she had decided to defile. Her upper arms had extremely colorful tattoos that depicted tigers ripping their prey to shreds. A warning? Julie ordered a lemon drop martini. I ordered a Heineken.

While we waited for our drinks to arrive, I noticed a small group in the corner at a table who evinced a similar Goth vibe; like the waitress. Lots of black leather, more piercings, less elaborate tattoos, but still kind of freaky. There were five of them. The one who seemed to be the leader was seated in the center with his back to the wall. He had shoulder-length, wavy black hair, no piercings, and no visible tattoos. He was taller than the others. Probably 6 foot 4. There were two men, both appearing 5-9, 5-10, and two women. All had extremely pale complexions and looked as though they had applied black mascara and eyeliner. Very early David Bowie.

One of the women had a long-sleeved black lace top that covered her from her neck to her wrists, I would learn later that her name was Karin. The other, Diane, had a leather bustier with a plunging neckline that forced her rather substantial breasts up and out for all to marvel at. Bare midriff to boot! What are women thinking of these days? Both women were handsomely decorated with tats and metal.

The two men were slight and emaciated, malnourished with a full complement of piercings and tattoos. Ian and Tony.

We drained our drinks and signaled to the waitress for another round.

She sauntered up with our new drinks. "First time here?"

"No. It's been a few years. The crowd seems a little different, but the music's still cool," I said.

"Changing nature of the state of man," she said, arching her eyebrow up and then turned and walked back toward the bar.

"Trippy crowd here," I said.

"Kids have always wanted to be different," Julie said. "Every generation feels the need to proclaim their uniqueness."

"I guess. Want to hit the dance floor again?"

"You bet," she said, leaping off her stool, grabbing my hand, and pulling me toward the dance floor to the pounding, churning mass of human flesh, attempting to achieve an orgasmic, ecstatic apotheosis of carnal expression and longing.

I loved the way the music throbbed and numbed my mind and body as we sought release through exhaustion and the depletion of perspiration. After 20 minutes or so I'd had enough and signaled to Julie that I'd like to rest. But she wasn't done. I waved a goodbye to her and walked back to our table, which was amazingly unoccupied. I got the waitress's attention to bring more drinks which she obliged quickly and then I noticed that Julie had been joined on the dance floor by the two men and two women I had observed earlier from the back of the club.

They were thrusting and churning and undulating with each other, taking turns pointing at and brushing up against

Julie. She laughed and they laughed back. Each coyly taking turn in touching her hands and then her arms. Then Karin, the woman with the long sleeve black lace top approached her from the rear and placed her hands around her midriff, grinding her pelvis into her ass. They moved and grooved to the music. Julie reached back and caressed the neck of her dance mate when I was startled to find that the taller man was standing next to me.

"Extraordinary display of decadence. Your girlfriend is quite beautiful," he said.

His language had a slight tinge of an accent. Was it Irish? Hungarian? Russian? His demeanor seemed way more sophisticated than his appearance. He sounded presumptive and arrogant, used to getting his way.

"Yes, she is." I offered him my hand. "Rick Jason."

"Victor Orloff," he replied, grasping my hand with his. I noticed he had a ring on the middle finger of his left hand with an enormous stone in it. It was oval and black with swirling clouds of bright red flowing to deep crimson.

"Interesting stone. Looks precious."

"An inheritance. A hand me down. An antique."

'It's beautiful. I've never seen another. What is it?"

"It's a bloodstone. It's been in my family a long, long time. Legend says the bloodstone was formed from the blood of Christ dripping on the earth and solidifying. It's purported to enhance the circulation of energy in the body, aiding the circulation of blood and increasing its owner's life energy."

"Does it work?"

Orloff snorted and grinned. "Some believe it does. Others..."

"Aren't you nervous that someone will try to steal it?"

Victor smiled wryly, his eyes sparkling. "Nervous? No. Never. I've found it possesses a power that captivates some, but always returns to me."

"Orloff. That's not an Anglo-Saxon name. What are you? Hungarian?"

"Romanian."

"Your friends. Are they Romanian too?"

"Ah. They are Americans with a sense of adventure and a pursuit of pleasure. We share both together. Perhaps you and your lovely friend would care to join us later in a bit of both."

"Well. I'm not sure…"

Just then Julie and Victor's companions came bounding from the dance floor to our table, laughing and giggling. Julie lifted her head up and shook it, sending droplets of perspiration into the air, beads of sweat on her face and neck. "God. I could use a drink and some air. Meet my new friends. Diane, Karin, Ian, and Tony. They've invited us to a private rave party. I've always wanted to go to one of these parties! It could be a lot of fun!"

"Julie. We've only just met these people. Don't you think…"

She lowered her head and adopted a pouty expression puffing her lips out, her eyes twinkling. "Please?" She pleaded with the cutest look on her face. She knew how to work me, I concluded. I caved.

"OK. But if it gets weird we'll go," I said glancing at Victor. He shrugged his shoulders indicating his lack of culpability in the situation.

Julie leapt forward and embraced me around my chest and almost purred as she kissed me next to my mouth saying, "Thank you. You're the best!"

"Well, should we get another round of drinks?" I asked.

Victor said, "Why don't we go to the after party. There'll be plenty of liquid refreshment and the night air will be invigorating."

It seemed to be a reasonable suggestion, but I went to the bar to settle our tab, and bought seven bottles of water, brought them back to the group, and distributed them.

Julie cracked hers open immediately and began to greedily consume it. I opened mine and began to drink. The others had failed to touch their waters. Finally, Victor reached out and took a bottle, opened it, and took a sip. The others followed suit and did as Victor did.

Victor gestured toward the door and said, "Perhaps we should be on our way now."

We all rose as Victor ushered us out into the cool night sky. The autumn air was brisk and invigorating. Victor was right about that. I was a bit nervous about embarking to an unknown destination with basically, complete strangers. But Julie wanted to go so badly. How could I deny her? I wanted to be with her. I wanted to make love with her. I was willing to do anything she wanted. Plus Victor promised liquid refreshment. That end of the rainbow I was ready for.

3

The sky was black and the moon was nearly full. We walked away from the neon and glitz of the party zone further and further into the depths of the city. We passed through a residential zone and finally into the essentially abandoned part of the city. I was grateful for the moonlight as the city doesn't power or maintain the streetlights in this part of town. Most of the lights had been smashed by thugs anyway.

"This doesn't look that great," I said. "Maybe we should be going back."

"Just a little further," Victor said. "The kind of party we're going to well... might not be appreciated in all parts of the city." I glanced at Julie. She seemed gung-ho, excited and ready to go. Did I say that I really liked her? A lot?

"OK. Just checking."

We walked through an abandoned business district filled with abandoned storefronts with smashed windows, burned out cars, and all manner of debris and filth on the streets, and headed to an abandoned six-story hotel that loomed before us.

"Just ahead now," Victor said. "Our destination."

Victor opened one of the grand double doors of the hotel and bade us enter. Upon entering I could hear the techno Euro-Trash pounding that had been the soundtrack of our earlier part of the evening. Victor led us up a staircase toward the second floor. As we rose the music became louder and louder. We reached the landing and then followed Victor up the next flight of stairs to the third floor where I could see lights and strobes flickering. When we reached the landing Victor led us forward to a large set of double doors and flung them open revealing the bacchanal inside a once ornate ballroom. Strobes were firing. Lights were flashing. Bodies were heaving. Music was pounding. It was a mind-numbing smack vibe with a chaser of cocaine. In the shadows, I saw people engaged in a variety of sex acts. There were others who appeared to be consuming drugs. The smell of marijuana was palpable. The sweat and the sex and rot were intoxicating, even overpowering. This was definitely the craziest party I'd ever been to. Did I forget to say decadent?

"You mentioned liquid refreshment," I asked Victor.

"Yes," he said and pointed to a table next to the DJ with dreadlocks smoking an enormous doobie.

"Thanks," I said and motored across the ballroom toward the bar.

The bar was manned, or should I say womanned by a skeletal heroin chic concentration camp survivor with an elaborate set of tattoos and an incredibly bizarre set of piercings. I swear, if women continue to insist on making themselves this unattractive, I'm going to swear off sex permanently.

"What've you got?" I said.

"Just what you see."

"Got any Champagne?"

She nodded and reached under the table, where I couldn't see, into a big plastic ice bucket and pulled out a bottle of Prosecco.

"Anything fancier?"

"This is it."

"That'll do. Pour me two."

She slapped two red plastic cups on the table, poured two generous pours, and said, "That'll be fifteen bucks." I grimaced, pulled out my wallet, and dropped a twenty.

"Keep the change?" she said.

"Hardly. I work for a living too."

She laughed and then dropped five ones. I left two for her.

"Thanks," she said as I collected the drinks and went off in search of Julie.

Even though there was plenty of light in the room, it was all flashing and really meant to be a freak-out distraction. I could barely make out anything. I did see Victor, though. As weird as he was, his height made him stand out in the room. I made my way toward him, surveying the room for any sight of Julie.

"You see Julie?" I asked Victor while holding the two glasses of Prosecco.

"I believe she's off in that corner with my four friends," Victor said, pointing to a spot of the room I hadn't yet explored.

Heading over there I finally could make out Julie and the four Goth freaks. How the hell we made friends with these guys I'll never know.

As I approached them I saw they were passing a glass pipe occasionally sparking up a lighter over the bowl.

"Hey! What's going on?" I asked as I witnessed Julie taking a huge toke while the freak known as Ian lit the flames.

Julie sucked in God knows what into her lungs, holding it in and banging her hands onto the floor repeatedly, her eyes turning into the back of her head, finally expelling the smoke saying, "Fuck. Fuck Fuck. That was fucking awesome! What a fucking rush! I can't believe you got me to do that!"

I said, "Excuse me, Julie. I got you a glass of Prosecco. I tried to get you Champagne, but this was the best I could do."

She leaped up and grabbed it out of my hand spilling some and hungrily gulped it down.

"Fucking awesome! Thank you! How did you know I was so thirsty?"

"Actually, you told me at the Far Gone. And then we walked here."

She came up to me, embraced me, and kissed me, opening her mouth, sticking her tongue into my mouth. I obliged her by intertwining my tongue with hers. It was a sublime moment. It made the whole bizarre evening seem worth it.

"It's time for us to proceed to the next phase of the evening," Victor said, giving me a start. I thought he was on the other side of the room.

"Come, children," he said as he turned and beckoned us to follow, which we dutifully did. We walked all the way to the back of the room and through a door, which led into a hallway with a dozen doors. Victor walked to the first one on the left, flung it open, unfurled his left arm rather flamboyantly, and beckoned us inside. We complied.

4

It was a large room that appeared to be a living room. There was a wet bar at the rear of the room and double doors that led to a bedroom. At the right side of the room, was a door that opened up to a similarly sized living room and I assumed another bedroom.

"The Presidential Suite," Victor announced as he walked to the wet bar, pulled out several bottles of liquor from a cabinet above as well as seven glasses.

"Any preference?" he said.

"What are my choices?" I asked.

"Cognac, Bourbon, Scotch, and a digestivo. I'm a little embarrassed, but it's made by my family."

"What's in it?"

"Old family recipe. Distilled eau de vie with herbs, seeds, berries, tree bark, roots, and extracts steeped for up to five years while aged in cask. It's been known to be a prophylactic against disease and promotes longevity. It's also quite delicious once you get used to it. Most people find it a bit odd at first taste, but grow to love it."

"What the hell. Pour me a glass."

"Excellent," he said as he poured three fingers into a highball glass.

"But digestivo. That sounds Italian. I thought you said you were Romanian. "

"I am, but I have lived in many places. I live here now."

He was right about the odd quotient. A strong eucalyptus mint aroma rose from the glass, plus a healthy alcohol burn to the nose. It reminded me of Vick's Vapo Rub in a glass with a twist of lime and coriander. On the palate, it packed a punch. Must have been 90 proof. Kind of like drinking cough syrup with a kick and a touch of weird. Which seemed absolutely appropriate considering present company and the crazy turn this evening out with my girlfriend had taken.

"How do you like it?"

I took another sip. "You were right. It does kind of grow on you."

"Good. Anyone else want a drink?"

"I'll have a shot of what he's having," Julie chimed in.

"Coming right up," Victor said as he poured three fingers into another highball glass and handed it to Julie. Then he poured one for himself and said, "To your health." We clinked glasses and sipped his odd brew.

"Anyone else?" he offered to Diane, Karin, Ian, and Tony.

"I'll take a Cognac," Tony said.

"Me too," followed Karin.

"The same," chimed in Diane.

"Better make that four," said Ian.

Victor raised his eyebrows slightly with a grin and reached for the bottle of Cognac and poured four glasses for his companions, who stepped forward to relieve Victor of their drinks. We all clinked our glasses again and settled into the serious business of consuming alcohol.

The heavy bass from the ballroom was still thumping through the walls as cries of ecstasy in the crowd reached our ears.

"Sounds like the party's showing no signs of slowing down," I said.

"Yes," Victor said. "We're going to have a more meaningful, more intimate party here."

"What do you do for a living, Rick?" Victor said.

I noticed to my left that Diane and Karin were in a hot clinch, French-kissing each other and running their hands over each other's bodies.

"Nothing important. I sell newspaper advertising. Not exactly a growth industry. My friends keep telling me to get involved in the internet. Something with a future. I don't know. Old dog. New trick."

"How bout you, Julie?"

by Randall Moore

"I write advertising copy. I work in the same office with Rick. I guess you could say we're having an office romance."

I was starting to feel a bit dizzy and I started to see double and then back to normal. Had I really had that much to drink? I then noticed that Diane was going down on Karin whose head was arched back in ecstasy. I looked at Julie and noticed that the color was draining a bit from her face. She was sweating rather profusely.

"What was in that drink?" she said.

"Just a medicinal brew. It's good for you," Victor said.

Ian and Tony moved in on Diane and Karin and began to caress the women who were now fully engaged in an erotic tryst.

"Perhaps you two should retire to the boudoir? You both look like the evening's taken its toll on you."

"Well. Maybe so," I said, stumbling forward, my head spinning now, the room spinning now. I don't think I made it. I don't remember hitting the floor. I just deduced that I did because when my consciousness returned in a drugged-out drunken stupor that's exactly where I was.

Conscious doesn't really describe my state accurately. I was in a fog, in a cloud. The room was swimming, turning in on itself. There was a deep gash in my left forearm and Diane had her mouth over the wound and was sucking on it.

"What the fuck," I said, trying to pull my arm away from her. She lifted her head up and I could see my blood all over her lips and face. "What the fuck are you doing to me?"

Three Victors merged into one as he approached. "Diane. That's enough. Ian! Tony! Get in here and get rid of him. We're taking the girl with us."

Ian and Tony grabbed me by the arms, dragged me out of the room, and into the hallway. Tony lifted me up to my feet and Ian leaned in with a nasty sneer on his face and started pummeling me, first in the gut then repeatedly in the face. Tony turned me around and Ian went to work on my kidneys. Close to collapse and excruciating pain, they continued dragging me toward the third-floor landing. When they got to the banister they lifted me up, Ian on my arms, Tony on my feet, and on three swings tossed me over the banister onto the second-floor landing. I crashed through the dry-rot-ridden floorboards and down to the first floor. That's the last thing I remembered until I woke up in a world of hurt this morning.

5

My head was throbbing and I was still hung over from whatever the hell Victor had given me. I must have hit the floor pretty hard because I couldn't close my jaw all the way. The hole in my shoulder throbbed in agony. The gash in my arm still hurt like hell. I was going to need to get it all cleaned up fast and get some fucking antiseptic in it. Who knows how many germs and bacteria that fucking bitch had gotten into my bloodstream? I needed to see a doctor bad. Maybe a witch doctor too.

And where was Julie? Where were Victor and his crew of murderous psychopaths? They had Julie and I had to find them and find them soon. Who knew how much time she had?

I dragged myself up. My left knee was really tender. My shoulders ached. When I stood my left leg shook, vibrated really. I could barely stand on it. I made my way down the hallway, leaning against the left wall, gingerly made my way toward the door. I opened the door. The front door wasn't here. I had crashed through the second-story landing down to the first-floor landing in another wing of the hotel. Maybe that's why nobody saw me. Or maybe they just assumed I was a drunk druggie down for the count.

I figured I needed to go left and walked down another long hallway. I could see the foyer from my position and the light of day filtering into the room. I made my way to the front door, pushed it open, and stepped into the light. I immediately felt a burning sensation in my uncovered skin. My cheeks were on fire and my hands hot as well. This was quite a trick as it was late October in Michigan.

I began to drag myself down the trashed sidewalk. I wish I hadn't caved so easily to Julie. I knew it was a bad idea and still allowed myself to be dragged into it. I felt like a grade-A chump. Now Julie was gone and I was fucked up bad.

And how the hell was I going to find them? I'd just been left for dead and I felt close to it. But a gnawing hunger rose up in my gut and burgeoning anger filled my eyes.

But first things first. I had to go to a doctor, get home, clean up, get something to eat, and retrace my steps from last night.

As I walked, my knee began to feel stronger, and I was able to pick up my pace. I finally got out of the abandoned part of town and into the residential section I had passed through earlier. Finally, I reached a street that contained shops, markets, liquor stores, and right ahead I saw what I was looking for: an Urgent Care Center.

I walked up to the front door, which slid open automatically, and marched inside. The receptionist looked at me with a start, but not completely surprised. I must have looked pretty bad, though.

"I need to see a doctor."

"I can see that."

"It's not for the bruises. It's for this," I said pointing at my left breast and unfurled my arm showing her the wound. "I got punctured. Somebody bit me. I need to get it cleaned up."

"Are you able to pay?"

"Take MasterCard?"

"Visa, Discovery, and American Express as well. Your name?"

"Rick Jason."

"Just sit over there and we'll get you in as soon as possible."

As I was the only one in the office I was hoping that was going to be pretty damn soon. Walked over to the chic plastic couch and sat down.

She picked up her phone and dialed an extension. "Dr. Morgan, there's a patient here who needs some treatment. Typical weekend behavior. I'll send Mr. Jason right in."

"Mr. Jason? The doctor will see you now. Just head through that door to your right down two doors to Dr. Morgan's office."

"Thanks."

"I'll be needing your credit card first."

"Sure," I said reaching into my pocket for my wallet. I pulled out my card, handed it over, she ran it through her card reader, and gave it back to me.

"We'll settle up the charges when you're done."

"Thanks."

I put my wallet away and went through the door into the interior of the clinic. Two doors down on the right and walked in.

"Dr. Morgan, I presume."

"That's me," he said cheerfully. "Looks like you had a bit of a bad night."

"That'd be putting it mildly. Forget the bruises, what I'm really here for is this." I pulled off my shirt exposing the puncture in my chest and showed him the wound in my right arm.

"That looks pretty nasty."

"I think my arm was bitten."

"Doesn't look like a bite wound. But it does look like it was opened with something blunt. The wound is very jagged."

"Can you clean it up?"

"Of course. But first, we need to get your weight, blood pressure, temperature, and rate of oxygen exchange. Please step on the scale." He adjusted the counterbalances and said, "Very good. 160 pounds. Have a seat."

He wheeled over a machine, clamped a clip over the fourth finger of my left hand, wrapped a sleeve over my left bicep, and pulled it tight.

He then hit a button and it started to squeeze my bicep harder and harder. I could feel my pulse pounding and pounding in my arm. He then stuck a plastic stick with wires attached under my tongue, waited, and pulled it out.

"I'm not sure I like these readings. Your blood pressure is extremely low and your temperature is 92. Way below normal. I think you need immediate hospitalization."

"I've got things to do, people to see. And I've got to do it quick. At least disinfect my arm and chest."

"All right," he said.

He then irrigated the wound with Betadine, injected me with antibiotics, proceeded to stitch it up, wrapped a bit of gauze around it, and taped me up.

He then rubbed antibacterial cream into my shoulder wounds and taped gauze over them.

"Thanks, Doc."

"Mr. Jason?"

"Yes."

"You need to seek medical care immediately. Go to the emergency room to be admitted for observation. I'll fax ahead to let them know you're coming. I'll call an ambulance for you if you like."

"Like I said Doc, I've got places to go and people to see."

I got up, shook his hand, and headed out into the lobby. The receptionist was on the phone. "Oh, Mr. Jason, we'll charge your card for $150."

"Thanks," I said as I walked out the automatic door and turned to head back to my apartment.

6

It was a relief to get back into my apartment as my face and hands stopped burning as soon as I got inside. I needed to eat something as the gnawing in my gut continued unabated, then bathe and change clothes. I made a ham and cheese sandwich with lettuce and tomatoes on rye with a liberal helping of yellow mustard. I took a big bite and started to chew. There was something decidedly unappetizing about it. I chewed and chewed, reluctant to swallow. Finally, I swallowed. My stomach churned as though it was turning over. It wasn't going to stay down. Then I vomited the food and continued with dry heaves. Waves of chills washed over my body. I'd never had a hangover like this before.

I rinsed my mouth out with water to get rid of the acid and foul flavors. I was still starving and craved to feed. I needed to try something else. Other times when my stomach acted up raw food had been easier to digest. I opened the fridge to see what other options there were. There was a chub of ground beef I'd been making hamburgers from. I lifted it up and smelled it. It smelled good. I grabbed a handful and shoved it into my mouth. This went down well and provided me some satisfaction as the gnawing sensation began to subside. I'd had steak tartare before. That's what this was like. I hungrily scarfed down several more handfuls of burger, rinsed my mouth out with tap water, and swallowed a bit. It all stayed down. I guess a little protein was what the doctor ordered.

I went into the bathroom, stripped, ran the shower water warm, pulled the shower curtains closed, got in the tub, and let the water rinse the filth and blood and pain of last night off my body, and down the drain, careful to keep my bandages dry.

How the hell was I going to find those fuckers and get Julie back from them? I thought about what they had done to me. It didn't make any sense at all. What jollies did they get out of kidnapping a woman and leaving a man for dead?

I turned off the water, got out, toweled off, and walked into my bedroom drying my hair, and surveyed my modest wardrobe. I selected a long sleeve black turtleneck sweater, a pair of cargo pants, and a black leather jacket. I pulled a pair of hiking boots out of my closet, the ones with the steel-tipped toe. I dug out a fedora and a pair of thin leather gloves out of the recesses of my closet. I opened my dresser and pulled out a large kerchief, and wrap around dark glasses. I got dressed and felt a little more armored than I had last night.

I went back into the bathroom, opened the medicine cabinet, and found a tube of sunscreen my sister gave me one summer. It was SPF 50+, the maximum sun protection factor permitted by law. It was the middle of a cold snap in Michigan in late October and I was putting on fucking sunscreen. I squirted a liberal amount into my left hand and started rubbing it all over my face and neck, making sure to go well beneath the collar. I then rolled up my sleeves to my elbows and applied a similar dose to my hands and arms.

I looked around my apartment for things I could use as weapons. In my utility drawer, I found a razor-loaded box cutter. If it was good enough for Al Qaeda it was good enough for me. In the kitchen, I found the obvious: knives. I selected my favorite chef's knife. Razor sharp with an 8-inch blade bolted through the handle for durability. I also selected an old-fashioned rod knife sharpener. It had a heavy hand and sturdy metal rod. I thought it might make a good striking weapon. I also had an ice pick with five points with a wooden handle. I then picked up a flathead screwdriver that had been sharpened like a knife. That might do very nicely.

I went back into my bedroom and on the dresser was a miniature souvenir baseball bat about 14 inches long, exaggeratedly thick at the end, tapering way down to the handle. It had the makings of a nice club. I then found my 3-inch buck knife. Not very formidable, but it had sentimental pre-9/11 appeal. I slipped it into my back pocket.

Next, I went out to my workroom and my tools where I found a ball pein hammer and my old Estwing rock hammer from my rockhound days. I brought them back into the house and collected my impromptu arsenal. My wallet and cell phone went into my left pocket. I dropped the box cutter into my lower right-hand pocket, the souvenir bat in my lower left. I then pulled out my daypack and put the chef's knife, rod knife sharpener, ice pick, ball pein, and rock hammers in.

After putting on my sunglasses, gloves, and fedora, I went onto my balcony patio where I kept my barbecue. I grabbed my lighter fluid and a box of strike-free matches, took them back into the house, tossed them into my daypack, and prepared to zip it up. "What the hell," I thought, went back into the bathroom, grabbed a bottle of hydrogen peroxide, isopropyl alcohol and the sunscreen, tossed it all in the daypack, zipped it up, put it on, and walked out the front door.

7

I was relieved that the sunscreen was working for me. If I had to protect my face with the kerchief, I would have looked like a fucking terrorist.

I started to make my way to the "Far Gone," the place where this nightmare had started.

When I got to the front door I pulled on it but found it was locked. I tried peering into the windows but it was some of that crazy quilt, frosted, deformed colored glass that you can't see through. There was no light emitting from the inside.

I walked down to the end of the block, turned left past a building, and found an alley. Turned left into the alley and looked for the back entrance to the "Far Gone".

There was a liquor delivery truck in the alley. The driver had a hand truck loaded with booze and beer, wheeling it toward the door. I jumped forward and opened the door for him.

"Thanks," he said and wheeled his load into the club. I followed him in.

Once inside I took off my sunglasses and looked around. The driver wheeled his load to a storage room in the back. I walked through the swinging doors into the club and looked around.

There was a man sitting at the bar going over what looked like financial records. He was early 40s, balding with a generous gut. He noticed me as I approached.

"Excuse me?"

"I was wondering if you could help me? I was here last night with my girlfriend. We met a group of Goth freaks. A tall guy named Victor, a couple of shorter guys named Ian and Tony, and a couple of chicks named Diane and Karin. Do you know them? Do you know where they live?"

"Why do you want to know?"

"They drugged us, beat the shit out of me, threw me off a high place, and left me for dead."

"Shit," he sighed. "I don't know what to tell you. These guys are into some bad shit. They pay well, tip well. I do know something about them."

"Tell me."

"First show me. Do you have any wounds from your encounter? Bite to the neck, bite to the wrist, ankle?"

"I pulled my left sleeve up to my elbow and showed the bandage to the man."

"Shit. You've been bitten."

"I saw the doctor. He said I wasn't bitten, just cut with a blunt instrument."

"Same thing. Screwdriver, fingernail, whatever. They ripped your arm open and bit you."

"I had the doctor fix me up with antibiotics before he stitched me up."

"Doesn't matter. You've been bitten and you're going to change. You're changing now."

I couldn't believe what I was hearing. "This is bullshit!" I shouted at him. "Tell me where they are!"

"I can't tell you where they are, but as you change, you will know exactly where they are."

"How do you know this?"

"I'm a keen observer of my customers and my bar. Most people are normal. Then there are the others. Those that live in the night. You're going to be one of them soon. You don't have much time, maybe 48 hours. Then you'll be one of them too. I won't want to see you then. I don't like seeing you now. I want you to leave now."

I reached out and grasped him by the throat and pulled him to me. I felt a hunger deep within rise up, blinding my eyesight. I felt the urge to rip open his jugular and watch his blood flood the bar and the floor below. His look was of terror and fear. My anger subsided and I released him.

"I'm sorry. I don't know what's come over me. The last 12 hours have been the worst of my life. I know you don't know me and I don't know you. They have Julie and I don't know what's become of her. I feel like what little grasp I have of reality is quickly slipping away."

"Please go away from here. Like I told you, as you change you will begin to hear and see things that are invisible to normal people. You are no longer normal. You are becoming a creature of the night."

I backed up dejectedly and surveyed him. There was a curious logic to what I was hearing. I thought about all the horror movies I loved as a boy and the books I had read. It suggested a crazy thought.

"Are you saying I'm becoming a vampire?"

He reached out and touched my right arm. "I'm sorry. It's so."

He reached into his breast pocket and pulled out a pen and paper. He wrote down an address: 666 Gehenna Street, and a name: Mama Midnight.

"Go see her. She may be able to help you."

I put my sunglasses back on and walked pensively to the back of the club and into the alleyway. When I reached the outdoors I fell to my knees weakly and prayed. "Dear God, don't let this happen to me! Help me find Julie!"

This is fuckin bullshit. Vampires aren't real! Those fuckers aren't vampires. They may be murdering psychopaths, but this isn't a fucking "Twilight" episode! What I was contemplating was insane. As much as I hated the "Twilight" series after the second installment, I began to feel the gnaw of hunger deep within my gut.

I went into the next supermarket I found, up to the meat counter, and found the reddest, bloodiest steak I could find. I brought it up to the checkout stand, paid for it, and walked out. I walked into an alley and took the steak out of the bag. I carefully removed the plastic wrap. It smelled so wonderful. I don't know why I'd never noticed the intoxicating aroma of blood before, but I was giddy in anticipation as I lifted the tray up to my lips and drank the blood down. It brought an infusion of energy into my body as I began to rip the flesh with my teeth and greedily chew it up and swallow it.

Refreshed, I began to walk forward to find the home of Mama Midnight.

8

It was on the way to the abandoned part of the city, in the residential section that ringed it. 666 Gehenna St. Another crazy address in my now crazy life.

I walked up the stairs to the door and looked for a doorbell. I couldn't detect one so I lifted the enormous knocker, knocked five times, and waited.

It took a bit of waiting but I heard some rustling from within, some creaking of the floorboards, and finally the latch in the door being extracted. The door opened, stopped by a chain. An olive-colored eye with wrinkled lids filled the opening.

"Yes."

"Are you Mama Midnight?"

"That's what I be called."

"The guy. I don't know his name. The guy at the "Far Gone" told me about you. Said I should see you. Said I'd been bitten."

Her eyelids squinted as though trying to see me more clearly. "How do I know this is not a trick to gain entrance into my home?"

"Fuck! Do I look like I know what the fuck I'm doing? Like I have a clue what is happening to me? All I know is last night five crazy psychopath motherfuckers threw me off a building and kidnapped my girlfriend. And now some crazy bastard is raving about vampires and how I'm changing into one. I need somebody to talk some sense into me. That crazy bastard sent me to you! Can you help me?"

"OK. Me thinks you not be going to rip my throat open so I's going to let you in my home. But beware. You try anything to hurt me. I have potent ways of hurting you back, but worse."

She removed the chain from the door and opened it. I walked in. She was a slight, older black woman with grey in her curly hair and her dark skin complexion had flecks of grey in it. She spoke with a sing-songy quality that made me think of Jamaica.

"I swear. I just need to know what's going on. The doctor told me that I should check into the hospital for hospitalization and..."

"Plain to see that's not gonna help you. You got the bite and you got it bad. You turn for sure in the next 36 hours."

"How can that be? I'm just a normal, regular guy. I'm horny. I want to fuck. I want to eat great meals. I want to drink booze and watch the Tigers on TV. I want to see the next Star Wars movie. Jesus! But as I say it, it sounds empty to me. I just want to save Julie. How can I save her?"

"The door is closing on your humanity. Your woman will be consumed if you fail to act."

"Let's say you're right. I'm turning into an undead thing."

"Oh, but you are. Don't you feel the bloodlust rising in your belly? You need to feed. You will feed. One way or another."

"What about Julie?" She doesn't deserve this fate."

"She may already have been consumed. Her only hope is to be held for ritual sacrifice. Tonight is the Hunter's Moon. Every Hunter's Moon some poor child is found mutilated by these demons. You don't have much time."

"How can I find them?"

"You know now. Close your mind's eye and give yourself to your bloodlust. You will soon see them. You will know where they are and whether Julie is consumed or to be sacrificed."

I closed my eyes and concentrated on the increasing gnaw in my gut and I could see them. Victor, Ian, Tony, Diane, Karin, and Julie in a room. It was dark, but flickering light was coming in through the windows even though they were covered with sheets. I felt my delirium overwhelming me and I collapsed.

"Did you see?"

"I saw something. I think I saw them, but I didn't see clearly enough."

"You need to feed more. Then you will see better."

"I've been eating raw meat."

"That's not enough. You need to eat life."

"I'm not killing anybody."

"Then you must eat cat, dog, possum, squirrel. Anything with life will improve your acuity. Then you will see and know where they are. Then you can help your Julie."

I was in a complete tailspin. I wasn't sure what to believe. But something clicked in my mind and I was in.

"OK, Mama. I'll do it. But if you're wrong, I'll be back."

"No. You don't be comin back. We done. I told you what you gotta do to help your Julie. You I can't help. If you come back for Mama Midnight, she gots something that will really hurt you. Make you dead again. Get out of my house, demon! Find the other demons and do battle."

I walked out the door and it closed behind me.

Looks like I needed a witch doctor after all.

9

I walked further down Gehenna Street, turned right, walked down two doors, and made another right into an alley. This looked promising. Tons of garbage, discarded appliances, automotive waste, the smell of rancid grease, and other filth.

I walked over to what looked like one of the cleaner piles of garbage and sat down in it, dragging the cardboard, plastic garbage bags over me. I reached into my daypack, and pulled out the chef's knife, let it drop to my right side, and pretended to pass out.

It didn't take long. There was rustling of my pile of garbage. Something was moving toward me. I felt it climb on my leg, sniffing me and coming up toward my face. Out of the corner of my eye, I saw an enormous rat, the size of a cat, its whiskers and nose vibrating furiously. It crawled cautiously up my chest until I could feel its nose on my chin. That's when I struck. In one movement I lifted the knife and plunged it into the neck of the disgusting creature. It struggled violently. I ripped the knife further and further into its neck severing its carotid artery. As it quivered while its life's blood flowed from its body, I lowered my lips to the squirting blood and began to suck it in. I felt a sudden surge of energy and a power I had never felt as I drained the creature of its life's blood.

I tossed the body across the alley feeling disgusted with myself. A strange calm and clarity came over me. I thought of Julie and it was as though I was suddenly transported through a grid of the city, down street after street up a set of stairs, and into a windowless room. I saw Julie, tied up in a chair, her face dirty, blood on her blouse with Karin sneering at her.

I then pulled out of the room, and through the window down to the street, and looked at the house. The number was 7353. I collapsed. I had the house number, but what was the street name? Was I gonna have to eat another rat? Well, it did feel good, and if I could get the street name, and save Julie it would be worth it.

I heard a mewling sound and saw a cat licking the neck of the nearly decapitated rat. This cat didn't seem like it belonged to anybody. Its fur was matted and missing in clumps. It had visible abscesses on its hind legs oozing pus. I crept up behind it holding my chef's knife behind my back. It turned suddenly and hissed at me. I made kissy sounds. "Oh! Nice kitty!" I said as I neared it. It seemed to relax a bit as I slowly knelt down to pet its head. It was as though I had willed it to calm itself. I then grasped the fur at the back of its neck and plunged the chef's knife through its neck. It struggled and shook as I worked the knife around, enlarging the wound, the blood flowing freely. It ceased to struggle as I placed the gaping wound in the neck to my mouth and drank in its lifeblood.

The rush I had felt before intensified as I thought of Julie. My mind rushed through the grid of the city, all the way to 7353 but I found I was able to pull myself back from entering the building where Julie was being held prisoner. My spirit settled in front of the number as I forced myself to drift back the way I had come till I got to the intersection: Corner Street and Gratiot!

I now knew where they had her. But I didn't know why.

10

I contemplated the incendiaries I had packed. Nice, but maybe not as intense as I could get.

I found another street with merchants and found a thrift store. They had a rag bin in the back. I bought some of those and a sturdy 3-gallon container I intended to fill with gasoline at the next gas station I encountered.

I next went into a convenience store and purchased a six-pack of Coors Light and a box of gallon-size recloseable food storage bags. I cracked the tops outside and began to empty the contents into the gutter.

"Man, that's just wrong," a homeless guy exclaimed. "You want to get rid of it why don't you ask me to help?"

As his logic was sound, I handed him the next bottle. "I just want the empties. Be careful."

"Oh, I will. I'm so glad I can be of help, sir."

The guy chugged it as fast as I could pour it out. Hell, I didn't want to get a buzz. I needed the fragile glass.

He finished the last one. Actually chugged four of them and handed me the empties.

"Thank you, sir!"

"You're welcome," I said, loading the bottles into my bulging daypack and headed across the street to a gas station where I filled my 3-gallon container.

I pulled out my smartphone and typed in Corner Street and Gratiot. The intersection was located and I punched in walking directions from my current location. It was going to take 45 minutes.

I took off down the avenue. The turn-by-turn directions propelling me forward, inexorably toward my fate. Why would they try to kill me and keep Julie alive? What horror did they have in mind for her? I mean I was already completely fucked up. Probably already was even before they got their hands on me. Pathetic suitor, loser. Couldn't step up and ask for her hand. That's it! Just go through the motions and agree to everybody's bullshit. Look where that landed us. Swimming in shit, coming up for air in hell.

I drew a bead on that fucker Orloff in my mind. He was at the bottom of whatever was going to happen. He had the digestivo the others avoided. How could I have been so stupid? He had the bloodstone. Maybe I should eat another rat or cat and think about the bloodstone. The more I obsessed on Victor and the bloodstone I knew there was a connection, a chance to save Julie. I might be lost, but if I could save her from Victor and his crew I would have at least accomplished one good thing in my life.

My smartphone alerted me to my proximity to Corner Street and Gratiot. There it was. Just ahead. Just needed to determine which street it was on. I walked onto Corner Street. It was in the 1200 block, couldn't be it. I walked back to Gratiot. It was the 7000 block. This was the place. I walked down the street, counting the numbers on the row houses until I got to 7353. I paused a beat and kept moving. I assumed they thought they had killed me but had doubts. I didn't want to arouse suspicion.

Besides, with my fedora, dark glasses, and leather jacket I looked nothing like I had last night.

I hadn't really noticed anything other than the number as I passed the address, but I knew they were in there and that they had Julie.

I walked around the corner, went a couple of doors down, and entered another trash-filled alley where I looked for an isolated spot to load up my Coors bottles with gasoline. I filled each one with gasoline, leaving the proper ullage for inserting the rags. I tore the rags into strips and carefully inserted them into the bottles, letting them soak up the gasoline and yet seal it in. Then careful to keep the bottles upright, I inserted each of the bottles into one of the reclosable bags and zipped them shut. As I was finishing the fourth bottle, I heard a vicious growling and looked up to see a drooling, angry Rottweiler slowly moving down the alley toward me. There was something wrong about the animal. It had a wound in its left side and another in its head. Maybe it had tried to fuck up the wrong person. Suddenly it charged.

I had no time to think. It leapt into the air, jaws open; incisors ready to tear the flesh from my bones. I shoved my arm down its throat, grabbed its trachea as it clamped down on my arm, and I ripped it out. It fell to the ground. I fell upon it and with my teeth, I ripped its jugular open and greedily drank its blood until it stopped quivering.

I knew I was ready for the next step.

I continued down the alley until I found the service entrance to 7353. Small garage. Abandoned car inside. I looked inside and saw the door. I walked back to the other side of the alley and looked up. It had three stories. In my vision, Julie was somewhere on the third floor.

Suddenly I began convulsing and fell to the street. Visions began to commence again. The bloodstone began to draw me to it and then I knew why Julie had been kidnapped. The Blood Moon, which for many heralded the possible return of Jesus to Earth and the beginning of the End Times. For Victor, it was a time of renewal, a time of sacrifice that would infuse him with life's energy a thousandfold from what he and his ancestors possessed. Julie would be sacrificed at the height of the Blood Moon Eclipse and the energy of the cosmos would course through Victor's being, renewing him and his coven. The bloodstone he wore on his middle finger was part of his ritual and could not be accomplished without it. The Blood Moon would come, but I had to ensure that Victor would not have the bloodstone.

It was about 5 o'clock in the afternoon. The light was softening. The colors were deepening. I looked for a window for a look at myself. I was a fright. Wrap around mirrored dark glasses, fedora covering my head, dried blood all over my face, and as I opened my mouth, my teeth appeared sharper, more dangerous than I had ever thought possible.

I filled up the last two bottles with gasoline and rags, covered them up, and decided to walk around the block again to the street entrance.

This time I walked slowly until I got to 7353 and walked up the stairs to the door. I knocked and waited. I heard steps walking on hardwood getting louder and louder, then the door latch unlocked, and the door opened slightly. It was Karin! Mama Midnight was right! I had found them!

11

"Can I help you?" she said.

"I was looking for Russell. He gave me this address, I think. Sometimes I'm kind of dyslexic and screw up the numbers. Is he here?"

"No Russell. And you're right about being dyslexic. This ain't the place," she said as she slammed the door.

Thank God it wasn't Orloff. Orloff might have recognized me even though my appearance was completely different from last night. I decided to take my chances through the service entrance.

I walked around to the back. *What the hell*, I thought, walked up to the back door and turned the handle. To my amazement, it opened! Unlocked! In Detroit! I don't care how dangerous these fuckers were they were really taking their lives in their hands by leaving their back door unlocked in Detroit!

I tiptoed back to my stash of gas bombs by the fence, brought them into the house, and set them down by the door.

I looked around and surmised that I was in a utility area. Washing machine, dryer, double sink. Definitely a work area. I took one of the gas bombs and set it behind the washing machine.

There was a small stairway into the house, which I decided to use for reconnaissance. I noiselessly climbed the stairs and slowly turned the latch. Making no sound, I pulled it open, stuck my head into the first floor of the house and listened. I tied my kerchief to my face. I expected to see Karin somewhere on this floor and moved soundlessly into the house to explore every room.

The first room contained the kitchen. It was a rather nice, spacious kitchen, putting my apartment to shame. To the right was the living room and to the left was a family room. At the end of the family room was a door. There was light shining from the gap between the door and the floor. Karin.

There was a stairway in the middle of the room leading into the upper floors of the house. Julie was up there. Orloff, too, I assumed. I had to be careful. I turned back to retrieve another gas bomb, returned to the kitchen, and placed it inside a cupboard next to the oven. I had four bombs left. I pulled out some matches and put them into my pants pocket and the remaining bombs into my daypack, careful to keep them upright, and walked into the family room. There was a planter to the right of the stairs. I placed the next bomb behind it. I carefully stepped onto the first step near the left banister and lifted myself up. There was no sound. I gingerly repeated my actions for each step and reached the second story landing. There was a door directly in front of me, one to the left, and one to the right. There was a planter at the base of the next flight of stairs. I carefully walked over to it and placed one of the bombs behind it. I lay down on the floor and looked at the bottom of each door, hoping to see light emanating from within the rooms. There was none. I pulled the chef's knife out of my daypack, and slid it into the planter, slowly, careful to not make a sound.

I then began to climb the final flight of stairs. When I got to eye level with the floor, I could see light coming from the two doors to the side. I placed another bomb to the right at the top of the stairway and proceeded to the door to the right. I could hear my heart pounding in my chest and wondered if others could as well. Crawling forward, I could hear muffled noises, heavy breathing, and the sounds of passion. It sounded as though the two inside were fucking. I put my ear to the floor to listen. The heavy breathing, moaning, flesh slapping against flesh. Definitely fucking.

I raised myself up and walked slowly, silently across the floor to the other room with light emanating from under the door and listened, quieting my breath and focusing all my concentration on my ears. I heard breath rise and fall and the occasional creak of a chair. There was a single person within this room. It was Ian, Tony, or Victor. Although I doubted Victor was in either room. That left the door in the center. I slowly moved toward it, grasped the doorknob, and slowly turned it till I felt the latch release from the latch plate, and slowly pulled the door open, and walked inside. The walls were covered with books. In the center of the room was a large skylight. In the ceiling over the door was an amazing, oval stained glass panel. Even in the declining light of the day there emitted from it a most ethereal light. A legend on the wall identified it as a reproduction of Leda and the Swan by Giovanni Francesco Melzi after the lost painting by Leonardo Da Vinci. The sensuousness of the woman's form and the swan's undulating body, seeming to caress the beautiful, ravishing form of the naked woman.

Growing accustomed to the light, my gaze dropped from the stained glass and saw directly before me the silhouette of a woman with long locks, her head bent. Could it be Julie? I placed my remaining gas bomb in a wastebasket near the right-hand door, fluffed trash over it to hide it, and rushed forward to the figure before me and knelt down before her. It was she! An overwhelming sense of relief washed throughout my body and mind. I embraced her. She was bound to the chair and seemed to resist consciousness. Her eyes seemed to flicker to life. She opened her mouth and gasped for breath. Her eyes slowly opened.

"Is that you, Rick?"

"Yes," I said tenderly, caressing her head, holding her neck in my hand.

"What's happening to us?"

"I don't know, but I intend to take you out of here."

"Oh, thank you, Rick. You came back for me. These people are horrible. They have hurt me and from the looks of you, they have hurt you even more terribly. I'm so sorry. I never should have insisted on anything more than dinner and dancing."

I reached around her and sought the source of her bonds. I found where they were knotted and released them.

"Shhhh. That's in the past now. Nobody knew anything. Most of the time we take a risk nothing happens. What matters now is that you are safe and we must carefully flee this house." I reached down and untied her feet.

"Can you stand?"

"I think so," she said as she lifted her body off the chair and took a few cautious steps toward me. She wrapped her arms around my shoulders and put her head into my chest. A soft whimpered cry emitted from her throat. "You didn't forget me. I thought you had forgotten me. I thought they had killed you."

"So did I. We can talk later. It's time to go."

We walked slowly forward toward the front door of the room. As we reached the threshold, Ian leapt from behind the door to our right.

"Where the fuck do you think you're going?" he demanded.

I reached into my pants for the souvenir bat, leapt slightly off the floor, bat over my head, and swung it viciously down into his temple. He dropped to his knee. I held it with both hands and smashed it into his temple again. He dropped to the floor. I then kicked his face with my steel-tipped boot.

I then heard stirrings in the room to the left and turned to Julie. "We'd better make a run for it."

We flew down the stairs to the second-floor landing when the center room doors flew open as though gale force winds propelled them and out rushed Victor.

I'd never seen a man move as fast or with as much agility. He leapt straight over me, grasped me from behind, lifted me over his head, and tossed me forcefully down the left hallway. My head smashed against the wooden walls. I think the wood cracked with the force of my head against it.

Victor grasped Julie and pulled her to his breast.

"Well, well. I thought my familiars had finished you. They told me you had a stake through the heart. Blundering idiots! You may have survived your own death this time, however, it was just a preview of coming attractions. Now, before your unfortunate demise, you will witness one of the true wonders of the universe: a ritual whereupon my power will be magnified a thousandfold!"

A door flew open upstairs. Footfalls hit the landing and rushed down the stairs. It was Diane and Tony. Karin came running up from the first floor.

"Seize him!" They rushed forward to me. Tony got close first. I swung an elbow and caught him in his right eye socket. It felt like something cracked. He fell over, blood coursing from his nose. Diane stopped and looked at me, stepping backward.

"Come to me!" I commanded. She took a step forward…

"Enough!" bellowed Victor. "Hold her!" He pointed back at Julie. Diane turned and ran back toward Julie while Karin rushed forward. Together they subdued her.

Victor then leapt from his position, soaring to the ceiling, bouncing off it behind my back, and struck my head and smashed it into the floorboards with great force. I lost all strength and became supplicant. My eyes closed. I'd never seen anyone move that fast before. I felt my ankle lifted above the ground and being dragged forward toward the stairs and then down, my head banging forcefully on each step until I reached the bottom. Victor reached down, grasped me by the neck, and lifted me up to his face. He hissed and grimaced and showed me his teeth. They were exceedingly sharp and fearsome. I shuddered as he tossed my head down again into the floorboards and proceeded to drag me into the kitchen over to a door in the wall I had not noticed before. He violently slid it down with a crack and tossed me into it. I fell down into a basement I didn't know existed. My head slammed to the floor. I again lost consciousness.

12

I began to regain consciousness. I had no idea how long I'd been out. All I knew was it was dark and I was trapped.

I looked around trying to familiarize myself with this new place. I could see very little as the sun had finally fallen. I had no idea if sunlight reached into this place. In the dark I began to feel for the walls, touching every surface, looking for any kind of a clue how to get out of here. There was a way in. There also had to be a way out. I knew one way for sure. I looked above and saw a faint wisp of light emitting from the door to my prison. I closed my eyes, and plunged myself into total darkness, and waited several minutes. I slowly opened my eyelids and discovered that the wisp of light from above was more than ample for illuminating my prison.

The floor had a thick layer of grit and dust. The walls and floor were made of rough-hewn stone blocks with mortar between them. The door was directly in front of me. I rose and walked toward it. There was no doorknob. It opened in from the outside. The hinges, though, were in here. I smiled and realized that I still had my daypack and all the makeshift weapons with me.

There were three hinges: top, middle, and bottom. Each hinge was held together by a thick metal pin that permitted the door to swing open and back. The pin entered the hinge from the top and completed the lock at the bottom. The trick was to remove the three pins and thus remove the door from its place.

I pulled out the sharpened flathead screwdriver and wedged it between the pin and the hinge of the bottom hinge. There were years of paint to be ground through, and after several minutes of grinding paint out, I reached the point where I believe I exposed only metal.

I then pulled out the Estwing. It was a fearsome-looking hammer. It had a flat head on one side for cracking rocks open, and the rear side was a long, sharp, chiseled edge that had been tapered into a blade for cleaving rocks in two. It was a single piece of forged steel with a layer of rubber to provide cushion where the hands gripped it.

I inserted the sharpened end between the bottom of the pin, and the top of the hinge with the handle above it, and pulled the handle down a little. I felt the pin groan and lift.

I then moved to the top hinge and repeated the process. Success! Then the middle hinge. Also movement. All I had to do was remove the three pins from their hinges, lift the door from its place, and move back into the house to save Julie.

Suddenly I heard footfalls outside the door. I quickly replaced my tools in my daypack and waited. The door flung open and Victor strode in. Scowling at me, he stepped forward, grasped me by the neck, and pulled me close to his face. His fetid breath was nauseating and made my skin crawl.

"You've created quite a problem here, Rick. Poor Ian. Smashed his head nearly in. And Tony, too. Crushed his eye socket. Given him quite a shiner. Neither of them is willing to come in here to punish you."

"What do you want with us, Victor? We did nothing to you. Let us go! I promise we won't tell anyone if you let me and Julie go!"

"A lovely plea. I've heard it before. I do respect you for what you did to Ian and Tony. If they had attempted to kill me and failed, I would have visited them one last time. But in your case, and Julie's case, it's an entirely different matter. Tonight is the "Hunter's Moon." I prefer to call it the "Blood Moon." I require the sacrifice and the power that Julie's death will bring to me. Your witness and demise will bring further glory onto my apotheosis."

"You're nothing but a piece of shit vampire, Victor," I choked out.

"Yes. But you are also becoming a piece of shit vampire, Rick. And then I will show you how a vampire dies."

He flung me toward the back of my prison. My head banged against the stone wall. My consciousness flickered, faded, and gone.

13

When I came to, I was alone. The door was closed and my daypack was gone.

I searched my cargo pants. They had found everything except my three-inch Buck knife. It was the only weapon I had left.

Reaching into my pants pockets again, I realized that I still had multiple strike-free matches left. So I had two potential weapons at my disposal.

My attempts at removing the hinges foiled, I focused my attention to the wisp of light above. The rough-hewn stones might provide footholds and handholds for a determined climber. I was determined to climb.

I reached up and grasped the gap between the third stone and the fourth, placed my foot between the second and third, and pulled myself up. This seemed like it was going to work. I repeated this until I reached the level of the kitchen's door to my dungeon.

I raised my eye up to where the light was coming through and looked into the kitchen. I saw nothing. I listened to the refrigerator fan humming and the utility lights burning.

I reached up to the door in the wall and pulled on it. It moved! It moved down!

I climbed into the kitchen. I was back in the house!

14

Listening to the hum of the refrigerator, I went to check the cupboard next to the oven. My gas bomb was still there.

I slowly moved into the living room and started up the stairs again. I heard movement behind me. Turning, I saw Ian and Tony emerging out of the shadows coming toward me.

"Victor! He's back in the house!" Tony yelled.

Victor sprung from the darkness of the second floor and grabbed me by the neck.

"Thank you, Rick. You've saved us the trouble of having to bring you up. Our ritual is nearly ready to begin and I want you to have a front-row seat."

He turned to Ian and Tony and said, "Get up here, bind him, and take him upstairs to the center room," he commanded.

They quickly moved up the stairs, grabbed my arms behind my back, and tied them tightly together with hemp twine. They then proceeded to forcefully drag me up the stairs to the third floor.

"You're gonna die tonight, scumbag," Tony hissed in my ear.

"Your blood will make a tasty snack," Ian growled.

They were both clearly enraged over the beating I had given them earlier. Victor was right. I should have killed them both when I had the chance.

They pulled the double doors open and rudely ushered me in. Then they proceeded to punch me in the face, head, sides, stomach, and kidneys. They pounded me down to the floor and began viciously kicking me. Ian kicked me in the face several times.

"That's for what you did earlier, fucker," he said.

Tony fetched my daypack from the other side of the room, pulled out my souvenir baseball bat, and cracked me over the head four or five times.

"You thought you could hurt Victor with these weapons?" he snarled. "We're going to watch Victor rip you apart and drink your blood. We'll be there for the table scraps, though. I can't wait till dinner time."

"I'm going to check in with the girls and see how far along they are," Tony said as he spun out of the room and bounded down the stairs.

Ian glared at me and walked toward the floor-to-ceiling bookcase on the right side of the room, selected a volume, sat in a wing chair, and waited.

I sat up and leaned forward. While my hands were bound tightly together at the wrists, I could still move my arms about.

I began to move my arms and moan. Ian looked up and smiled at my agony, and returned to his book.

I reached my right hand into my right rear pocket, wrapped my fingers around my buck knife, and carefully lifted it out. I cautiously found the indentation on the blade and pulled the knife into the open position. It snapped into place with a soft, but audible click. I skipped a breath, fearing Ian had heard. I looked over at him and he displayed no interest in me. I sighed, relieved that I wasn't completely finished yet, and began to saw the blade over the hemp twine that bound my hands.

After about ten minutes or so I could feel strands of the twine snapping as the knife began to cut through my bonds.

All of a sudden Victor strode into the room, looked at me, and then at Ian.

"It is time. The Blood Moon rises. Get Tony and the women and bring up the sacrifice."

Ian jumped up, quickly left the room, and went down the stairs.

I noticed that Victor was now wearing a black, silk robe with his chest exposed. He had hard, rippling muscles. He was standing over a chair in front of the fireplace. He lifted his hands up and unfurled a large, rough-hewn knife with jagged sides almost shaped like a lightning bolt, but more jagged. It looked like stone, obsidian actually. Razor-sharp and shiny, capturing light, and reflecting it back off the uneven surface. It reminded me of some Indian arrowheads I'd seen as a boy. It looked like it would make a nasty cut, rather easily. Probably what they used on my arm.

I heard several feet climbing the stairs. First Ian and Tony strode in and took their places on each side of Victor. Then Diane and Karin entered. Between them was Julie. She was dressed in a white lace dress with an elaborate appliqué resembling vines with multi-colored flowers sprouting from the ends. The neckline was plunging. Her décolletage quite revealing. She looked stunning. Her hair had been styled into ringlets and flowers had been pinned into her hair. She was wearing garlands of flowers around her neck. A strong scent of jasmine and lavender filled the room. I felt intoxicated with the heavy scent. She moved as though in a dream. They must have drugged her.

Victor raised the knife above his head and looked up through the skylight. I looked up as well and could see the moon directly through it. It was glowing red. The room was bathed in crimson. I looked at Victor and at his ring. It was glowing red. I thought I could see the red in the stone swirling like clouds.

"Astaroth, Moloch, Valefor!" he bellowed. "Infuse us with power. Honor our sacrifice."

The bloodstone began to emit red slivers of luminous light upward to the Blood Moon. Luminous threads of red light from the Blood Moon descended and reached through the skylight. The two sources of energy reached out to each other and met just below the skylight and a glowing red orb of dark energy began to grow. My ears trembled with what sounded like an approaching train and the skylight shattered, sending slivers of glass throughout the room. Victor brought the knife toward Julie and sliced her upper left arm and then her upper right arm. He then sliced her abdomen and the skin of her left breast near her heart. They were not deep cuts, but all drew blood. Lightning bolts of energy emitted from the orb into her wounds.

A lightning-like bolt of energy entered me, and I started convulsing. I looked up and could see that Ian, Tony, Diane, and Karin were convulsing as well.

Multiple bolts of energy descended from the orb into my arm, into the wound in my left breast, and into the wounds in my face. I felt an incredible surge in strength and energy. The bonds I had been slicing through felt like a puny obstacle as I felt a superhuman rise of energy and power within me. I pulled my hands apart with all my strength, my bonds snapping, and I rose and leapt with demonic fury toward Victor as he prepared to plunge the knife into Julie's heart. I leapt with a force I had seen Victor display. Grasping his knife hand and throat, I drove him into the wall. Victor lost grip of the knife and it dropped to the floor. I reached down and picked up the knife as Ian, Tony,

Diane, and Karin rushed toward me. Four quick slashes from the blade dropped them all.

"So your transformation is nearly complete. Shame we didn't complete the job earlier. It will just be a little harder now. I told you I'd show you how a vampire dies. Prepare yourself."

Victor lifted his ring hand, pointing the bloodstone at me. Vicious bolts of red lightning shot into my abdomen. They seemed to pass completely through me, emanating through my hands and eyes. I was in absolute agony. My body was vibrating as I began to levitate above the floor. The knife shot away from my hand onto the floor in front of Victor. He pounced on it, leapt through the air, and plunged it into my chest as I simultaneously grasped his ring hand and throat. I flung him mercilessly against the far wall. I had ripped his ring off his finger. Energy still flowed through the bloodstone. I grasped the knife and pulled it out of my chest.

"Thanks for the knife, Victor." I felt the power Victor felt when he possessed the bloodstone and I knew I could direct it. I sent bolt after bolt of energy into Victor. He began to fall to his knees. I moved in on him and sliced open his jugular vein and his blood began to drain from his body. I walked over to the wastebasket where I had hidden my last gas bomb, and removed it from the resealable bag. I pulled a strike-free match out of my pants and struck it. It hissed and burst into flame. I held it up to the rags that drank the gasoline and they burst into flame. I hurled it with all my strength at Victor. It shattered, igniting the gasoline. Victor was completely engulfed in flames and began to scream with an unholy cry of unspeakable agony.

"Thank you, Victor, for fulfilling your promise to show me how a vampire dies!"

I went to Ian, Tony, Diane, and Karin, and plunged the knife into each of their hearts, and then cut off their heads. Next, I neared Victor's flaming carcass and sliced off his head as well. We don't want to give them another chance, you know.

I then went to Julie. "Can you hear me?"

"Rick. Rick. Is that you?"

"Yes."

"Can you tell me what just happened?"

"Later." I led her down to the first floor, and into the kitchen. "Wait here. I have one more thing I need to do." I opened the cupboard next to the stove, retrieved the gas bomb I had hidden there, and headed up to the third floor, and the scene of unholy carnage. I removed the bomb from the bag, lit another match, ignited the rags, and smashed it on the floor amidst the five headless bodies. The flames rose with a fury. I could feel their heat on my now cold skin. The wood was now burning. The house should be an inferno soon. I flew back down the stairs, swept Julie up into my arms, carried her outside into the alley, and ran to the next street. She seemed so light to me that carrying her was nothing. I had never felt so strong. I was not winded. I rushed down several more streets and slowed down. I had the sudden sense of needing to appear more inconspicuous. The light of the Blood Moon bathed us.

"Can you walk with me?" I asked.

"I think so."

"Do you remember anything?"

"I'm not sure. I think they must have given me a sedative and maybe a hallucinogen. I feel I'm barely here."

"Let's keep walking. The exercise will help get the drugs out of your body."

We walked for about nine miles. It must have been about four in the morning. I looked at Julie and felt a predatory urge rise in my breast. I pictured ripping her throat open and draining her of blood. I stopped.

"We're almost at your apartment. Do you think you can make it the rest of the way?"

"I think so."

"Good."

"When will I see you again?"

"I'll come by tomorrow."

"Alright."

We turned and walked away from each other. When I reached the shadows I turned and followed her to make sure she made it home unmolested, all the while keeping a safe distance from her. I then left for a bad part of town in search of food.

I went to a part of town that was known as a place to score drugs of all kinds. I walked by an alleyway and heard the repeated smack of fist on face, and gurgling choking on blood. This seemed as good as any place to lose my virginity. I turned and walked into the alley. There was a fierce-looking man with bulging biceps with cobra tattoos and a serious five-o'clock shadow. He was standing over the man he had just beaten into submission, going through his victim's wallet, taking the money and credit cards. He dropped it, turned, and saw me.

"Well. Looks like this ain't your day, mister," he said and ran toward me with an ugly sneer twisting his face into a mask of torment. He had quite the stench as he neared me. One flick of the knife severed his jugular. He fell to the ground trying to hold in his blood. If he could have stopped his heart he might have had a chance. I lifted his hand away from his neck as his blood coursed out of his body and into my mouth. I felt a renewed sense of energy and power. I was sated. For now. I then severed his head. Don't want any more bloodsuckers running around this place than there already are.

TEN YEARS LATER

The sun had begun to set. It was that wonderful time of pre-twilight. Colors seemed richer and more saturated than at noon. Julie was in her home office working on her blog. The door to her office flung open and in rushed two beautiful little girls who leapt upon their mother who showered them with kisses. A car pulled into the driveway of the lovely house in the suburbs with the white picket fence, rhododendrons, hortensias, roses, and daisies. The garden a riot of color. Quite beautiful. A man wearing a business suit got out of the car holding a briefcase, walked to the front door, and entered. The man entered her office. She rose up, embraced him and they kissed warmly. The girls hugged their parents with delighted, satisfied smiles on their faces.

I was in the tree across the street watching her. That was supposed to be me with her. But for one cruel night, it might have been. I now had to view her from afar. I guess it broke her heart that she never saw me again. It took her two years before she started dating again. But I was always there, in the shadows, watching out for her. I always made sure I was sated before I came near her.

Like today. Earlier I came upon a pimp who was using a razor on his girl. It wasn't a hard call. I grabbed him, ripped open his throat, the girl ran away, and voila! Dinner!

The police were looking for me. The FBI too. Their profilers had a serial killer on their hands. Slit throats, bodies drained of blood, and always the heads severed by a jagged instrument forensic experts couldn't identify. Courtesy of Victor's former knife. But they would never find me.

I suppose her husband was a good choice for her. I mean, she did deserve happiness. If it wasn't me who was to make her happy, I had to have a say in who would. I stalked all her dates to learn who they were, to see if they were good men, honest, upstanding, kind-hearted, and generous. He was the best choice for her once I was out of the picture. There were several that were made to exit her life. Liars, cheaters, thieves, all had an encounter with a fearsome creature in the dead of night. I didn't kill any of them. Except for the mobster. I did have my standards. I had no desire for normal people, regular people, even though I hungered for them and could have easily fed on them as well.

I have a code I live by. I might be a monster, but if I limit myself to committing monstrous acts only on those who perpetrate evil, in a way I serve the living in society. At least that's what I tell myself. I mean, society hasn't been able to find the will to kill Richard Ramirez or Charles Manson. Leave it to me to take out the trash. I was always good at rationalizing, my shrink once told me. I've even developed a lucrative internet business that serves a dual purpose: protecting innocents while finding scumbags to satiate my unholy compulsions.

I've found a comfortable, quiet place to rest during the days. It's not much of a life, though. Watching over Julie has given me some purpose, but it cannot fill the hollow gaping maw that once was my heart.

Falco the Dark Angel

I walk in the shadows. I live in the night. I am a creature of the night. I need to feed daily, but I am very selective about my victims. If you are a killer, a torturer, a brutal thug, and a thief you'd better look out for me. You think you're someone's worst nightmare? Well, I'm yours and I can't wait to meet you. There's nothing better to do and I'm hungry to make your acquaintance.

by Randall Moore

Part 2

FALCO

1

I got out of my car and looked at the house. This was the place. The porch light was lit and I could see the number 6016. It was a modest two-story home with lace curtains in the windows. Light was emitting from the windows. I walked down the front walk, up the stairs to the porch and knocked five times. I heard feet on floor approaching the door.

"Who is it?" said a man.

"Falco," I replied.

I heard the door unlock, the chain unlatched from the door, and the door creak open.

"Come in Mr. Falco," said a balding man with unkempt hair and a pockmarked face. He looked like he hadn't shaved for days. His body odor suggested he hadn't bathed either. He wore a weathered bathrobe over sweat clothes. He smelled like he'd been drinking.

"Thank you, Mr. Girard. Falco will do."

"You can call me Bill."

I looked over the front room. There was a coffee table behind which sat a comfortable looking sofa with end tables on each side. There was a slight looking woman with long, straight dirty blonde hair that reached halfway down her side. Her visage was gaunt as though someone had sucked the joy out of her soul.

"Mrs. Girard?" I said approaching her with my hand extended. She reached up and grasped my hand. It felt cold. Her breathing was short and tight sounding.

"My name is Edith. Get Mr. Falco a seat, Bill."

"Of course."

Bill went into the dining room, retrieved a chair, and brought it into the living room, set it next to the coffee table near Edith. I sat down.

"Do you have what I asked for in my email?"

She pointed to a photograph on the coffee table of a beautiful little girl and slid it over toward me. The girl looked like she was nine or ten when it was taken. She had a lovely smile with sparkling eyes, high cheekbones and a dimpled chin. He hair was tied in pigtails and fastened by checkerboard-patterned ribbons.

"Is this a recent photo?"

"About six months ago. Katy's her name." Edith said.

"And the other thing?"

"Bill, can you get it? I'm so weary," she sighed.

Bill turned and left through the door opposite the dining room and returned with a sweater.

"I don't know why you need this. But here it is..."

"Like I said in my email, I need a recent photograph and a personal item to determine if I can help you."

Bill walked over to me and handed me the sweater. I lifted it to my face, up to my nose, and breathed in deep. I could smell the scent of her body, her sweat and grease and hair. I closed my eyes and suddenly psychically rushed out of the house, down the street about six blocks to the child's school, back two blocks down an alley, up a fire escape to a third-floor room. Inside the room was a weak-chinned man, about 22 years old with little muscle definition and an empty, dull look on his face.

My spirit rushed through his apartment to a utility room. There was a freezer lying on the floor. Inside were Katy and another little girl. Both dead.

I put the sweater back on the coffee table.

I shook my head. "I'm sorry Mr. and Mrs. Girard, but I'm afraid I'm not going to be able to help you."

"I suppose you'll be expecting to be paid," Bill said gruffly.

"That's not how I work. I only ask for compensation when I think I can be of service. I'm so sorry Mr. and Mrs. Girard. I can only hope that the police will find out your lovely little girl's fate. I can let myself out."

I got up, walked to the front door, and strode back into the night. When I reached my car I decided to walk in the direction my vision had led me. If I couldn't save this little girl I could salvage the evening with a meal.

The initial years following my transformation were difficult. My feedings were opportunistic, spur-of-the-moment affairs. Often times in high-risk situations. Not that I thought I couldn't escape, but control of the situation and discretion dictated that a little privacy was more than prudent.

So I thought I'd become more entrepreneurial. I decided to take my old friends' advice and get involved on the Internet. I created a website that advertised my newfound psychic abilities. I even created a one-word name that would sound mysterious and spooky. I mean Rick Jason didn't exactly sound like someone who could conjure up spirits from beyond, so I chose the name Falco.

HAVE THE POLICE AND THE FBI GIVEN UP ON YOUR LOVED ONE?
CONTACT FALCO.
I MAY BE ABLE TO HELP.
INITIAL CONSULTATION FREE.
FEE NEGOTIABLE.
ONLY DUE AFTER RETURN OF YOUR LOVED ONE.

There was a dramatic picture of only my head with my face in shadows and my eyes lit as by spotlights. There were rays of light emanating out of my head. The background was billowing purple satin.

Interested parties clicked on the contact button, which brought my email: falcofinder@falco.com.

My email was routed through several servers first in Europe, then China, then Australia, then Canada, and then back to the good ole USA.

I didn't want anyone finding my home base, which after the success of my website was set up pretty nicely for a person of my persuasion.

I was one of the first tenants of an abandoned office building, the Broderick Tower, a mix of Neo-Classical and Beaux Arts that was built in 1928. I took a sixth-floor space and had it outfitted to my specifications. The walls, floors and ceilings were reinforced with steel. Closable steel shades were installed over the windows and doors. I had a secret room constructed at the end of the unit and walled up as though it was the end of the room with a retractable steel door that looked as though it were part of the wall. It was all protected by steel plates. This was my hiding place.

The rest of the apartment was done up handsomely with black leather, glass and steel. The kitchen countertops were granite and I had marble floors with thick throw rugs strategically placed. There was a faux fireplace, luxurious sitting area and a workstation where I kept my main computer. I often took my laptop with me on the road to jobs.

My service provided me with two things I needed: an income to provide me with the means to protect myself, and hopefully, a steady supply of worthy victims to sate my unholy desires.

I thought about that as I walked toward the location I had seen in my vision. Billy Barky, callow child rapist and killer. And not the first time either. This would be the last, however.

I reached the alley I'd seen earlier and turned down it. I walked toward the fire escape at the end, leapt up and landed noiselessly on the bottom platform, and began to climb up to the third floor. Upon reaching the third-floor landing I looked into the window. Billy was in another room. I tried the window and slid it up carefully and stepped in the apartment and looked around. My sense of smell had become quite acute and I could smell that the sweaty, greasy, foul Billy was in the room to my left. I walked in and turned right, facing him. He was sitting at a dinette in his kitchen. He moved to jump up but I instantly rushed over and had him by his neck. I opened up my mouth and displayed my sharpened, fearsome teeth and hissed at him.

"Well Billy, I think you've been a very naughty boy. It's time for your punishment."

I dragged the whimpering Billy into the utility room, flung open the freezer exposing the corpses of Katy and the other poor little girl.

"Please! Ple…" he attempted to plead. But it was too late. I had sliced open his carotid artery and begun to drain the life out of his evil soul. After I finished, I separated his head from his body with my obsidian knife and left the way I came in.

2

The meth lab was in the second floor of an abandoned engine parts factory. The first floor had high ceilings and what was left of the massive machines that pumped out parts for Detroit's once dominant auto industry. The machines had been stripped of whatever could be pulled off, salvaged and scavenged. What remained are primarily the large heavy forged steel bases. The second floor is a large office complex, part of which is now devoted to the production of crystal. The third floor sits on top. Not as wide but with high ceilings and floor to ceiling windows. This is where the executives had been located. There is a large lobby that one time served any manner of social occasions and company parties. The large stone façade at the top of the building had giant raised letters in art deco style that read: MADISON MANUFACTURING. It was located near the intersection of Hastings and Piquette.

"Brock the Rock" was milling about looking out the window. Brock Sikonalski was a gigantic six-foot five-inch bundle of fearsome, paranoid (he had a taste for crystal), muscle-bound ball of anger waiting to explode. He had recently gotten out of prison where he had apparently managed to lift heavy weights the last seven years. He had prison tats, a tightly cropped moustache and a goatee.

"You guys hear from Knoxie?" Brock said.

"Give him time, big guy!" Brenda Berkowitz said.

"Shut up, Brass," Brock snapped.

"Come on Brock. You know Knoxie always comes through."

Brock sighed. "Well, I guess you're right. I'm just so impatient," he said, shaking his head.

"So what else is new?" Brass snapped.

"He's on his way," Pete the Creep said quietly from the sofa. "We'll get to the bottom of it."

The stairway into the lobby creaked open. Mouse, Jimmy, Dred, and Bigsy walked in, removing their gunner's headgear with deck helmet and oxygen masks. Got them at the local army surplus store. Looks like they'd just finished cooking a batch of crystal.

"I could sure use a cold one," Mouse said.

"Don't look at me," Courtney Darling (Sweetcakes) said.

"I'll catch up with you later, hot stuff," said Mouse.

The others laughed. The four meth cooks walked over to the cooler that was under the conference table, opened it up, pulled out four beers, cracked the tops, and started drinking.

"Man! I don't know how many more times I'm going to be able to stand wearing this shit," said Bigsy, a slight, smart, geeky and funny guy who had a close personal relationship with his .357 Magnum.

"Here he comes now," Pete said as a pair of headlights pulled into the factory's driveway and parked in front. "He's got a guy by the collar. He's dragging him inside."

Brock looked out the window, furrowed his brow and said, "Time to deal with a rat. Gangsta and Shank. Come with me."

Jeff O'Reilly, otherwise known as Gangsta Jeff, and Jimmy Franklin otherwise known as Jimmy the Shank got up and followed Brock to the stairway down to the first floor.

They made their way to the supply room in the center rear of the building and opened the door. Mike Knox (Knoxie Rocksi) had Ron Beckman, Brock's former roommate, with his arms lashed to a steel chair with electrical cords.

Brock eyed Ron Beckman contemptuously while walking around him. "Well, well. If it isn't my old pal Beckman the snitch. Because of you I just spent the last eight years in prison."

"You don't know what you're talking about, Brock. I told nobody nothin!"

"That's not what you told Sweetcakes," Jimmy the Shank said as he put a ten-inch tactical blade next to Beckman's right cheek. Beckman's eyes opened wide in terror.

"Please! Please! Don't cut me!" he said as Jimmy sliced his cheek open from his chin to his eye. He repeated the cut on his left cheek and crossed both lines with additional cuts. Beckman was screaming.

Brock pulled out a glass pipe, popped a rock in it, sparked up a lighter, and let the flame dance over the rock as he sucked the poison into his lungs.

"I got this piece of paper that swears I told the cops nothing!" Beckman exclaimed. "Don't you want to even see it?" He started crying.

Brock exhaled slowly and looked down at Beckman. "Want a toke?" he said as he offered the pipe to Beckman.

"Sure. Just let me go. I'd love a toke."

Brock looked over at Gangsta Jeff and said, "Shoot him."

Jeff cocked his Glock and pumped four rounds into Beckman's chest.

3

It was mid-afternoon. The sun was shining brightly. Butterflies and sparrows were flying around and alighting on surfaces. A large lawn sprinkler methodically shot long jets of water to the lawn interrupted by a piece of metal interrupting the stream and increasing the reach of the water.

Dan Stone sat in a patio chair on his back patio watching his wife Julie gardening while daughters Lucy 4 and Susan 6 helped.

Their romance had been kind of a whirlwind. Their path to happiness seemed positively greased. Six months after they met they married and moved to Bay City. Six months later they had Susan.

It was much nicer out here. Safer too. The TV news was a constant reminder of what they had left and both were glad for it. But there was something about Julie that had always bothered him. She seemed to conceal a deep sadness and sense of loss from him that never seemed to abate. He had asked her to confide in him many times, but she always denied that there was anything wrong. She was happy with her life, she would exclaim. He always accepted her admonition and relaxed with her assertion. But there were the late nights, the dreams, the terrible dreams. He would wake up and watch her, sweat pouring out of her as she would writhe in her place and moan silently. There was a terrible torment that operated beneath her placid demeanor that bedeviled him. He had been unable to penetrate her secret.

The girls were digging in the dirt with their toy shovels and pails while Julie was tending to her flowers, trimming off the dead and sick leaves and stems and fluffing up the ground at the bases of the plants to help create a catch basin for water.

"Darling?" Julie asked Dan. "Do we have any lemonade for the girls?"

"Of course. I'll bring it out to you."

The girls began squealing for lemonade, jumping up and down. Lucy jumped on Susan. "I can drink more lemonade than you," she boasted.

"No you can't!" said Susan.

Julie was beside herself with delight. "Now you girls get along with each other. You don't know how much you will need each other one day."

"Need Susan? No! I'm big! I don't need anybody!"

Susan walked behind her smaller and younger sister and wrapped her hands, playfully around her throat and gave it a little squeeze. "Not so fast you little shrimp!"

Lucy squealed and tried to get away. "Mommy! Make her stop!"

Julie could barely contain her smile. "Susan! Let her go," she pleaded.

"But Mom! She's such a brat!"

Just then the sliding glass door opened and out came Dan with a tray filled with a pitcher of lemonade and four glasses. The girls rushed over to the patio table as Dan filled up four glasses. The girls greedily gulped down the elixir as fast as they could, leaving splashes on their faces and tops. Julie joined them, picked up her glass and lifted it to Dan.

"To the best husband a girl could ever have."

They clinked glasses.

"Hey!" exclaimed the girls. "We want to clink too!" said Susan.

Julie and Dan knelt before their darling girls and all clinked their glasses together.

4

The yellow tape said CRIME SCENE. DO NOT CROSS.

Lieutenant Frank Kowalski of Special Investigations Divisions (SID) approached from the stairway. He ducked under the crisscross of yellow tape sealing the door and walked inside.

"Hey, Frank. Looks like it could be your guy."

Frank looked up and found the voice. It was Rafer Johnson, a six foot two black guy, who was the kind of guy you wanted on your team in a pickup game of basketball and a helluva detective.

"Where's the stiff?"

"Through here. Utility room."

They walked through the front room, then the kitchen into the back room where they saw it. The body on the floor. The head separated. The freezer door lifted up. Frank walked past the body and peered into the freezer. Two bodies. Two little girls. He stifled a pique of rage and put the deep sorrow he felt to the back of his heart and mind.

"CSI get the blood work?"

"Yeah. But there's not much. The body's pretty much drained."

"Time of death on the girls?"

"They were in the freezer, Frank. It's hard to tell now. CSI will give us a better idea later. It does look like one of them was in there longer than the other. CSI will give us a good guess."

Frank looked at the body and the severed head. He looked at the scene deep in thought.

"Looks like your guy, Frank. Body drained of blood, head chopped clean off. I don't know who this guy is, but some of the guys in the department approve of what he's doing. No trial. No prison. He's just gone and no other pretty little girl will die at his disgusting puke hands."

"We need the DNA to be sure."

5

I awakened to the strains of Mozart's Divertimento: "Eine Kleine Nachtmusik" (a little bit of night music). A completely appropriate piece considering my present condition.

I opened my eyes in my sealed room, hit the switch, causing the steel plates to retract, rose, and walked into the room. I stretched my arms out and yawned. Even vampires need their beauty sleep.

I walked over to the refrigerator, opened the door, selected a bag of blood, poured some into a juice glass, and took a sip.

"Ahhh!" I sighed. That should calm the bloodlust for a while.

I took my glass over, sat at the computer workstation, and settled in.

"Let's see. Do we have a new job or two to attend to tonight?"

The computer woke up and the monitor came to life. I clicked on my email account, entered my password and my email list came up. One was asking for help finding their runaway teenage girl, one was asking for help finding a missing husband and the other was asking for help finding a missing college student.

Intrigued, I opened the missing college student email again.

We've lost track of our daughter Marie. The police say she doesn't qualify for missing person status, the FBI told us to go to the police. We hired a private detective who doesn't seem to know anything.

She's a good girl. She's never done anything like this before. We're convinced something may have happened to her. Can you help us?

My name is Richard Vickers. My wife's name is Gloria.

I clicked the reply button.

I may be able to help you. Can we meet? I will need a recent photograph and a personal item. Once I can examine them I will know more.

I hit send and waited.

I got up and luxuriated in the Mozart. Such a joyous sound! Such genius! It made me feel almost human!

There was a beep from my computer. I walked back to it and saw that I had a reply. I clicked on it and opened it.

We want to meet. We will have what you need. Our address is 26518 Franklin Avenue.
Richard Vickers.

I will come to you in one hour.
Falco

I closed down the computer, went to the closet, selected my leather jacket, leather pants, and fedora. Before putting on my jacket, I put on the shoulder harness that held swords, which actually rest on the inner side of my arms. The harness was a spring-loaded contraption that would propel the swords into my hands. There was a sheath at the back of my neck that held my obsidian knife. I put a couple of loaded Nighthawk Custom Bob Marvel 1911 .45s in custom-made shoulder holsters that hung on my sides. I put on my leather jacket and dark glasses, locked down the apartment, and made my way down the elevator into the basement garage.

When I hit the floor, I walked out and walked over to my parking spaces. There it was. The Aston Martin Vanquish! What a machine! Anytime you needed to disappear in style this was the vessel. Tonight, however, required something a little less conspicuous.

I unlocked the door to my 2001 Honda Civic, got inside, powered it up, drove to the exit, hit the boulevard, and headed toward Franklin Avenue.

After turning left on Franklin, I looked at the numbers. 28000 and going down. I slowed down and watched the numbers drop. I reached the 26000 block and halfway down, found a parking place, parked and turned off the engine.

I got out, locked the door and walked down the street till I found 26518.

It was a large, ornate house. Perhaps at one time, it had been the lair of one of the movers and shakers of the industry. Now? It was a shadow of what it had once been.

I walked up the steps, found the doorbell and rang it.

I heard shuffling within the house coming closer to the door and a voice demanding, "Who is it?"

"Falco."

"Hold on."

The chain was lifted from the lock, the latch released and the door flung open.

"Mr. Falco?"

"I get that a lot. It's Falco. Like on the website."

"OK. Can you help us?"

"I'll tell you after I examine your daughter's photo and personal item."

Gloria Vickers waited by the fireplace, which was fully engulfed in flames, and emanating heat throughout the room. She walked forward. "Mr. Falco? There are blogs on the internet that extol your extraordinary powers."

I shrugged my shoulders, frustrated by my attempts to be known only as Falco.

"I'm not sure I can fulfill all that has been promised of me, but I'll try to accomplish what I came here for."

"Good," said Richard. "What do you want?"

"Only what I asked for in my email. A recent photograph of your daughter and a personal item.

"Gloria? Can you get them for him?"

Gloria walked from the hearth through the double doors leading into the heart of the house. Several minutes later she returned carrying a snapshot and a shawl.

She brought them to me, set them on the table in front of me, and sat down in a chair near me.

I picked up Marie's photograph. I studied it. A lovely young woman. Perhaps an earlier version of her voluptuous mother. She had raven black hair, pouty lips, dimpled cheeks and black eyes that reflected the light like spotlights. She was a beauty.

I picked up her shawl and like so many before, I lifted it to my nose and face and breathed in deep. I inhaled her scent, her grease, her essence, her hair and whatever else was there. With a crash, I was psychically transported out of the house, down the boulevard and out to the interstate. Miles beyond the interstate out of town I went. Maybe 60 miles I went until I came upon a collapsing barn to my left and I followed it down a long country road until I came upon a cottage with inviting lights shining out. I was, however, drawn to the darkened barn to the right of the cottage. Into the shed, I saw the door in the floor and the dungeon beneath. Marie was at the bottom in chains, weeping."

I broke off my trance short of breath and attempting to rest.

"Well?" Gloria said. "Can you help us?"

I nodded. "Yes. I think I can."

I pulled out escrow papers. "This is standard. I ask that you put $50,000 in escrow. When Marie is restored to you, the money is deposited into my accounts. If not, it reverts to you."

Richard Vickers looked at me, trying to decide whether or not he could trust me. Gloria came up to Richard. "It's an escrow account, Richard. What do we have to lose?"

Vickers called his after-hours banker to make the arrangements, and then he and Gloria signed all copies of the documents. I pocketed mine and gave them theirs.

"Alright. If all goes well, the next time you see me will be with your daughter."

Gloria's mouth opened in a state of awe. "If you can accomplish that. We will have spent well."

I arose. "Time's a wasting. I must go now."

I turned and walked out the front door into the street, got in my Honda Civic, powered it up, pulled a u-turn, and headed for the interstate and out of town to where Marie was held captive by an FDS: Future Dead Scumbag.

6

I had been propelling my Honda Civic for 50 minutes now. I was getting close. I looked ahead and could see that this was not yet it. After 9 more minutes, I slowed down and noticed a notch in the road and the collapsing barn I had seen in my vision. I took a left, which took me onto a rough road into the hills. After several country miles filled with road ruts, I slowed up and came upon the cute little cottage I'd seen in my vision. Lights emanating through the windows, smoke pumping out of the chimney. All was at peace. I looked to my right toward the barn I had seen in my vision.

I walked toward it, opened the door and walked inside. I saw the door in the floor. I knew Marie was in there. I also knew that the scumbag who put her in there was nearby. I knelt down by the door and lifted it. Marie and another woman were in the pit, consciousness gone.

I lifted my consciousness to the room in front of me.

And then I saw it! The undulating mass of humanity rising up and forming a rich, copulating, vibrating and thrusting force of flesh.

They were alive! All would live but one.

I climbed swiftly down to Marie and the other woman and released them from their chains. I gently lifted Marie up. Her eyes flickered and opened.

"Are you my angel?"

"No, I'm not an angel."

"Then, what are you?"

"Something else. Your father and mother asked me to find you. I've kept the first part of our bargain. You need to make sure I keep the second part by staying alive. Are you ready to join your family again?"

"Yes."

"Then rise."

Marie and the other woman rose slowly and agonizingly. They reached their feet.

What's your name?" I said to the other woman.

"Cynthia."

"OK. Marie and Cynthia come with me," I said, putting my index finger to my lips in a plea for silence.

I cracked open the door to the barn and looked into the night. All seemed at peace in the cabin, but something bothered me.

"Stay here for now. I want to check something." I pulled out a .45 and handed it to Marie. "Just in case." I showed her the safety and slipped outside.

I glided noiselessly up to the cabin and peered through the window. I saw no one in the room with the fireplace. My acute hearing detected the soft grass behind me being compacted, and in the reflection in the window, I saw a man approaching with a shovel in his hand getting ready to throw a blow, which he commenced to do. As the blow flew toward me I leapt about 15 feet into the air and landed behind him. I grabbed him by the throat, ripped the shovel from his hands and flew into the forest with him in tow. I stopped in a small grove of Eastern White Pine trees and tossed him up against one of them.

"Looks like you're at the end of the line. Got a name?"

"Fuck you!"

Not too friendly sounding, but I've dealt with worse.

"I was hoping you'd let me try out my latest thing." I clicked the switch projecting the sword into my right hand.

His eyes became full of fright. "What are you gonna do?"

"Really, Fuck You? I think you know." I flung the sword across his throat, severing his veins and arteries. He fell to the ground vainly attempting to quell the flow of blood from his body. I knelt down and gently removed his hands from his throat. "There, there. It's all for a good cause. I can't have you molesting any more young women," I said as I brought my lips to his neck and drank my full from the sanguine fountain he no longer possessed. Sated and satisfied he was dead. I severed his head.

I flew back to the barn and whispered, "It's OK. You're safe now. Come out."

The door creaked open and the two young women emerged from the barn, Marie holding the .45. "I'll take that," I said as I gently pulled it from her grasp. They were both trembling and sobbing as I led them to the Civic. I opened the doors and bade them enter. "Wait here. I've something else to do."

"OK," Marie said. "Just don't be long."

I grinned. "Back in a flash."

I walked out of their sight and then flew to the corpse of Fuck You, grabbed his head and body and flew toward the cabin, went inside, tossed the head in the fireplace, and put the body in front of the hearth. I ripped his sofa cushions open, pulled out the stuffing, spread it on his body, and looked for an accelerant. Out behind the barn was a gas-powered lawn mower and a gas can. It was about half full. Perfect for my use. I took it back into the cabin, doused the body, and poured a generous trail into the fireplace, which immediately started to burn furiously, engulfing the room in flames. I walked out toward the Civic. The girls were looking back in horror at the cabin, which was now a raging conflagration. I walked over to the driver's side and got in.

"What did you do?" Cynthia asked.

Without looking at her, I said, "He's not going to hurt anyone else ever again." I turned the key, turning the engine over, popped it into gear, and drove back down the rutted country road to the interstate and back to the city.

7

Dred looked out the window from the executive lobby of MADISON MANUFACTURING. "Somebody's coming…"

Brock leaped up and angled for a view.

Dred said, "From the looks of that Cadillac STS, I'd say Frank's come to pay us a visit."

Brock looked at Dred with some annoyance and nodded his head.

The car parked, the door opened, and Frank Morgan stepped out, attired as always in a finely tailored suit, diamond cufflinks and a snappy pair of Italian shoes. He looked up at the eyes peering at him from the third floor and walked into the first floor.

Brock and the others waited in the executive lobby and listened while footsteps grew closer and louder up the stairs until the door opened and Frank walked in.

"Good evening," he said with a satisfied smile. "I've got something for you."

Brock walked over to Frank slowly, reached out his hand, which Frank took with his and they shook vigorously.

"What's the deal, Frank?"

"We've got a thriving little enterprise here, but it's come to my attention that some lowlifes are trying to horn in on our dope business. The head office takes care of the crystal distribution, nasty business, but these scumbags are in our turf stealing customers from us."

"What do you want us to do?" Brock said.

"Go over to their house, steal their stash and dough, break their legs and let them know they're crapping in their own house, and they're about to be buried in shit if they don't stop."

"Sounds like fun," Dred exclaimed.

"Any girls in the house?" Pete the Creep asked.

"Should be a few," Frank says nonchalantly.

"Got an address?" Brock asked.

"Sure. 56718 Chattanooga Avenue. Take a solid crew. You know what to do."

Frank turned and walked toward the door, stopped and turned back toward the gang. "How many pounds of crystal have you cooked?"

"About 12 pounds," Mouse said.

"Keep it up and make sure you have 20 by the end of the week for delivery." Frank opened the door to the stairwell and disappeared from view, the sound of his steps fading as he made his way to the first floor.

Dred watched from the big windows as Frank got into his car and drove off.

Brock looked up at everybody with a sneer and said, "You heard what the man said. Knoxie, Dred, Creep, Gangsta, and Shank. Saddle up. It's time to go bust a nut."

"How come we don't get to go?" Mouse said.

"You and Bigsy need to keep your nose to the grindstone and cook the rest of that crystal Frank needs."

Brock picked up two Sig Sauer .45s and a couple of extra clips, which he slid into his pocket, the .45s in his belt. Knoxie Rocksi checked his Glock 9, then massaged his brass knuckles. Dred picked up a Tromix 12 gauge Saiga AK Semi-Auto Shotgun with spotlight and 20-round drum terminator. Gangsta Jeff picked up his favorite: the MAC-10 with a 50-round clip and a spare. Pete the Creep selected a Mossberg 500 Chainsaw pump-action shotgun and loaded it with six 12-gauge shells. He packed a bag with 18 more. Jimmy the Shank pulled out his favorite weapon: a Gil Hibben Extreme Survival Bowie knife with a 10-inch blade and powerful sawback teeth. He also picked up a couple of United Cutler Sub Commander Black Mini Boot Knives and slid them into his boots. He then picked up a Ruger LC9 Lightweight Compact 9mm Pistol. The kicker was it was loaded with 9mm shotgun shells.

The men filed down the stairs, walked out of the factory and headed to a black Escalade with blackout tint.

Brock took the wheel. Knoxie took shotgun. The rest of the men poured inside. Brock fired up the engine and they tore out of the lot.

8

I pulled into an empty space near 26518 Franklin Avenue, got out, walked to the passenger side, and opened the door for Marie and Cynthia. They both gingerly exited the vehicle. I reached out for their hands. They grasped mine. We held hands as I walked them to the front door. I stopped and rang the doorbell.

Gloria Vickers asked through the intercom "Who is it?"

"Falco."

"Do you have any good news to report?"

"Open the door and see."

I heard the chain being lifted from its spot and the door opened. Gloria Vickers' eyes filled with tears as she exclaimed, "Marie! Thank God! I thought we'd lost you forever!" she said, breaking down with emotion and weeping profusely.

"Mother!" she sobbed. "I thought I'd never see you again. I thought I was going to die! That man. He was so horrible. But this man. He's so wonderful. How did you find him?"

Gloria came forward and embraced her daughter, tears flowing down her cheeks.

"Thank you, Falco," she said with a quivering in her voice. "I had no idea what they said about you was true."

"Before you get too emotional, remember the escrow account."

"Of course. I'll have Richard release the funds to you. You've done a great thing for us. Your payment is small compared to what you've done for us."

"This is the service I provide and nothing more. I am at your service, Gloria."

Gloria walked up to me and held my face in her hands.

"I don't know who you are, or how you got to be the man you are, but I am so thankful that you are who you are." She wept openly. Marie and Cynthia also wept.

"I need to go now," I said, pulling away.

"Won't you stay? If only for a little while?"

I shook my head. "No, I'm done here. Cherish each other."

I turned, walked away from the house, got into my car, and drove off.

9

Lt. Kowalski opened the door to the morgue, ushered in the Girards and approached the attendant.

"We're here for a viewing, to see if we can get an ID. This is Bill and Edith Girard. Their girl has been missing for three weeks now and they deserve an answer."

The attendant walked over to the refrigerator doors that held the bodies of the dead.

Lt. Kowalski said, "Please Mr. and Mrs. Girard, come with me. I know this is painful and difficult but you can help with the case."

Kowalski turned to the attendant and said, "Open it."

The attendant opened the refrigerator door to D16 and slid out the sled that held one of the two victims pulled out of Billy Barkey's freezer."

"Take a good look, Mr. and Mrs. Girard."

They both gasped with relief. "It's not her!" Bill said.

"I cautioned there were two. The second?"

The attendant opened the refrigerator to D17 and pulled out the sled.

Bill Girard's face turned pale, his mouth hanging open, an empty look on his face. Edith started trembling as tears began to stream down her cheeks. "It's her. Katy. My poor, dear Katy," she said as the sobs began in her abdomen and spread out throughout her body.

"Thank you, Mr. and Mrs. Girard. I know this is a difficult time, but you've helped us immensely. I'll visit you soon. I want to ask you about anything else involved with this case, no matter how unrelated it seems to be."

"But what about the monster who did this to our Katy?" Bill blurted out, clearly enraged, barely containing his anger.

Kowalski said, "We're close to making a break now. I'll update you when I see you next."

"Alright," Bill said, all the fight leaving his body, as he led Edith slowly out of the morgue both sobbing in suppressed tones, giving into the fullness of their grief periodically as they walked through the door to the morgue and into the hallway.

Kowalski turned to the attendant. "Show them to me."

"You always want to see them. But CSI can help you more."

"I owe it to them. I want to see how they look in death so that I can find justice for their memory among the living."

The attendant opened the doors to D-16 and 17 and slid out the sleds that held the corpses of the two little girls. They were pale. Both had ligature marks around their necks. Apparent strangulation. Kowalski stood there contemplating their corpses and imagining the unspeakable horror they had had to endure until a monster ended their brief lives. What a waste! He shook his head, did the sign of the cross over their bodies and pulled back slightly.

"Okay," he said, his eyes misting up. "I'm done, Murphy."

Murphy slid the sleds back into place and closed the refrigerator doors.

"Thanks again, Murphy."

Kowalski turned and headed out of the morgue and over to the basement floor elevator and pressed the call button. After a solid minute, the elevator reached the bottom with a clunk. The door whirred open; Kowalski walked in and pressed 3. The door slid open on the third floor. Kowalski walked out and down the hallway to CSI and walked in. He looked up and saw Bill Signorile, the agent in charge of his case, walked over to his desk, pulled up a chair, and sat down.

Kowalski said, "What do you have for me?"

"The first girl had probably been dead for about six months. The second, 3 weeks. Both had their hands tied tightly behind their backs. Both had semen in their vaginas. Both had been strangled."

"Any DNA match?"

"Yes. One William Barkey, a 99.9% match with the semen extracted from the girls and what was left of his blood. Looks like we've got a dead perp. Your other concern is a bit more difficult to explain. Who killed Barkey? There was no evidence in the apartment to provide the slightest clue to suggest a perp. What we do know is most of the blood was drained from his body and then his head was severed with a sharp jagged blade. Messy affair. I know this is your real case. I don't know what to think. Somebody going around murdering scumbags the law can't find? I'm not sorry he did this one."

"Can't say I disagree with you. Still, vigilantism went out of style with the Old West. Email me a file of your report."

"Will do, Lieutenant."

"Thanks."

Kowalski walked out of CIS and down the corridor to the conference room next to SID, unlocked it and walked inside, shutting the door behind him. The walls were covered with bulletin boards with dozens of photographs from crime scenes displaying corpses whose heads had been severed from their bodies. The Barkey killing was of a piece with the rest of the disgusting array of death and dismemberment. Barkey belonged on the bulletin boards not just because of how he had died, but in what he was. Kowalski viewed the rogue's gallery of killers, child molesters, petty thieves, thugs, pimps, crack dealers and meth dealers. All scumbags of the first order and all dead. Maybe Johnson and Signorile were right. This guy was doing a better job than they were.

10

Raymond Chang poured out a nice bit of coke on the small bamboo cutting board he had brought for just this purpose and started to chop it up.

Raymond's mother was Vietnamese Chinese and his father was black. They had been lovers when his father was stationed in Vietnam. His father married her and managed to bring her back to the states in 1975 when Raymond was born. Shortly thereafter Raymond's father left. He never knew him. Consequently, Raymond's mother retained her family name: Chang. It was a name Raymond wore proudly.

Marcus Carter lifted his 1911 Desert Eagle .45 caliber handgun and laid it on the table, pulled a pack of Camels out of his back pocket, pulled one out, and lit it.

"Still after that shit?" Raymond said.

"Fuck. Gotta die a somethin. This ain't shit," said Marcus, a light-skinned black. Definitely too black to pass but closer to white than black. Hell, he had freckles plain as day. The darker-skinned ones would require a microscope and an infrared light to find theirs.

Raymond separated a couple of lines of coke, pulled up a straw and snorted the closest one, slid the board over to Marcus who picked up a straw and snorted it up. "We should smoke some."

"We start smokin coke and we gonna have to pull Brad and Jerry out of the back room and share with them. Those fuckers have serious work to do on our shit."

"You guys doin coke again?" Rhonda said from the couch in front of the TV.

"Just go back to your shows," Raymond said. "Unless you want a taste."

"I can't sleep when I do that shit. Couple more bong hits and a shot or two of Vodka and I be fine."

"Good girl. Know what you like & do that."

Raymond pulled out his vial, poured out another load of coke, and started to chop it up and shape the lines.

"That was a nice little score we made today. Half a kilo!" he said pointing at the stack of cash on the table.

Marcus started fingering the money, cracking a smile. "We're just a little closer to the next level."

Raymond called out, "Say, Rhonda? Cindy tell you what she's doin?"

"She's takin a nap. She's in the back bedroom."

11

The black Escalade rolled slowly down Chattanooga Avenue looking for 56718.

"Two doors down," Knoxie said, pointing ahead.

"Got it," Brock said. He pulled the Escalade to the curb and the men poured out.

"Gather round boys. Jeff. You, Pete, and Shank, go around the back. I'll send you a text when we're about to breach the front door. You go in the back. Wait a sec." He moved to the back of the Escalade, opened the rear and pulled out two 31 pound Zak Door Rams, handed one to Shank and the other to Knoxie.

"When you get my text, knock in the back door. We'll be coming in the front."

The house was modestly sized with a large porch. It was surrounded by an aging wooden fence with gates on each side. There was a home to the left, but to the right was only a driveway with a 5-car carport at the rear. Pete the Creep, Gangsta Jeff, and Jimmy the Shank made their way toward the carport and discovered an old picnic table in one of the carport spaces.

They lifted it and walked it over, next to the fence. They used the table to leap over the fence and made their way to the back door, Jimmy the Shank carrying the 31-pound Zack Door Ram. Pete the Creep stood next to him holding the Mossberg Chainsaw Shotgun.

Meanwhile, Brock, Knoxie and Dred walked up to the front door, Knoxie holding the ram, Dred flanking Knoxie with the Tromix Semi-Auto 12-gauge.

Brock sends a text "Showtime". He nods at Knoxie who pulls back on the door ram.

The door rams hit nearly simultaneously, startling the occupants, shaking the house. Dred eyes Rhonda through the now open door. She starts screaming. Marcus quickly pulls up his 1911 Desert Eagle that was sitting on the table as Raymond pulls out his Heckler & Koch Compact .45 from his waistband at the small of his back.

"Don't think about it fucker," Pete the Creep yells from the kitchen, pointing the Mossberg Chainsaw at Raymond and Marcus. Marcus turns to fire on Pete who lets a blast go, catching Marcus full in the chest and face, shielding Raymond from the full force of the blast. Dred comes through the front door, whirling to his left and fires four quick shotgun blasts in Raymond's general direction, shells ejecting automatically with a fresh round chambered as fast as the trigger can be pulled. The blasts blow a hole in the dining room table and blow out serious chunks of drywall.

Brock steadies Dred. "We're not here to kill em all."

"Why not? I love this gun!"

The sliding door from the back room opens and Brad starts firing his Barsa Thunder .32, hits Gangsta Jeff in the left shoulder.

Jeff says "Cool," and opens up in full auto with his MAC-10 on Brad, cutting him down handily.

Brock walks over to Raymond with Knoxie standing sentry at the door. Jerry is sneaking into the hallway from the back room's other door, keeping low, his Beretta Tomcat .32 out in front. He starts to draw a bead on Knoxie, when he feels the cold steel of Jimmy the Shank's 10-inch blade up against his neck.

"Give me a reason. I'd like this."

Jerry drops his weapon.

"Good choice," Jimmy says, keeping the knife to Jerry's neck, motioning him to get up and walk into the living room.

"Look what I found!"

Rhonda's still screaming.

"Somebody shut her up," Brock says. Rocksie walks over to her and slaps her face and grasps her by the mouth and says, "I'm only going to ask you nice once."

She stops screaming but continues to blubber and whimper, tears & snot flowing down her face.

───────────

Cindy awoke with a start as the house shook at the breach of the front and back doors. Shotgun fire rocked her sensibilities. The firing of the MAC-10 pierced the wall to her room. Petrified, she only thought of running. She slid the window up on her side of the house and started to climb out.

In the kitchen, Pete the Creep heard the sound of the window slide up, ran out the back door, into the backyard and into the side yard only to see Cindy as she was about to reach the gate. Pete ran toward her as she struggled with the latch and grabbed hold of her.

"Leaving so soon?" He looked her over lasciviously and licked his lips. "Looks like this little party's about to heat up." He grabbed her arm and forcefully led her back into the house.

"You're hurting me!" she complained.

"That's nothing. I'm going to really hurt you later. You'll see. Now get inside."

Pete the Creep led her back to her bedroom through the back room and shoved her down.

───────────

Brock knelt down, regarding Raymond.

"What are you? Some kind of Nigger-Chink mix?"

"Fuck you, Nazi," he spat.

"I think you don't understand this situation. You're dealing to my customers in my part of town. This was inevitable," he said while grandly unfurling his arms to the room. "Now what I want is your money and your stash."

A gurgling sound emitted from Marcus.

"That fucker's not dead yet?" Dred exclaimed. "I thought Pete would have had trouble handling that thing. Where's Pete?"

"Where do you think?" said Knoxie.

Dred smiled. "Didn't see the other cooze. Pete always had a nose for pussy."

"What's your name Chinker?" Brock said.

"Raymond Chang."

"OK, Raymond. Tell me what I want to know and I'm going to forget you pulled your gun on us."

"OK. Got this dough here. Got a floor safe in the back room."

Brock cocked one of his .45s and motioned Raymond up. "Show me."

Raymond walked slowly into the kitchen ahead of Brock and into the back room.

"Shit," Raymond said viewing Brad's bullet-ridden corpse. "It's back here in the closet."

"Allow me," Brock said, opening the closet door, peering in.

Raymond said, "There's a safe in the floor, under the carpet."

"Let's get to it."

Raymond lifted the carpet from under the rear baseboards and pulled it through the doorway, the carpet still fastened at the front. There it was. An Amsec Square Door Floor Safe.

"Nice," Brock said admiringly.

"There's a gun in it."

"That's a good career move, Raymond." He pointed his cocked .45 at Raymond's head. "Open it."

Raymond twirled the combination wheel backward and forward until he hit the last number. "Do you want me to open it?"

"Jimmy! Get in here! Watch this guy!" Jimmy came running.

"I'm thinking Raymond here is not as dumb as he looks, but just in case, watch him while I get their shit."

Jimmy pulled out his Ruger and points it at Raymond. "The loads in this are 9mm shotgun shells. I'm itchin to try them out on a living target. Make a wrong move and you'll be the first."

Raymond raised his hands up and shook his head.

"Good.'"

Brock, looking at Raymond and Shank, turned to the floor safe, flipped the latch and opened it up.

"Gotta say, Raymond, I admire your style," he said as he pulled out a Walther PPK .38 auto. He reached in and pulled out stacks of cash. "This is a big fuckin safe, Raymond. Nice choice!" At the bottom, he pulled out some sealed bags. They looked like a kilo each. There were ten of them. "What's in these?"

"Heroin. It's Afghani. Through Cambodia."

"You're helping your cause, Raymond. Looks like you had your boys weighing out and bagging some coke and weed. Where's the rest?"

"Front bedroom closet. Got a footlocker."

"Show me."

Raymond rose and walked toward the front bedroom with Brock right behind him, opened the closet, Jeff taking up the rear.

A wailing rose up from the back bedroom. Cindy.

"Please! No! Please! No!"

"You know how to turn me on bitch. Try and hurt me!" said Pete the Creep.

"I don't want to hurt you," Cindy protested.

"God doesn't like a liar. You *do* want to hurt me. You want to kill me, you bitch! Before I get through with you, you'll confess it to me!"

Brock turned back and opened the footlocker, pulling out sweaters and shirts. He next pulled out three sealed bags of sensimilla, about a pound each and four kilos of coke. "Jackpot! Nice!"

Raymond sighed, his shoulders slumping in defeat.

"Now you know I'm supposed to fuck you up. But I'm thinking... Shank! Bring in the cash."

Shank ran back to the back room and came back in.

"Sorry Brock. It's too much. Had to find a shopping bag to hold it."

"How much do we have here?" said Brock.

"It's about 450K," Raymond said. "Six years of my life."

"Well, I'm taking your cash and your dope. You can't do business under our noses anymore. That 450K was mine from the beginning."

"Can't you leave me something? Leave town. Buy a new start somewhere else? Away from you?'"

"I got better ideas for you, Raymond. You got connections I want. We should form a partnership."

"What kind of partnership?"

"Think of it as a hostile takeover."

12

Kowalski parked his car and looked out to the house number: 6016. This was the place, a modest two-story home with lace curtains in the windows. Kowalski walked up the stairs to the porch and knocked. The door opened. A gaunt woman appeared.

"Mrs. Girard?"

"Yes. Lieutenant Kowalski. You said you'd have news. Come in."

"Thank you, ma'am."

She opened the door wide for him and he walked in, his hat in his hand.

"Is your husband in?"

"Yes."

Would you mind getting him? I'd like to talk to you both."

"Not at all. It'll just be a moment."

She disappeared into the house. Kowalski got up and looked around their living room. Over the hearth was a family portrait. They all looked so happy. Now... not so much. *The murdered are gone forever*, he thought. *But the murder and the loss continues on in the lives of the survivors forever. They live with the loss and the regret and despair and sorrow for the rest of their lives. As bitter as it was, the child's suffering was over. Her parents? Their suffering was just beginning.*

Bill walked into the living room. Edith followed carrying a tray with a bottle of Bourbon, a pot of tea, and several glasses.

"Please sit down Lieutenant. Care for a drink?" Edith said.

"A cup of tea will do Mrs. Girard."

Bill poured himself a double shot of Bourbon. Edith poured a glass of tea for Kowalski and herself.

"You said you had news?" Bill said anxiously.

"I do. The case is solved. Your daughter was murdered by a man who lived in the neighborhood near the school."

"My poor dear Katy!" Edith started sobbing. She steeled herself. "I'm sorry Lieutenant."

"Is he in custody?" Bill asked.

"No. He's dead."

They both gasped.

"How do you know he's the one," Bill asked.

"DNA. 99.9 percent certainty. Blood type. Hair"—*he didn't mention semen.* "He kept her in a freezer in his home. The other girl you saw in the morgue? She was also in his freezer. I only wish you hadn't seen her. It gave you false hope."

"But he's dead. How did he die? I mean, I'm glad he's gone but how did he die? Did you kill him?"

"No, we did not. That's not our task. Society asks us to investigate crimes, collect evidence to be presented in court where the accused is either convicted or exonerated. Justice is meted out by the jury and the judge. The police are the tool of the court in theory."

"Did someone else kill him?"

"Yes."

"I wish I would have killed him. Am I a suspect?"

"I know you would. But no, you're not a suspect."

"Why not? I would like to be a suspect!"

"The way in which he was killed. It followed a particular pattern. One, which we have been following for several years now."

"Pattern? What do you mean?"

"It's not important. But what I need to know from you is was there anything unusual that happened from about the time your daughter disappeared until this moment?"

The Girards rested back on their couch and breathed out with a collective sigh.

Edith spoke first. "Well, after the Police told us they didn't have any idea or suspects in the case, and when we learned that the FBI wasn't interested in our daughter's case, I did some research on the internet. I found this website that claimed that he could help when the police and the FBI couldn't."

"He? Do you have a name?"

"Yes. Falco. I sent him an email. He responded. He asked for a recent photograph and a personal item of our daughter's. He came here and sat in the very chair you're seated in. He looked at our daughter's picture and breathed deeply through our daughter's sweater. He went into a trance and when he came out of it he said he was sorry and couldn't help us. He didn't ask us for any money. He just left. He seemed genuinely sorry that he couldn't help us."

"Falco. You're sure."

"Yes. He made a point of it. Whenever we addressed him as Mr. Falco, he seemed annoyed and insisted we address him as only Falco. Does this help Lieutenant Kowalski?"

"I don't know where or how this connects with your case. But you said it was a website."

"Yes. Just Google Falco find lost children. His email address is on his website. It was memorable: falcofinder@falco.com"

Kowalski rose. "Thank you for the tea and thank you for this bit of information. I don't know if it's significant or not but it's something I'm going to look into. I have to say, I find this information intriguing at least.

"Mr. and Mrs. Girard, Bill and Edith, once again permit me to express my deepest sorrow and profound grief at the loss of your daughter. Please forgive my departure."

"Dear Lieutenant!" Edith said. "You've been the kindest of all the policemen who've visited us."

"Thank you, ma'am. Bill?" Kowalski said as he extended his hand to Bill Girard. They shook hands. Kowalski turned and left.

13

Julie had been having the dreams again. She was tied up in the house. Rick was there. Victor was there. There was a pulsating orb of red light over her head that emanated bolts of lightning in all directions. It exploded. Victor was gone. Only Rick was there. In front of her. His eyes glowed red. He smiled and displayed a mouthful of sharp teeth. She looked at the floor. There were five headless bodies there. One was engulfed in flames. Rick effortlessly lifted her as though she were weightless. A shroud of darkness engulfed her and she was back in her old apartment. She woke up.

She was breathing quickly with a sheen of perspiration on her forehead, neck and shoulders. Her mouth was dry. She reached for the glass of water she kept on her nightstand, took eight gulps, returned it to the nightstand and lay there in the dark. The dream was so vivid. It took her back to that night ten years ago. The ordeal that she and Rick shared. She had been drugged much of the night and much of what happened seemed shrouded in fog. What she did know was that Rick had saved her from being murdered, and saw her almost all the way home, and then disappeared from her life. Thinking about Rick opened up a hollow spot in her heart. *Where did he go? Was he still alive? Why didn't he return as he promised?*

Dan stirred and rolled over. His eyes were open. He was watching her.

"Can't sleep?"

"I had another dream."

"What was it about?"

"A nightmare. Monsters were trying to kill me. Someone from my past stopped them."

"Rick?"

"Yes. Rick."

"You should tell me about it. It might help."

"I don't know. I'm not ready," she said as she got out of bed, walked over to the chair she dropped her clothes on, picked up a long nightshirt and put it on. "I think I'll work a little while. Then come back to bed."

"Don't stay up too late, honey. It'll screw with your natural rhythms."

"My natural rhythms are already screwed," she said as she walked from the bedroom and into her study where she sat down before her computer monitor and keyboard, touched the keyboard, typed in her password and looked at the screen. She opened her browser, opened the Google home page, and typed in "disappeared persons find," and a page of results came up. A lot of ancestor websites and places that asked for a fee to search their database. Then there were police department websites by city as well as the FBI and missing persons listed by state.

She typed in "missing persons psychic help," which brought up a list of psychic websites. One of the sites caught her attention. CONTACT FALCO.

HAVE THE POLICE AND THE FBI GIVEN UP ON YOUR LOVED ONE?

She clicked on it and it loaded Falco's page. There was something piercing about his glowing eyes. The message read like this was a place of last resort. She clicked on the contact link and it brought up the address falcofinder@falco.com.

She typed: *I have a dear friend who disappeared ten years ago. I am wondering if you can help find him. Please let me know.*

Regards,

Julie Stone

She hit send and sat pensively for a moment. She then quit her browser and returned to bed.

14

Back in the executive lobby of MADISON MANUFACTURING, Brock was pacing impatiently. Suddenly he stopped and bellowed, "Hey, Brenda! Go down and check on Bigsy and Mouse!"

"Aw. Why me?" She looked really annoyed.

"Cause you're here and I told you to."

Shaking her head, she said, "Shit. Can't you do this shit by yourself?"

"We're not going to have a problem are we?" he said, challenging her.

"You better do something nice for me," she demanded.

Shaking his head in disgust, he snapped, "Just do it!"

Brenda picked herself up off the couch, stubbed out her cigarette, walked over to the door to the stairwell, and walked down to the second floor.

Brock found himself thinking about his dead brother Chris. Chris, the smart one. The attorney. The guy who had all the angles figured. The guy who made all the connections. Chris had class and style. Brock admired him. After Chris was murdered, that prick Frank Morgan stepped in from the gangsters Chris had connected with to expand their business. *Hell. I was in jail before all this went down*, he thought. *I'd of suspected Frank and the mob of the murder, except for the way it went down. Chris's body drained of blood. Decapitated. Fucking ugly. Nobody deserved that. It was like that fucker Zarqawi. The prick who decapitated Nicholas Berg in Iraq. As bad as the mob was, they weren't into beheadings...yet. The Mexican drug cartels, they adapted Zarqawi's methods to strike terror into the hearts of their enemies.*

The stairwell door opened. Brenda walked in.

"They're almost done. Nearly twenty pounds of crystal cooked, your highness."

"Don't be so smartass, Brass."

"That's why I gots the name!"

"Shit," Brock shook his head and suppressed a smile.

"Tell them to come up and see me when they're done."

"Don't have to. They're coming up. They're done."

Brock heard the footfalls on the stairway leading up to the third floor. The door opened and in walked Bigsy and Mouse sans protective gear.

"Got that fucker done! I need a beer and a joint!" said Mouse.

"Ditto that motherfucker!" said Bigsy.

"You guys get some refreshments and come and see me. I've got something important for you to do," Brock said.

They walked over to the fridge, opened it and each pulled out a beer, cracked it and chugged it. Tossed the empties in the garbage can next to the fridge, reached in and pulled out another beer each and cracked those and then walked over to Brenda, who had commandeered a huge bag of weed.

"Give it up girl!" Mouse exclaimed. "You got papers?"

She reached into her purse and tossed a pack of Zig Zags on the coffee table.

"Help yourself."

"Thanks. Don't mind if I do."

Mouse pulled out a paper and loaded it with a huge load of sticky marijuana flowers and rolled it up, just barely closing it. He licked the glue and fastened it to the other side of the paper. He sucked the joint into his mouth and coated it with saliva. First one end, then the other. He examined his creation. The ends were open with a large amount of weed exposed. Not one of those thin pussy joints that were twisted closed.

"Give me a light, Brass."

Brenda reached into her purse and flipped a Bic lighter toward Mouse, who swept it up and sparked the flame to the blunt. He sucked on it and it was slow to light due to the thickness of the resins in the dope. But it finally caught fire and he sucked the sweet smoke deep into his lungs, holding it in and passed it to Bigsy, who followed suit.

Mouse exhaled his hit and felt the rush of intoxication envelope his mind and body.

Bigsy finished his hit and did the same.

The two walked over to Brock with their beers and the joint.

"What's up boss?" Mouse said.

"I got something I want you to look into."

"What's that?" said Bigsy.

"It's about my brother Chris. I want to find out who murdered him. I want to rip out his living guts and shit down his throat. You guys are good with the computers. You're great at stealing identities that we can sell. I want you to get some leads for me to follow up on. I'm hot to do this. It's been too long."

Brock sighed and continued. "All I know is that he was getting serious about a chick named Julie Rivers at the time he was killed. Maybe there was somebody in her life that didn't want her to be with Chris. Find her and maybe we find him."

Bigsy and Mouse looked at each other and then at Brock.

"It's been a while," Mouse started. "But we'll see what we can dig up."

"Thanks. Let me know what you get."

15

I woke up from my rest and flipped the switch that automatically opens my tomb. I rose and walked in the kitchen, the hunger palpable, gnawing at my center. I opened the refrigerator, pulled out a bag of blood, poured some into a juice glass and sipped. It felt so good going down. The pangs of hunger receded. I put the blood bag into the refrigerator. I'm going to have to lay in an additional supply of this stuff. Kill opportunities seem fewer and far between. I don't have to descend into savagery.

I sat down at my computer workstation, brought it back to life and logged onto my email account. There was a message from a woman in Indiana who wanted me to contact her dead aunt. I deleted it. There was a message from a man in Northern Michigan who was looking for his long-lost father. I deleted that as well. There was a message from a woman in Port Austin who asked me to help her find her missing boy. I clicked to respond and sent her my standard request for a personal meeting with a recent photo and personal item. The next email startled me. It was from Julie. She was asking Falco to find me! I felt the old longing that I suppressed as well as I could. I wanted to see her in person again. But it had been so long. She couldn't know. My heart rate increased. My breathing accelerated. I breathed in deeply and exhaled slowly, relaxing me. I frankly wasn't sure how to respond. I clicked to advance to the last email. It intrigued me. It was from a Lieutenant Frank Kowalski of the Detroit Police Special Investigations

Division. He had met with poor Edith and Bill Girard about their late daughter Katy. He said their daughter's murder was solved, but he was trying to tie up some loose ends regarding the investigation. He wanted to interview me regarding my meeting with the Girards.

I leaned back in my chair and wondered. Who is this Kowalski and what is he investigating? Could he possibly suspect that I am the killer's killer? I clicked the reply button and wrote him that I would be happy to meet and help resolve his investigation. I told him I doubted I could be of any help but was willing. I clicked send.

16

The sound of the truck was growing and growling. Brock looked out the window of the executive lobby of MADISON MANUFACTURING and saw it. It was a Mack Truck towing a huge flatbed trailer loaded with pipe. It barreled into the lot, horn blaring and pulled up in front. Brock took off downstairs and burst through the first-floor front door.

"What the hell is this?"

Dred and Jimmy the Shank hopped out of the cab. "Construction site," Jimmy said. Security guard's got a couple of extra holes in him. This load of pipe ought to be worth something to Frank and his friends.

Brock put his hand to his chin, deep in thought. "It was a helluva a bad idea to bring it here. What if the cops are looking for it? Drive it off-site, someplace remote, and call me. I'll call Frank and see what he wants to do."

Dred and Jimmy hopped back into the cab, started the truck up again and drove it back into the street.

Brock speed-dialed Frank, who picked up on the first ring.
"Morgan."
"Frank. It's Brock."
"Yeah. I got caller ID. What's up?"
"Dred and Shank just highjacked a load of pipe off a construction site. They got the truck too. What do you want them to do?"

"Shit. This is kind of short notice. But we might be able to use that shit. We got a warehouse near Dearborn. Have them drive it there. They can park inside and we can figure out what the score is."

"How do my boys get back?"

"Send a car." Frank gave Brock the address and hung up.

Brock dialed up Dred. "Hey, Dreddy. Drive the rig down to Dearborn. 6660 Wessex Ct. I'll send a car to pick you up."

"Solid."

They both hung up.

17

Detectives Rafer Johnson and Tony Rodriguez pulled up in front of 56718 Chattanooga Avenue in their slickback: police slang for unmarked car. Yellow CRIME SCENE DO NOT CROSS tape crisscrossed the front door and the side gates. There were several black and whites parked with their multi-colored light bars flashing. Uniformed cops were in the front yard and inside the house.

The detectives walked up to the first uniform they saw on the lawn.

"What's your name, officer?" Johnson said.

"Ronald Carter. And you?"

"I'm Rafer Johnson," and then pointing to his partner. "This is Tony Rodriguez."

"What the hell happened here," Johnson said.

"Neighbors called it in after it was over. They were afraid to call it in while it was happening. Didn't want to be next, I guess. Apparently, there was some serious ordnance being fired. Three stiffs inside. Apparent home invasion."

"Who's in charge?" Rodriguez said.

"That'll be Sergeant Perez." He said pointing to the uniformed officer directing traffic on the porch.

"Thanks." Johnson and Rodriguez walked down the walkway and up the steps onto the porch, and pulled their badges out.

"Sergeant Perez?" Rodriguez asked. Perez nodded.

"Looks like we're taking over this crime scene."

"Good. Happy to hand it off to the suits. We like the O.T. but I'll be happy to sleep in my bed tonight.

"What's your take, Perez," Johnson said.

"Well, it looks like we had a coordinated door breach of the front and back at the same time with shooters coming in from both doors. Stiff in the front room looks like he took a 12 gauge full in the chest and face from the rear door. Then it looks like somebody came in through the front door and fired 4 shots from a 12 gauge, blowing up part of the dining room table, the other three rounds into the drywall. I'd guess he was shooting at somebody who walked out of here."

"Carter said there were three stiffs," Rodriguez said.

"Let's go inside," Perez said.

Sergeant Perez walked through the front door. Johnson and Rodriguez followed and turned left around the splintered front door and looked at Marcus's ruined corpse.

"Looks like he pulled on someone who had the drop on him," Perez said.

"Why do you think he pulled a gun on somebody?" Johnson said.

"Look at the table. The bamboo cutting board, the razor blade, the straw. Somebody was cutting and doing lines of coke. Based on other parts of the house I'd say these were drug dealers who were in the process of being taken down by a superior force. Guys like this are never unarmed. The perps probably took the guns. They're worth a lot of money."

"You guys keeping this pristine? Has CSI been called?"

"Cleaner than a virgin on prom night. CSI is on the way."

"Show us more."

Perez led them into the kitchen. There were bullet holes on each side of the door to the right into the back room. They walked in and saw Brad's bullet-ridden body."

"Jesus!" Rafer exclaimed. "What do you think they used here?"

"I don't know. Something converted to full auto. Maybe a MAC-10. The pattern of bullet holes in the body, the walls entering the room, and the walls on the far side of the room suggests something difficult to control. The MAC-10 is notoriously hard to control, but fires a lot of bullets fast."

"And the last?" Rodriguez said.

"Through here."

Perez led them through the back room's other door, left down the hall to the last bedroom.

"There it is," Perez said.

"Not leading us in Sergeant?" Johnson said.

"You go first. I've already been in there."

First Johnson, then Rodriguez entered the room, Perez following, and they saw her. Cindy lying on the bed. Massive contusions to her face. Black spots on her ribs and breasts. There was a huge wound from above her navel through her vagina to her anus. Her throat had been slit and the bed was soaked in her blood.

The hardened police officers gasped and choked as they viewed this scene of unspeakable cruelty and sadism.

Johnson turned and left the room. Rodriguez followed. Perez taking up the rear.

"I've seen a lot of evil shit. But that just might be the topper," Johnson said.

Perez was holding his throat, a tear running down his cheek.

"Let me show you the rest."

He led them back into the back room and led them to the closet and the empty floor safe.

"Looks like the guys in this house had something to hide. What do you think it was?" Perez said.

"Money. Dope. Dope. Money." Rodriguez said. "That's a big fucking safe."

"That's probably what the perps said," Perez said. "Then there's one last stop. The front room closet."

Perez led them back into the hall, this time turning right into the front bedroom and the closet with the footlocker opened and empty.

"I'm guessing there was more dope and money in here. The guys who took this place down had a serious motivation to put these guys out of business. I'm figuring they were low-level competition who had gained too much market share."

"Perez! You ever think about taking the Detective's exam? I don't disagree with a single thing you said!" Johnson said.

"Fuckin A," Rodriguez said.

"Nah. I like the street action. I'll let you brainiacs take care of the tough stuff."

"Glad to make your acquaintance, Perez. You're making my job easy. I'll be glad to see you on any case I'm assigned to," Johnson said.

18

Bigsy and Mouse were locked into their laptops, performing multiple searches on public data websites, news articles, social media websites, and email servers.

Bigsy had written a worm that could break through firewalls and extract sensitive data, including deleted data from databases on a variety of private and public websites.

He was just waiting for it to compile the data he had asked for: Chris Sikonalski, Julie Rivers, decapitation, Michigan. Chris's body had been found on Beaver Island. Bigsy wanted to eliminate Michigan before expanding the search to the 50 states and Canada.

"Hold on. I think I'm getting something," Bigsy said.

His window said it was compiling. It was 38% complete. The progress bar was moving slowly, but moving up to 39, 40, 41%.

"Shouldn't be long now."

Mouse looked up at Bigsy.

"I hope you're right."

"Oh yeah. I've got something for sure."

19

I walked into the Starbucks at 10 Mile Road and Michigan Avenue. I looked at the patrons and approached the middle-aged, world-weary man with the expression of a basset hound.

"Lieutenant Kowalski?"

"Falco?"

I reached out and shook Kowalski's hand and sat down.

"Can I order you something?"

"It's too late for coffee for me. I prefer something more nourishing this time of night."

"Well. Thanks for seeing me, Mr. Falco. Sorry. Falco. The Girards mentioned you were sensitive on the topic."

"I don't think about it anymore. I'm becoming accustomed to being addressed as Mr. It's a sign of respect. I welcome respect."

"OK. We've solved the murder of Katy Girard. The Girards told me you were unable to help. The testimonials on your website grant you with extraordinary insight and ability in helping recover your clients' loved ones. Assuming all the claims are true, why did you refuse to help the Girards?"

"I didn't refuse to help them. I only told them I couldn't. I saw that their daughter was dead. Telling them served no purpose. They were better off with false hopes. I had no hope for them."

"How did you know she was dead?"

"I have some skills. Skills I have acquired. I have learned how to direct them. I use them to help the living. The dead I cannot help."

"You're an unusual man, Falco."

"Do you have any more questions, Detective?"

"I suppose not. How do I get in touch with you?"

"Email's best. See how quick this meeting transpired?"

"But what if I need to meet you quicker than email?"

"This is my preferred method of meeting."

I stood up. "If there's nothing more, then I have business to attend to."

Kowalski stood up and shook Falco's hand. "All right Mr. Falco. Sorry. Falco. You intrigue me. I have a case that you might be able to help with."

"Case?" I said.

"It's a serial killer case. We're up against dead end after dead end. A parade of scumbags. All drained of blood and decapitated. Would you be willing to come to my office and view the photos?"

So it was as I suspected. Kowalski was seeking my help in capturing me. Did he suspect me? I didn't think so. I should probably accept his request to help. At least I'd find out how much he knew.

"Serial killer. How gruesome. Like I said. I have a greater connection with the living. But if you think I can be of help, I'll look at your investigation."

"Thank you, Falco. Perhaps you could accompany me downtown to the station to see my exhibit?"

"I told you I had business to attend to. Perhaps tomorrow. Send me an email."

"I will."

20

Bigsy watched as his program reached 100%. "Bingo! Got it!"

He hit the file with the cursor. It opened and flew down to fill the screen and he scrolled down to the bottom.

"I got her! Name's Julie Stone, formerly Julie Rivers of Detroit, MI. Married Daniel Stone, stockbroker seven years ago currently living at 13657 N. Monroe St., Bay City, Michigan!"

Bigsy sent the file to his wireless printer. Jumped up and waited for it to spit out the page. It slowly churned out. He grabbed the page and briskly walked up the stairs to the third-floor executive lobby.

"Paydirt!" he exclaimed, handing the page to Brock. "This is her name and address. And her husband's too!"

Brock looked at it with satisfaction. "Nice job, Bigsy. I think we got a girl to see."

21

Kowalski walked out of the Starbucks behind Falco. He started to tail him. He couldn't quite put his finger on it but there was something about Falco that troubled him.

The guy was very slick. The leather jacket and pants. The shades and the Italian shoes. The slicked back hair. The shades.

Something about the shades. They hid his eyes. It was night and he wore shades. What was he trying to hide?

Falco reached a car. A Honda Civic. Kowalski stepped into an entryway of a shop to avoid detection.

Rick was amused at Kowalski's inept tail. He had a sixth sense that Kowalski could never imagine. He got into his car, powered it up and drove away.

Kowalski ran down the street to his car, unlocked it, jumped inside, started the motor, and peeled out in search of Falco's civic.

After a couple of blocks, he thought he spotted a Civic that looked like Falco's. He settled back in traffic three vehicles deep.

Rick smiled. Kowalski was following him. He would lead Kowalski far away from his lair, lose him, and double back.

He took the exit to the 15 and punched it. His speed increased to 70, 80 and 90 as he flew down the highway. Kowalski attempted to follow suit, but Rick had beaten him to the punch. Rick took it to 110 and took the next exit. Kowalski cruised past doing 80 and continued up the 15.

Rick turned the Civic around and headed back into the city.

22

Rafer Johnson sat across the table from the Detroit PD's gang expert, Lee Taylor.

"OK. We've got a home invasion robbery and murder at 56718 Chattanooga Avenue. We think rival drug dealers got into it and one of the gangs was put down, permanently."

"On Chattanooga? There's only one crew that would be interested in taking down a bunch of cockroaches in their backyard. That'd be Brock Sikonalski's gang."

"Who are they?"

"Exceptionally bad guys. Doesn't matter what you worry about. They doing it. Drugs, stolen goods, robbery, prostitution, murder. These badass motherfuckers are into it all. Take the Chattanooga Avenue case. One of those fuckers mutilated a woman. Imagine! One of God's most beautiful creatures mutilated! I don't understand how a man could treat a woman like that."

"S'allright Lee. I don't either. What we gonna do is figure about how we're gonna find this motherfucker and burn his ass into the ground."

"Fuckin A."

23

Kowalski logged into his laptop and hit Falco's email address.

Per your request. Let's meet at police headquarters so we can go over my investigation photos. 9pm tonight?

He hit send and waited. A reply came back.

9pm it is.

Kowalski closed the computer and walked over to the cafeteria. It had been a while since he ate and he decided to eat some of what was available.

He got a cup of coffee, two creamers, one sugar. One turkey on rye with lettuce and tomatoes. A cup of chicken noodle soup and a slice of lemon meringue pie. He grabbed 3 packets of mustard and took his tray to an unoccupied table.

He dug into the soup first. *Unremarkable, but nourishing.* Next, he tore open the mustard and squeezed it onto the rye bread and took a bite. *Bland, but satisfying.* He consumed it all, wiped the mustard from his cheeks, and dug into the lemon meringue slice. It was wonderfully tangy with a creamy texture. It went well with the coffee that washed it all down.

He thought about Falco and his purported psychic powers. He'd read the testimonials on his website. They were quite powerful. And if true, Falco had impressed a great number of people of his provenance. Kowalski would wait for his turn.

24

After parking my Civic on the street, I proceeded through the front door of the Police Station. An act I'd assiduously avoided. Well, maybe as a child I had had my run-ins with the police. But once Mother no longer cared what I did, and I had ceased to care about the rules, my only interest was in not getting caught.

I walked up to the receptionist and asked her, "What floor is Lieutenant Kowalski on?"

"Third floor. Just take the elevator up to three. It's room 316."

I pressed the call button and waited. The door slid open and I got in. It rose two floors to three, opened, and I got out. I looked to the left and then to the right, chose right and walked down the hallway. I came upon room 316 and knocked.

There was no answer.

I opened the door and entered the room. It was a large conference room. There were bulletin boards and large easels at the far end of the room. Each vertical surface was adorned with a photograph of a headless torso with a head in the background. Evidence of my feeding. I was alone in the room. There was on display a tableaux of death and decapitation on the walls. My victims.

The door opened up and Kowalski walked in.

"Sorry, I'm late, Falco. But thanks for coming. I'm pursuing a long-shot. Maybe you can help me."

"I'll see. What do you want me to do?"

"I want you to look at these pictures and tell me if you can find a unifying factor."

I feigned absorption in the photos. They were obviously my handiwork. It was like viewing meals consumed in the past. Some were memorable. Some were not.

"These are very disturbing pictures. All these decapitated corpses. What could I possibly tell you that you don't already know?"

"I want to know the identity of the person who did this. That I don't know."

I looked at Kowalski. "I don't think I'll be able to help you. These people are already dead. I specialize in the living."

"Thanks anyway for humoring me, coming down here and considering my request."

"You're welcome."

I left.

25

Kowalski ran down the stairs to the first floor, cracked the door, and waited for Falco to emerge. His explanation had sounded reasonable enough, but there was something not quite right about him. He wanted to find out more about him, where he lived, what made him tick.

The elevator door opened, and Falco walked out into the lobby, through the door to the outside, through it and into the car he had parked on the street. He got in and drove away. Unbeknownst to Rick, Kowalski had planted a GPS bug under the rear bumper. It didn't matter how many successful evasion maneuvers Rick made, Kowalski would always know where he was.

by Randall Moore

Part 3

ABDUCTION

1

The black Escalade with the blackout windows was parked in the next block down from 13657 N. Monroe St., Bay City, Michigan. Brock the Rock, Knoxie Roxie, Bigsy, and Courtney Darling sat waiting patiently for their opportunity.

After several days of recon, they had learned the pattern of the house. Each morning the husband, Dan, would drive the kids to school, one to nursery school and the other to a public school. Each afternoon Julie would pick them up and bring them home. Since she always entered and exited through the garage with a roll-up door, they concluded it would be risky, but possible to grab her in the garage if someone ran into the garage as she drove in.

Abducting her with the children in tow would be too complex. Dealing with kids would be a mistake. The best solution was to grab her while she was alone. Bigsy had tried to coax her into opening her front door but she had responded through an intercom from her home office. Apparently, she had a webcam watching the front door and probably other entrances to the house.

They did notice that she occasionally would run an errand in the middle of the day before she picked up her girls. It was decided that this was the best chance for a clean grab. So they waited for their opportunity to appear. Every day they would show up at nine and wait until three. Then back to the motel.

They'd been at it for a solid week. They'd take turns watching Julie through binoculars.

"This might be our chance coming," Knoxie said, looking through the binoculars. "She's getting up and moving out of the office. It's 1 pm and she leaves to get her kids at 2:30. Wait a minute. She picked up her purse. This is going down now."

They watched and waited. Brock was breathing hard. His hard look hardened. His grip on the armrest increased.

They watched as the garage door rolled up, and her Prius backed up into the street, and drove forward.

"Let's go," Brock said. "But take it easy. Don't get too close. Let's find out where she's going and try to catch her alone."

"Roger that brother," Knoxie said.

The Escalade pulled away from the curb and began to follow the Prius, always careful to keep 2 blocks behind.

The Prius took a left turn on Center Avenue, a right on N. Lincoln Avenue, a right on Columbus Avenue, drove all the way down to Cass Avenue, turned left, and arrived at Tuthill Brothers Food Market. She pulled into the lot, parked, and walked inside.

The Escalade slowly pulled into the lot and parked near Julie's Prius.

"Bigsy. I want you to distract her. When her back's turned, I'll take her," Brock said. "Knoxie. Stay in the car and get ready to go once we have her inside. Let's go."

Brock and Bigsy got out of the car. Bigsy stayed in the Escalade's shadow while Brock moved over, next to a dumpster, and waited. The automatic door whirred open and out came a dark-haired Hispanic woman with a child in the shopping cart seat. She pushed the cart over to a Chevy HHR, loaded her groceries into the back, put her boy into the back seat child-safe seat, got in, and drove off.

The door whirred again and this time it was Julie pushing a cart toward the Prius. As she got close, Bigsy emerged from the Escalade's shadow and said, "Excuse me, Mrs. Stone, I was wondering if…"

At that point Brock came up from behind her, shoved a rag into her mouth, and dropped a knapsack over her head, bear-hugged her, pulling her off the ground, and walked her toward the Escalade. Julie attempted to scream but was thwarted by the gag, which Brock held firmly in place. The back door opened. Brock threw her in, slammed the door shut, and got into the front passenger seat. "Drive."

Knoxie took off. He turned right out of the parking lot.

Julie pulled the gag out of her mouth, screaming hysterically, and lifted the knapsack off her head but Brock slapped her hard, coming into the back seat.

"Go better for you if you calm down." He then pulled out a pair of flex cuffs, cuffed her wrists behind her back, and fastened them tight. "If you promise to be quiet I won't put this back on," he said threatening her with the gag. She nodded her head in agreement. He then returned to the front seat.

Courtney reached out and stroked her shoulder from the middle row. "It's not so bad. Just calm down. There're things we want to know. That's all. We find out. We let you go.

2

The phone rings at Dan Stone's desk. It's 4 pm. He picks it up.

"Mr. Stone. Your wife hasn't picked up your daughter. She's very upset. I think you need to pick her up."

"What do you mean she hasn't picked her up?"

"Just the way it sounds. I'm sorry but we won't be able to keep Susan indefinitely."

"I'm sorry. I'm just confused. I'll be right there."

He hung up the phone and dialed the nursery school.

"Hi, this is Dan Stone. By any chance has my wife picked up Lucy?"

"No, Mr. Stone. Lucy's here in our office waiting to be picked up."

"I'll be right by."

Dan grabs his briefcase, and with a sense of urgency approaches his boss, and tells him "I've got to go. My girls. My wife." He stifled a tear.

"Don't worry about a thing, Dan," Norbert, his supervisor said.

"I've got to go."

Dan practically ran to the elevator, reflecting on how slow the damn thing ran. When it finally reached the ground floor, he exploded out the door, into the parking deck, and into his car, peeling out of the lot, and off to get his girls.

3

Knoxie worked his way through town, finally turning left on 7th, taking the bridge over the Saginaw River all the way to the cloverleaf entrance to the 75 South back to Detroit.

"Do you know who I am?" Brock asked Julie. She shook her head.

"Maybe you remember my brother Chris. Chris Sikonalski."

"Yes. I do. We dated about 6 months before I met my husband."

"Do you know what happened to Chris?"

"No. He just never called again. He disappeared. What happened to him?"

"He was murdered."

Julie gasped and held her hand up to her mouth. "I had no idea. Why are you kidnapping me?"

"I'm betting whoever did this is going to be very interested in finding you. When he finds you, we find him."

"Why don't you go to the police?"

"We did. The cops don't care. I care."

4

Dan Stone had his girls in their car seats in the back seat as he sped back to their home. He hit the garage door opener as he pulled into the driveway. Julie's car was gone.

"Where's Mommy?" Lucy asked.

"I don't know. We're going to try to find out."

He got out of the car, opened the back door to help the girls get out of their car seats, and brought them into the house.

"Why don't you girls go out in the backyard and play for a while? Daddy's going to try to find out where Mommy is."

They looked at his face with a forlorn look, slowly turned, and walked out into the backyard.

Dan pulled out his cell phone and dialed the Bay City Police Department.

The phone picked up on the fourth ring. "Bay City Police. How may I direct your call?"

"I'd like to make a missing persons report."

"Who's missing and how long have they been missing?"

"My wife, Julie Stone. Just a few hours ago. She was supposed to pick up our girls at school around 3 pm and she never showed up. She's just disappeared."

"Look, Mr. Stone. We can't report anyone missing before 72 hours. We usually find that the person comes back sooner than that. Did you guys have a fight?"

"No! You've got to be kidding me! This is completely out of character for her! Her car is gone as well. Can I report it stolen?"

"What kind of car is it?"

"It's a 2011 Prius. It's white. The license plate is personalized. It's IBLG4U."

"I'll put out a note to our officers to look out for a car that matches that description. In the meantime, cool your jets. She's probably coming back soon. Anything else I can help you with?"

"I guess not, if that's the best you can do. I'll see if I can find any clues around here. Thank you, officer."

"Give her a chance. She's probably on her way home now."

"I certainly hope so."
"Goodbye, Mr. Stone."
"Goodbye."

Dan called her cell phone again and it went straight to voicemail, just like the last ten times. He was feeling really panicked. He went into her office and started looking at all the surfaces, desperate to find a clue. Seeing nothing he woke up her laptop, which brought up the login page. He typed in her password and the home page came up. He launched her browser and brought up her recent history. Mostly pretty normal stuff related to arts and entertainment. He clicked on show all history for the last 14 days and began to scroll down the list. Ten nights ago there were searches for missing persons. One of them had a curious name: falco.com.

He selected the website and up it came.

HAVE THE POLICE AND THE FBI GIVEN UP ON YOUR LOVED ONE?
CONTACT FALCO.
I MAY BE ABLE TO HELP.
INITIAL CONSULTATION FREE.
FEE NEGOTIABLE.
ONLY DUE AFTER RETURN OF YOUR LOVED ONE.

He noticed the link to an email address.

He next launched her email account, typed the password, and entered. He clicked on the sent folder and it opened. And there it was. Ten nights ago at 2:47 am, there was an email to falcofinder@falco.com. He clicked it and Julie's email came up.

I have a dear friend who disappeared ten years ago. I am wondering if you can help find him. Please let me know.
Regards,
Julie Stone

Dan read her email and wondered. *Ten days ago she sends an email to a missing person specialist and now she's missing.* He wondered if there could be a connection. He went back to Falco's home page, clicked the email link and wrote:

by Randall Moore

My name is Dan Stone. Ten nights ago, my wife, Julie, sent an email to you asking about a friend that disappeared ten years ago. Now she's gone missing. This is a strange coincidence. Were you working on anything for her?
Dan Stone

Dan went into the kitchen to prepare a meal for the girls. Julie had made a big batch of macaroni and cheese two days ago. He pulled it out of the refrigerator and began to dish it up when his landline rang. He looked at the phone. Caller ID said UNKNOWN.

He picked it up.
"Hello."
"Dan Stone?"
"Yes. Who's this?"
"Falco."
"How did you get this number?"
'Never mind that. How long has Julie been missing?"
"I leave at 8 and take the girls to school and then go to work. Julie picks them up at 3. So I guess any time between 8 and 3. I tried to file a missing persons report. They won't do it until she's been missing 72 hours."
"The police are like that. They have rules. I don't."
"Can you help me find her?"
"Yes."

5

At 3:55 pm the black Escalade pulled into the driveway of MADISON MANUFACTURING and parked near the entrance. Brock the Rock and Knoxie Roxie got out followed by Courtney and Bigsy.

"Come on out, darlin," Brock says, gesturing Julie up and out.

She gets up and is trapped by the second-row seats. "My hands are tied behind my back. How do I get this seat out of the way?"

Brock flipped the seat release lever and it popped forward. Julie squeezed forward to the second row and out the back door, Brock grasping her arm.

"Let's bring you upstairs."

The group strode through the wrecked and filthy first-floor machine shop, and up the stairs to the third floor. They walked in. Brenda was on the couch with Mouse and Shank. Sitting across from them was Pete the Creep, Dred, and Gangsta Jeff. They were passing a bong around.

"Hey, Boss! Long time no see!" said Brenda.

"A little bit of recon and we brought back a prize."

Julie looked disheveled and emotionally burned out. The group looked at her as though they knew something bad was about to happen and they were going to enjoy it.

"Let's make a little movie," Brock said, and led the group into one of the third-floor executive offices.

6

Raymond Chang was pissed. He couldn't believe that all his hard work had been destroyed and stolen by that scumbag Sikonalski. He resolved to pay him back and then some.

OK. Sikonalski had spared him for his drug contacts in the Far East. He had agreed to do that. There was a business opportunity for him there, but he wanted to cut Sikonalski out of that deal and work exclusively with the higher-ups in the mob.

He dialed up Jerry Jaworski. The call went to voicemail.

"Jerry. It's Raymond. Call me. It's important." He hung up.

Two minutes later his phone rang. "Raymond," he answered.

"Jerry. What up cuz?"

"You need to get over here. I got some bad shit I need to cook up and I need your help."

"Be there in 20."

"Cool."

Raymond Chang was boiling in a pot of rage and revenge for what they had done to his friends, and to him personally. And then they cut him loose like he was a harmless punk. He was going to show them how stupid they were. He dialed a number.

"This is Franklin."

"Hey, Mack. Raymond Chang. I want to organize a hit on the motherfuckers who hit us and murdered your sister. Are you in?"

Franklin Mack seethed in anger and hate. Blinded by Cindy's suffering.

"I'm in."

"Get over here in an hour."

Franklin next dialed up William Mosely. Mosely had grown up with Marcus Carter and had been an important street force for their operation, both in distribution and retribution.

"Mosely."

"Bill. Raymond Chang here. I want to help organize a hit on the motherfuckers who took Marcus out. Are you in?"

"Abso-fucking-lutely."

"Be here in an hour."

Raymond next dialed up Wardell Reed, street warrior and buddy of Marcus and William.

"Reed."

"Dell. Raymond Chang. I want to fuck up the Sikonalski gang. Are you in?"

"What do you think?"

"Be here in an hour."

Lastly, he dialed up Rick Griffith, a tight partner of Brad Jensen.

"Griffith."

"Rick. Raymond Chang here. I want to organize a hit on the Sikonalski Gang. Settle some scores. Interested?"

"More than you could possibly know."

"Be over here in an hour."

"See you."

Within the hour Franklin Mack, William Mosely, Wardell Reed, and Rick Griffith were gathered in the apartment of Raymond Chang. Jerry Jaworski was already there.

Raymond had laid out some blow, and a bong, and threw down some weed.

"What's the plan, Raymond?" said Franklin Mack. "I want to cut their balls off for what they did to Cindy."

"I thought about it. I thought how satisfying it would be to directly assault those cocksuckers. But then I realized it would be no good."

"What do you mean no good?" Mosely said.

"We got this deal going. Sikonalski's bosses want my contacts in the east. I said I'd help them. I still want to burn down those motherfuckers for what they did to our friends and the money they stole. I just don't want them to connect it to us. And they will if *we* do the job."

"What do you have in mind?" Wardell Reed said.

"Spread the word on the street. There's 25K for a hit on the Sikonalskis. Find some gang bangers with no connection to us. We'll pay them or kill them when the job's done."

"I like it, Raymond," Mosely said.

"I'd still like to be there, ripping their guts out," said Franklin.

"I know how you must feel. I was there and heard her screams. I want those fuckers as dead as you do. This is a chess game. It's gotta be we win, they lose. You'll have your revenge. Only it will have to be vicarious."

"OK."

"Alright. It's agreed. Go out and recruit some animals to do a savage's job."

"I got just the crew in mind," Reed said, reflecting on a group of dangerous men he used to move product for him.

7

After putting the girls to bed after dinner, Dan Stone had his laptop open and was typing into a Microsoft Word document everything he knew about his wife, her personal history and proclivities, grasping desperately to find some connection that might make sense of this nightmare when an alert tone from his Outlook account rang. He clicked on Outlook and saw the new email. It was from Wandls Higbl. He opened it. It said click on link for a surprise. He clicked and was redirected to a video file that started to load. He clicked play.

The image was pointed at the floor and a pair of shoes, and slowly panned up to reveal first, a barefoot woman who was gagged, her hands fastened behind her back with welts on her face, and dark streaks running down her cheeks. It was Julie!

There was a man behind her with a large knife. It looked military. He was pressing it into her cheek and lowering it down to her neck. She was whimpering, tears running down her cheeks.

A voice began singing. "Oh, Danny Boy, the fates are finally calling, calling you here to witness her demise." The singing stopped. An extreme close-up of a man filled the screen.

"Danny. We have something you want. We want you. We'll tell you when and where. No cops." It faded to black.

He was frightened and angry and alone. He clicked to forward the email and sent it to Falco.

8

Wardell Reed drove his car down East Warren Avenue, parked just outside Perrien Park, and rolled down his windows.

A group of four blacks ranging in age from 13 to 23 came upon him.

"Hey, Dell! Got any shit you want us to move for you?" said Venom, about 17 years old.

"Always got shit for you." He tossed them a couple of bags of dope. "I got a business opportunity for the right crew. We need a bunch of badass motherfuckers to do a hit on some pieces of shit who ripped off some friends and cut a bitch in half. They wasted pussy, man! That should never happen!"

"What do you think, Little Evil?" the 23-year-old known as Big Evil said to the 13-year-old.

He had a hollow look to him, as though any empathy had been removed from his soul.

"I think this man's found his crew. What's the deal?"
"Kill these motherfuckers and you get $10,000."
"$10,000's chump change, punk. I want $25,000."
"$15,000. It's as high as I can go."
"What you think Venom?" he said to the 20-year-old.
"I think the man's lyin to you," Shadow interrupted.

Little Evil turned to Reed and said, "OK. I want $20,000 and you can go prison fuck yourself in the ass. My niggers'll do it for you."

"Let me make a phone call," Reed said. He pretended to make a call. He made their demands clear and feigned to hang up.

"OK, bitches. You got your deal. $20,000."

"What's the setup?"

"It's an abandoned factory. MADISON MANUFACTURING. There're some cocksuckers in there who need killing. $20K. Take four of you that's $5K for a few minutes of work."

"How do we know you pay us when we done?"

"C'mon? This is Dell talking here. I ever stiff you for the shit you move for me?"

"No. But this ain't shit we moving. This be cappin motherfuckers. Don't pay us the cash, we find you. It ain't pretty for your ass then."

"You do this for me, we tighter than ever. Tell you what. Here's $2K up front," he said, handing a couple of K to them. "Get some more guns and ammo and call me on my cell. We'll make a plan. We gonna conquer."

They all fist bumped and high-fived him and walked off.

Wardell dialed Chang. "I think we got our crew."

9

Dell's cell phone chirped. He answered. "Wardell."

"Sup, Dell. It's Big Evil. We ready."

"OK. Bring your crew to Perrien. I'll pick you up and take you to them."

"Solid."

Dell drove over to Perrien Park, parked, and waited. After about ten minutes he saw the crew walking through the park to his car.

"Get in, niggers."

"Hey! I'm a blackatino," Venom said. "Show a little respect."

Dell laughed. "OK. Niggatino."

The four got in. Big Evil up front. The other three in the back. Wardell then put the car into gear and took a left on

Grandy Street, a left on Ferry, and right on Russell, and a left on Piquette, right under the I75, and nearly to Hastings, and parked. He got out, the others following suit, and walked to the rear of the car.

"OK. Show me your weapons."

Big Evil pulled out two .45s and laid out 4 clips. Little Evil pulled out an Uzi Sub Machine Pistol. Venom had a Magnum, and Shadow had a Glock 9.

"Keep all your shit. It's all good. But I got some other shit you may want to use."

Dell opened the trunk and lifted the tarp that covered his contribution to the arsenal. There was a fully auto AR-15 with three 50-round clips, and an Armsel Striker Shotgun with a 12-round revolving cylinder and a box of extra shells. He tossed an extra 50-round clip and a bag of shells on the table. "Go kill these motherfuckers."

Big Evil grabbed the shotgun. Little Evil motioned for Shadow to grab the AR-15.

"Keep the Glock. That's your backup." Little Evil advised.

Dell said, "OK. Here's the plan. You work your way slowly through the parking lot and gain entrance to the ground floor. Work your way upstairs and cap these motherfuckers. Any questions?"

"Just one. Where are they?" Little Evil said. The others whooped in approval.

"Great. Go get em. Kill everyone you see."

They nodded their heads in determination and headed into the parking lot of MADISON MANUFACTURING carrying their weapons.

———————————

"Shit! We got company," Mouse exclaimed, surveying the parking lot from the top floor.

Brock looked down and sneered. "Looks like these bangers are here and hot for us. Everybody grab your weapons!"

———————————

Shadow took point and walked carefully to the entrance. Venom, Big Evil, and Little Evil followed suit. Venom entered the first floor and looked around. The others followed and took cover behind support pillars and the huge metal dinosaur fragments of a dead era of manufacturing.

They all took cover as they heard the upstairs horde rushing down the stairwell when they burst into the room. Dred was first into the room with the Tromix 12-gauge Semi-Auto with the spotlight blazing. He scanned the ground floor. Gangsta Jeff was next with his MAC-10. Bigsy came in with his .357 Magnum. Shank ran down the hallway to the rear stairwell and worked his way silently down.

Venom lifted the AR-15 and fired off an extended burst in their general direction. They all dove for cover behind the ruined machines and support pillars as the bullets slammed harmlessly into the wall behind them, ricocheting off the machines.

Big Evil poked his head around the machine directly in front of the entrance and Bigsy fired off a round from his magnum, which ricocheted off the machine as Big Evil fell back. He quickly jumped out and fired a shell to where he thought he saw the gun being fired from. The pellets slammed into the pillar Bigsy was hiding behind and into the wall.

"Shit! He's got a 12-gauge! Fucker came a little too close for comfort! Dred? Little help?"

Dred moved to his right with the Tromix Automatic Shotgun raised, spotlight on. He caught a glimpse of Little Evil firing his Uzi in his direction. He fired off three rounds at Little Evil who jumped behind a machine.

Big Evil exposed himself and fired at Dred. Gangsta Jeff came up with his MAC-10 from the machine to the left of the stairwell and fired off 25 rounds at Big Evil who fell to the floor, dodging the fusillade. Bigsy fired his Magnum at Big Evil. It slammed into a machine just 4 inches from his head. He crawled behind the machine.

Shadow worked his way forward, and got behind a machine closer to Gangsta and Bigsy, and pressed the trigger, emptying the magazine at them. They dove for cover, the bullets bouncing harmlessly off the machines and pillars.

Venom worked his way to the left side of the room and saw Dred peek out from behind one of the pillars as he pulled the trigger sending a powerful cartridge toward him. The bullet slammed into the wall behind Dred's head. Dred quickly turned toward the spot where the shot had come from and squeezed off a round. Venom had already ducked behind an obstacle.

Shank had worked his way downstairs from the back of the building and made his way to the front of the building behind the gang bangers. He silently crawled behind Big Evil, rose up, and knifed him in the back. Big Evil fell, coughing up blood. Next, Shank worked his way over to Venom and stabbed him in the neck, angling the blade toward his heart. He was dead before he hit the ground. That left just Little Evil and Shadow. Gangsta Jeff moved to his right, detected movement, and fired off 50 rounds from his MAC-10 in the general direction of the movement. He slapped in another 50-round clip and ran to his right. He saw Little Evil and Shadow unprotected and fired off another 50 as they turned toward him. Before they could get a shot off, multiple rounds hit them both with punishing force. They fell from the merciless fusillade in agony, the bullets had missed their vital organs.

Shank worked his way behind them. Bigsy sought cover behind a CNC machine directly in front of them. He stood up and calmly shot Shadow in the head. As Little Evil lifted his gun toward Bigsy to return fire, Shank rushed forward and plunged his knife into Little Evil's neck, angled down toward his heart, and pierced it, killing him instantly.

10

I looked at the video Dan Stone had forwarded me. I felt the bloodlust rise in my spirit. The unholy power I possess began to grow exponentially. In the case of Julie, I don't need a picture or a personal item. I have her face permanently imprinted into my psyche. I conjured up her visage. As for a personal item. I remembered the last time we kissed. It was at Victor's crazy after party. She had kissed me, stuck her tongue into my mouth and I returned the favor, wrapping my tongue around hers. It was a sublime moment. One for which I would do anything to repeat. And then it happened. My spirit rushed out of my condo and sped through the grid of the city until I came upon a building: MADISON MANUFACTURING. I saw Julie. I saw the men who held her. I knew what to do. And it couldn't wait.

I put on my harness with the 2 spring-loaded swords. I dropped my obsidian knife into its sheath. I put on my shoulder holsters and put 2 loaded .45s into them, donned my black trench coat and shades, and headed down to the parking garage.

11

Officer Patrick Clark was patrolling his normal route in his squad car and was making a detour through one of the abandoned parts of the manufacturing district when he witnessed what looked like gunfire coming from the first floor of the MADISON MANUFACTURING building.

He turned on his radio and got the dispatcher. "I've got what looks like a firefight at MADISON MANUFACTURING at the corner of Hastings and Piquette. Probable major crime scene. Request assistance.

Knoxie had opened a window on the third floor and was aiming a sniper rifle at Officer Clark. Brock was looking on.

Brock said, "Cap the cop."

Knoxie fired a powerful round that smashed through the windshield, ripping through Clark's right shoulder, knocking him to his right and below the dashboard.

"Did you get him?" Sikonalski asked.

"I don't see him. I think he's gone."

Clark, seething in agony, reached for his radio. "Officer down! Officer down! Request immediate backup at MADISON MANUFACTURING building at the intersection of Hastings and Piquette!"

12

Kowalski drove to the Broderick Tower, the location of Falco's Civic. People had begun to move back into the place after having been abandoned in the 1980s. He parked his car and began to walk toward the building. As he reached the entrance to the parking garage an Aston Martin Vanquish pulled up to the exit. Kowalski looked inside. It was Falco!

The Aston Martin Vanquish peeled out of the parking lot and roared as the engine opened up and achieved a remarkable rate of speed as it zoomed into the darkness.

"Who is he? Fucking Batman?" said Kowalski.

He rushed to his car but was too late to catch up with Falco.

Still, he started his engine and peeled off in chase of where he thought Falco had gone.

His radio chirped. "Officer down. MADISON MANUFACTURING. Hastings and Piquette. Major crime scene. Need Help immediately. All officers in vicinity report."

Kowalski punched down the accelerator and rushed to the scene. He knew exactly where it was and he knew he had a decent chance of being the first cop on the scene.

13

I sped down the boulevard, bloodlust and hate churning in my veins. I contemplated the animals that had Julie and smiled to myself as I thought about what I would do to them. *God, I loved driving this car. 120 mph and it felt like it had barely warmed up.* One of these days I was going to see what it was really capable of.

I called Dan. He picked up on the second ring.

"Yes."

"Dan. I've got a bead on Julie. I'm going for it."

"Are you sure? Maybe we should talk to them."

"Forget it. I know what needs to be done with them. Julie's coming home when I'm through."

"Are you sure?"

"Never more certain."

14

This was supposed to be a pleasure vehicle. But now rushing to the rescue and retribution of Julie's abductors, I felt more anger and hate than I knew possible. And I had marinated in plenty over the years. The angry growl of the engine as it changed gears, the squealing of the tires as it changed lanes and made turns. It was as though the car was a wild, vicious beast at my beck and call. And like a good and loyal servant, no matter how predatory its nature was, it would not be happy until it delivered me to my ultimate destination.

I drove the Vanquish until I came to the place I'd seen in my vision: MADISON MANUFACTURING. Julie was in there and I was going to see that she came out alive. I skidded to a stop and got out. In my vision, I had seen Julie on the third floor. That was where I was headed.

15

Dred, Gangsta, Bigsy, and Shank bounded up the stairs and burst into the executive lobby.

"Bad guys four, Punks zero," Bigsy exclaimed.

"I'm proud of the little guy," Shank said. "Capped one of those motherfuckers himself. Me, on the other hand," he said as he pulled out his bloody knife, "took care of the other three. I gotta go clean this thing off," he said as he walked down the hall to the bathroom next to the rear stairwell.

"Nice work, boys!" Brock said. "We're gonna have to dispose of the bodies. Then there's that cop car out there."

16

I walked to the front of the building, looked up, and leapt up to the third floor, shattered the floor to ceiling plate glass window, and stood on the ledge looking at my next victims.

"What the fuck!" Brock yelled. "Who are…? How the hell did you do that?"

"I'm your executioner."

"Shoot him!"

They opened fire simultaneously at the spot I had vacated. I bounced off the ceiling and ripped the throat open of a white man with dreadlocks carrying a shotgun while extending the spring-loaded sword into my right hand, I cut his head off and slit the throat of a short man holding a .357 Magnum as he was turning toward me. I then flew across the room at the man with a MAC-10 as he was turning in slow motion to me as I plunged my sword through his heart and extended my left-hand sword. I turned and took in the room. There was a small man and two women backing up to a door. Probably a stairwell. There was a big man, six foot five, I guessed, holding two smoking .45s, turning toward me, and a stocky man about six foot two, turning at me holding a Glock 9. As they prepared to open fire at me, I leapt across the room behind the women and the short man and cut them all down. I heard a trigger starting to be pulled from behind me and leapt in the air just as the shotgun blast fired. I landed behind him and ripped his throat out with my teeth. His corpse fell to the floor. I beheaded him. As the last two in the room started turning toward me, I flew at the wall to my right, bounced off it and landed behind the man with the Glock 9, and severed his head. I next retracted my swords and flew at the big man who was turning, once again too late to get me, and grasped him by the throat and squeezed hard, sinking my fingernails into his flesh.

"Where is she?" I demanded. My eyes aglow, the blood dripping from my teeth down my chin. He was trembling in fear. *Good*, I thought. *No sense in prolonging the inevitable.* I sank my teeth into his neck, and spit out a hunk of his flesh and veins, and drank deep as his heart pumped his blood down my throat as I drank my fill of this vile creature's life.

17

Kowalski pulled into the lot and looked on in amazement as he saw Falco leap from the ground and up to the third floor, shattering the plate glass window of MADISON MANUFACTURING.

He ran into the first floor and saw the dead gang bangers and cautiously moved across the room to the stairwell on the far left and started to walk up to the third floor. He heard automatic gunfire, shotgun blasts, and the reporting of .45s. He slowly opened the door and ran right into a man with a 10-inch tactical knife pressed into the throat of a blonde woman, who looked disheveled, bruised, and beaten.

"Back off fucker!" Shank said.//
"I'm the guy with the gun. Drop the knife!"
"I'll cut her!"
"Then I'll kill you for sure." Kowalski fired a round over Shank's head.

Shank said, "I warned you!"

Suddenly there was a rush of air. Julie's hair blew off of her face. Kowalski felt pushed back by an unseen force. Then Falco appeared suddenly behind the man with the knife, pulled the knife arm down, away from Julie's throat, and snapped the man's arm at the elbow, Julie falling forward. As she began to turn a sword ripped through the man's torso and quickly retracted as he fell dead to the floor. Julie collapsed, weeping in relief. Falco knelt and touched her hand. She looked into his face. "Rick? Is it really you?"

"It is and it isn't." He turned to Kowalski. "Thank you."

There was another rush of air and he was gone. They heard an engine turn over and the powerful engine of the Vanquish roared, accompanied by the squeal of tires as the sound of the engine began to fade and disappear into the night and police sirens grew louder as the police and ambulance approached.

18

I parked the Vanquish in its spot in the parking garage of the Broderick Building and took the elevator up to the sixth floor. I disabled the security and entered my apartment and locked the door behind me. I went into the bathroom and washed off my face and looked at myself in the mirror. Tonight was both a success and a disaster. Julie was safe, but she knew I was alive (well, sort of). I had underestimated Kowalski. As I was driving out of the parking garage this evening I saw him walking toward my building from my left. As I peeled out I saw him run back to his car and start to give chase. I outran him utterly. Yet he still found me. Still, he did help save Julie, and he could be trusted to take care of her and return her to Dan.

This place. This perfect place I had invested so much time, effort, and money in, may now be compromised. Once they complete the crime scene investigation at MADISON

MANUFACTURING, Kowalski will know the identity of his serial killer and where he lives. I'm going to need a couple of more places I can rotate between.

My website was still usable. But it no longer protected my real name as Julie, and now Kowalski knew that Rick Jason was alive (sort of).

I fired off an email to my real estate agent and told him to provide me with a choice of similarly situated properties I could purchase and develop in disparate parts of the city. I also wanted to consider some rural properties. Preferably remote locations. I hit send.

19

Kowalski drove Julie to a hotel they used for witnesses, parked, got out and walked over to the passenger side, and opened the door for her.

"Please follow me. We use this hotel for witnesses we're trying to protect. It's safe. You can clean up, get something to eat, and rest."

She got out, taking his hand. He shut the door and they walked through the main entrance and up to the desk.

Kowalski thought about the tearful conversation she had with her husband. He did find it curious she had called Falco, Rick. But to her husband, she called him Falco.

Kowalski said, "I'll call you in the morning. There are some details I'd like to ask you. Don't worry about the charges, though. It's all on the Detroit Police Department. Back there at MADISON MANUFACTURING, you called Falco, Rick. Why's that?"

"Ten years ago I had a relationship with a man named Rick Jason. He disappeared. Ironically, I contacted Falco to find Rick Jason. Now I learn that they are one and the same."

"Thanks, Mrs. Stone." Kowalski extended his right hand and they exchanged a warm handshake.

"No, Lieutenant Kowalski. Thank you."

"Just doing my job. See you tomorrow. He turned and walked out of the hotel lobby, got into his car, and drove off.

His phone rang.

"Kowalski."

"Frank. It's Rafer. I'm at MADISON MANUFACTURING. I think you'd better get over here. It looks like your guy's been busy."

"OK. See you in a few."

20

Detectives Rafer Johnson and Tony Rodriguez drove up to MADISON MANUFACTURING near Hastings and Piquette and parked on the street. There were five black and whites with lightbars flashing multi-colored lights in the parking lot in front of the building. There was a black and white in the street with a hole blown through the windshield. They walked up to the car and looked inside. There was blood on the passenger side seat.

"This must be the officer's car who was shot. I hope he's going to be OK," Rodriguez said.

They turned and walked toward the main entrance with crime scene taped all over it. They pulled their badges out and showed them to the first officer they encountered.

"Detectives Johnson and Rodriguez. What's your name officer?"

"Officer Robert Pecota."

"Can you tell us who's in charge?" Rodriguez said.

"That'd be Sergeant Franklin Perez."

Johnson and Rodriguez smiled. "We know him. It'll be a pleasure to see him again. Do you know where he is?"

"He could be anywhere in the building. I'd start on the first floor."

"Thanks, Officer Pecota," Johnson said as he and Rodriguez walked toward the entrance. As they neared the entrance, Perez walked out. He recognized them immediately, smiled, and offered his hand in greeting.

"Detectives Johnson and Rodriguez. Here to take over again? It's a real pleasure to see you gents."

"The pleasure is all ours, Sergeant," Johnson said as the men exchanged handshakes.

"Care to give us a walkthrough?"

"With pleasure. We've got a boatload of stiffs. Four on the first floor and ten on the third. Follow me."

They followed Perez into the factory level and saw four corpses strewn about. They were all black, wearing gangster garb. Their weapons lay near where they fell. One of them looked like a kid.

"The kid and two others were killed with a knife. A really big knife. I think it's upstairs. Somebody blew this other kid's head nearly off with a high-caliber handgun."

"Any ideas about what went down?"

"From where I sit these guys came in to do a hit and were just outclassed. These were street punks. Drug dealers probably trying to graduate to a higher level of crime. Someone probably offered them big bucks to do a hit. Didn't even make it upstairs.

"They had some serious shit with them. Street Sweeper Shotgun, an AR-15, probably fully auto based on some of the bullet holes in the concrete at the back of the room, little kid with an Uzi. The opposition reminds me of the weaponry we saw at the home invasion. Probable MAC-10, automatic shotgun. Most of the kills up close and personal. I'd say this was a one-sided gang war. Upstairs is a different story."

"Lead us up, professor," Johnson quipped.

Perez smiled and walked toward the central stairway and up to the third floor. Johnson took out his phone and rang up Kowalski on the way upstairs. After speaking to him he hung up.

When they arrived. Johnson and Rodriguez surveyed the scene of carnage.

"Holy shit! What the hell happened here?" Rodriguez queried.

"These killings are completely different. Most of them were killed with a sword or a large knife. Some of them look like they were killed by a wild animal. A lot of them were beheaded. The big guy over here looks like he's been drained of blood."

"You said three of the bangers were killed with a knife. Could it be the same guy?" Johnson asked

"Totally different wounds. Those vics look like somebody plunged in one of those military tactical knives with the sawteeth to rip their guts out as it's withdrawn. The vics up here were cut by something extremely sharp and clean. What I don't get is these guys had a serious amount of firepower at their disposal and somebody with a sword gets the better of them? From the looks of the room, they fired a lot of ordnance and hit nothing but the walls and ceiling. It's like an army of ninjas attacked them with a pack of rabid wolves. I've got no clue. Looks like CSI's going to earn their money this time."

"You said something about a knife."

"It's back here. Follow me."

They walked down the hallway, and turned right to the rear stairwell and came upon Shank's corpse. His ten-inch tactical knife lay on the floor next to his body. There was a gaping wound in his chest. His right arm snapped back at the elbow.

"Somebody with amazing strength did this to his arm. "

"And then shoved a sword into his back through his heart," Rodriguez said.

"Who's this Kowalski you called? You said this looked like his guy's been busy."

"Lieutenant Frank Kowalski. He's in SID. He's got a serial killer case he's working on. Bodies beheaded, drained of blood. Thing is, all the vics are scumbags, like these guys."

"Well, well. How're you ladies doing?" Lee Taylor asked, Detroit PD's gang expert, as he entered the room and walked up to his fellow policemen.

"Better than these stiffs. Any idea who they were?" Johnson asked.

"This is the late great Sikonolski gang. The probable perpetrators of the home invasion massacre of the other night."

"Any idea who the vics were downstairs?" Rodriguez asked.

"No idea. Just some useless punks itchin to get to the finish line before their time.

"Whoever did this did us a big favor. No lawyers. No juries. No long stays on death row. No endless appeals. Oh yeah!

Saved society a boatload of cash and saved a lot of lives to boot."

Just then Kowalski entered through the back stairwell.

"Detectives Johnson and Rodriguez. How's it going, Lee? Can you introduce me to the officer?"

"Sergeant Franklin Perez. Meet Lieutenant Frank Kowalski, SID," Johnson said.

Kowalski and Perez shook hands.

"Pleasure to meet you, Sergeant."

"Pleasure is all mine, Lieutenant. The detectives tell me this looks like the work of one of your perps. Tell me about it, if you don't mind."

"Not at all. The city's had a series of killings going back nearly ten years. Bodies beheaded, drained of blood. The primary thing the vics have in common is they were all scumbags and had it coming. We wanted to take them all down, but this guy got there first. You told me this looks like my guy. Can you show me?"

"Sure thing," Johnson said and ushered Kowalski back to the lobby area to view the carnage.

Part 4

A PROPOSAL

1

In the morning Kowalski arrived at the hotel. He had called Julie earlier and arranged to meet in the coffee shop for breakfast. He had some important questions to ask. He walked through the front doors and over to the coffee shop. Standing at the entrance he saw her waving from the back of the room. He nodded acknowledgment and walked to her table.

"How are you doing this morning, Mrs. Stone?"

"A lot better than last night. But I'm still pretty shaken."

"Is your husband coming to get you?"

"Later. I told him to take the girls to school and go back to work. That I had things to wrap up with the police."

"You told me Falco's real name is Rick Jason. That you knew him ten years ago. Can you tell me about him?"

"He was a man I was serious about. We both worked in the same office. I was in advertising copywriting and he in advertising sales. We went out to dinner and dancing and met a group of Goth types who invited us to a rave party in an abandoned hotel. Rick didn't want to go. I really wanted to do something different and exciting and insisted we go. Rick said okay and we went. I wish I'd listened to him. To make a long story short, Rick was savagely beaten and I was abducted."

"How did you survive?"

"Rick found me somehow and saved my life. I remember some things clearly and others in a fog. Their leader was a tall man named Victor Orloff. He moved with incredible speed and agility against Rick as he was trying to help me escape from the house I was imprisoned in. Now Rick is able to move as Orloff did, even faster. They drugged me and dressed me up in a beautiful lace dress with an appliqué of vines sprouting beautiful flowers. They pinned flowers in my hair and I was scented with lavender and jasmine.

"There was a terrible struggle, and I may have been hallucinating, but I saw orbs of power emitting lightning bolts into my body, and into the others. I lost consciousness. But I remember five beheaded bodies on the floor and one on fire. I think Rick killed them. I remember the house on fire and the moon was colored red: the Blood Moon. I remember Rick carrying me effortlessly, going so fast. It felt like I was weightless in his arms and he was flying. He then stopped and put me down. He asked me if I could walk. I said yes. We walked several hours back to my neighborhood. Rick told me to go the rest of the way by myself, which I did. He told me he would come by in the morning. I never saw him again, until last night. I think something terrible has happened to Rick and somehow I'm responsible."

"I saw Falco, er Rick do superhuman things last night. I saw him leap from the ground floor through a plate glass window on the third floor. Ten heavily armed, hardened criminals are all dead, all hacked with a sword or an inhuman bite. The ones with the bite were all beheaded. We saw the last man die. The way he snapped that man's arm at the elbow, I didn't know was possible. We saw the sword that killed the others. I heard a tremendous amount of gunfire. Still, Rick managed to kill all of them before saving you again. There were four more dead on the first floor."

"Do you think Rick did it?"

"No. They were gang bangers. I think the guys upstairs did it. One was shot in the head with a .357 Magnum. The other three were knifed, one in the back, two in the neck. No, the guy who did that was the one holding the 10-inch tactical knife to your face. The one Falco killed with the sword."

"I want to see him."

"I do too, but not for the same reason."

"Do you know where he lives?"

"I think so."

"Can we go today?"

"Alright, but I'm not sure he's up yet."

Kowalski was a rational man. He dealt in facts, not fantasy. The facts suggested a fantastic interpretation. That something happened to Rick ten years ago that turned him into Falco, a creature possessing superhuman powers with a thirst for blood and a sweet tooth for retribution.

2

Kowalski drove Julie to the Broderick Building. He found a parking space on the street near the front and got out. He and Julie walked to the main entrance and over to the elevator.

"Excuse me," the man behind the desk in the lobby said. "There's restricted access to this building. I'm afraid if a tenant doesn't approve you. You can't go up."

Kowalski walked over to the reception desk and pulled out his badge.

"I'm here on official business and I could use your help."

"Officer?"

"We're looking for someone and have a reasonable belief that he is a tenant here. Do you have a list of tenants?"

"Yes. But it's confidential. Our owners have spent a considerable amount of money to guard their privacy."

"Could you please share the list with me? Don't make me get a warrant. I can't stand the delay, BS, and red tape that entails."

"Okay, Lieutenant."

"Thanks."

by Randall Moore

The receptionist/security guard pulled up on his computer a password-protected gateway. He typed the password and entered the page that showed the layout of the Broderick Building, the units occupied and their location.

Construction on the Broderick Building began in 1926 and was completed in 1928. It was 35 stories tall and at the time of its construction was the second tallest building in Detroit. It was originally named the Eaton Tower after Theodore Eaton, Jr., an importer and dealer in chemicals and dyes. The Eaton Tower was purchased in 1945 by David Broderick, an insurance broker who changed the name of the building. He created the Sky Top Club on the 33rd floor of the tower, which was a private club used for entertaining Broderick, his associates, and guests.

"Can you print me a list?"

"It's going to be pretty big. We have roughly 150 tenants."

"Just give me the men and the corporations."

"That will leave us with 117."

"Big number," Kowalski said, glancing over at Julie. "That's a lot of doors to knock on. You want to attack this the old-fashioned way?"

"Yes," she said nodding. "I have to know more."

"Okay. But first I need to send Falco a message."

Kowalski pulled out his smartphone and typed an email to Falco.

We need to meet. It's not what you think. I think we could help each other. I'm in the lobby. I'm prepared to knock on every door. You'd make the job easier if you'd tell me which number to come to. What you did last night? Amazing, incredible, admirable.

Lt. Kowalski

I was in my tomb when the email alert beeped. I had forgotten to leave my smartphone in the main apartment rooms. My eyes blinked open. I pulled it out of my pocket. It was a message from Kowalski. I read it and sighed.

This is accelerating faster than I'd expected. He's going to find out soon enough. I might as well let him in and hear him out. I could still kill him. I'd never killed a cop before. But we're talking about survival.

I sent him an email:

606. Was hoping for 666, but the room numbers don't go up that high.

I hit send.

Kowalski's phone chirped. He opened the email, read it, and showed it to the receptionist. "Looks like an invitation to me."

"Okay. I'll open the elevator for you and give you access to the sixth floor."

"Thank you very much," Kowalski said and smiled while walking with Julie toward the second elevator door, which had opened for them. They got in, pressed 6 and rode up.

I pressed the switch to open my tomb, rose from my short, slumber, and climbed out. As I had slept in my clothes from last night, I decided to change. I stripped naked, walked into the bathroom, rinsed my face, hands, and arms with water, and dried off with a hand towel. I then went to my dresser and selected black silk trousers, a crimson silk shirt with plunging neckline, and a long flowing black silk robe. I pulled out Victor's bloodstone ring and put it on the middle finger of my left hand.

I next walked over to the refrigerator, pulled out one of the bags of blood I kept, poured a juice glass full, drank it down, felt the energy course through my veins.

I sat at my computer workstation and brought up my webcams, watched, and waited.

The elevator finally reached the sixth floor, stopped with a thunk and the door opened. Kowalski and Julie walked out.

"What room is it again?"

"606."

They walked down the hallway and arrived in front of room 606. Julie walked up to the door, reached her arms up, touching the top of the door, uncertain what to do. She looked for an eyehole but saw nothing. She stepped back and spied a black dot above the door. She looked up with tearful eyes.

"Rick! Rick! Let me in! There's so much I need to know. There's so much I now remember. Please, Rick! Please! You broke my heart! I moved on. I got the life I always wanted. But there's something missing! Let me in and let me see you. Prove what I saw last night isn't another hallucination!"

Kowalski stepped up and looked into the webcam silently.

I was stunned. Julie was here. The woman I had secretly protected for the last ten years. I had been her guardian angel or devil, whichever may be correct. I had protected her from dark forces and saved her from dark forces again. I loved her, but I knew I could not have her unless it was in the loathsome bloodlust that now consumed my heart.

Kowalski. Sly Kowalski. He must have surmised that Julie would soften my black heart. I looked at him on the computer screen and saw an intelligence and cunning I had missed on our earlier meetings. Perhaps I was too arrogant: Victor's flaw. Overconfident: Victor again.

No. I would listen to Kowalski and to Julie. I owed her the truth and Kowalski would know as well.

I walked to the front door and hit the switch that unlocked it. The security doors retracted. I opened the door and welcomed them in.

Julie approached me and attempted to embrace me. I glared at her and shook my head, and motioned for everyone to enter the living room and take a seat.

"I could offer you coffee. I don't drink it myself, but I bought some years ago. Keep it in the freezer just in case. I don't have very many visitors."

"Sure. Coffee sounds great," said Kowalski.

"Me too," Julie said.

"That settles it. Coffee for two."

I opened the freezer and pulled out a can of coffee beans, measured 4 tablespoons into the grinder, and ground it for about fifteen seconds. I reached into the cupboard and pulled out a filter, loaded the coffee from the grinder into it, put it into the filter basket, slid it in the coffee maker, filled it with about four cups of water, and turned it on. I next put the coffee beans back into the freezer.

"Falco. Or should I call you Rick? Julie says that's your real name. She's got some catching up she wants to do. I have a proposal for you. It's kind of crazy. But I think it might make sense for both of us."

I looked at the two of them. I had conflicting emotions. The blood from the bag had toned down my bloodlust, but it was always beneath the surface. I considered the two requests and chose Kowalski, as Julie's presence here was so unsettling, I felt I had lost my mind.

"Lieutenant. Tell me your proposal."

"Well. You possess an ability to see things no other man can see. You also have agility and strength that is beyond anyone I have ever heard of. I think we should work together. I seek the worst of the worst in society. From what I witnessed, so do you. I would never have believed it until I saw you leap through the third-floor window of MADISON MANUFACTURING from the ground floor! And the way you dispatched the man with the knife who held Julie? He never had a chance. And I'm glad he didn't.

"I want you to help me solve particularly heinous crimes. We try to serve society the best we can, but cases bog down in the courts, lawyers argue technicalities. Sometimes the innocent go to prison. Sometimes the guilty go free. I want you to help me balance the scales of justice so that the guilty never go free."

Kowalski's proposal resonated with me. "Interesting proposition. Something I've been practicing in the shadows for the last ten years. I do have a certain hunger that needs to be sated. Is that included in your proposition?"

"Yes."

The coffee was just finishing up. I got up and got out two mugs, and poured each a cup and brought them to the coffee table. I then reached into the cupboard, and pulled out some non-dairy creamer and sugar, and placed those on the table as well.

"Not terribly fresh, I'm afraid."

"It's no problem. I drink it black," Kowalski said.

Julie took some of the creamer and sugar and stirred it into her cup.

"And you, Julie?"

"I've pieced a lot of it together. I remember more than I'd let myself remember from the time with Victor. I know it was you who saved me. I know it was you who took Victor's power and killed him and his servants and rescued me. I'm afraid I now know and maybe always knew why you disappeared. You broke my heart, Rick. I now know that I love you, that I've always loved you, and will always love you. I want to kiss you the way we kissed before our ordeal. My heart will always be yours."

I trembled at her words. This was more than I had ever dreamed I'd hope for. Love was not for my kind. Retribution and vengeance in the service of bloodlust were how I'd channeled my unholy desires. But the love of a woman? Impossible.

Yet I had been devoted to Julie and her happiness from before the time of my change. I couldn't deny her then. I couldn't deny her now.

"Julie. I have made many sacrifices for you. I am a creature that drinks the blood of the living. There is a thin veneer that keeps me from drinking yours. It's a trick I play on myself. A sleight of mind. I take my ordinary unholy bloodlust and seek its satiation in the life of a killer. Most like me don't know this trick. It's far easier and more savage to feast on the first thing in front of you. I suppose I'm unusual for a vampire. I actually have standards and discipline," I said while laughing aloud and shaking my head.

"Vampire?" Julie said.

"Afraid so. That's what Victor and his crew were. They'd nearly killed me, but I now have this," I said displaying the bloodstone ring on my left hand. "I also have Victor's knife."

I leaped up, pulled open a drawer in the living room, and pulled out Victor's enormous and jagged obsidian knife, and showed it to them.

"Victor took it from an antique dealer he killed in Mexico City. It belonged to an Aztec High Priest who used it to cut the hearts out of sacrificial victims."

Julie's eyes widened as she looked at the obsidian knife. A look of terror flashed across her face. She calmed down.

"I remember. You killed them all. You had become as powerful as Victor and destroyed him. I can't believe you're as evil as him! There is good in you! I know it!"

"Good? Does good slaughter an entire room of human beings?"

"Give yourself a break, Falco," Kowalski said. "Those guys were scumbags and needed killing. You killed them and I say thank you very much."

I dropped my hands, and lowered my gaze, and then looked up.

"You guys catch me at a particularly vulnerable time. I would like to get some more rest. Perhaps we can continue this chat in the evening?"

"Thanks for seeing us, Falco. Remember my proposal."

"Of course, Lieutenant."

They rose and let themselves out. I closed the security door and returned to my tomb.

3

I awoke at 8 pm. The sun had gone down. It was my time now. I walked into my living room and approached my workstation, woke up the computer, and logged into my email account. There was a fresh email from Kowalski. I clicked on it.

Falco. I have a case I need help with. I don't care if I solve it. I just want the perp stopped. Can you meet me to discuss?
Kowalski

I typed a reply:

How about the Starbucks at the end of my block? Say 9 pm? Falco

I hit send and waited.
A minute later I got his reply:

I'll be there.

This turn of events caused me some concern. I mean, I had this serious gig as a Psychic finder of lost children with a pot of blood at the end of the rainbow. Still, I felt in danger. Kowalski was looking for me. I was the serial killer he was looking for and he now knew who I was. He couldn't subdue me or overpower me, but he was still a danger to me. I decided to meet and hear him out. I dressed in my leather and shades, let myself out into the hallway, and walked down the stairway to the lobby and into the night.

I walked down the street toward Starbucks and peered through the window. Kowalski was there. I walked inside and sat at the table opposite him.

"Well, Lieutenant?"

"Thanks for coming, Falco. I need your help. The city needs your help."

"What do you want from me?"

"I have one particular case that has haunted me for years. I'm in SID. I'm in charge of special investigations. Your case was on the front burner. I wanted to find you and arrest you, but now that I found you, I can't deny that I admire you. That I approve of what you've done. You've provided justice that society has voted 'present' on. I've closed the file on the bloodless beheadings cases. There are a lot of cases in the backlogs, but there's one particular series of killings that has perplexed me for years. The fact that the victims were all prostitutes has led to a systematic neglect of their value as human beings, but I always felt that they deserved dignity, justice, vengeance and retribution. I think I have a fresh new victim tonight. Would you care to accompany me to the crime scene?"

"Have a trap for me? You could never hold me."

"Falco. You misread me. I want your help. I want you to find the monster who's been doing this, and you know, do what you need to do."

"So you won't interfere?"

"That's why we're here. An impossible puzzle. All minds stumped. The brilliant genius, Falco, solves the case and eliminates the perp. Justice served."

"What do you want from me?"

"Come with me to the latest crime scene."

"Okay."

I got into Kowalski's car and rode deep into the city. I paid no attention to where we were. We pulled up to a house surrounded by cop cars, lights flashing, yellow tape surrounding the doorway. Kowalski parked and got out. I followed suit and we walked to the front door.

"Hello?" the cop at the door said.

"Kowalski. Lieutenant, SID. This is one of my cases. This is my consultant."

He looked at Kowalski's badge, at him, and then at me skeptically. He dropped his eyes, and lifted them up again and said, "OK. Go on in."

We walked through the front door and into the house. It was ugly. There was blood on the sofa and blood smeared on the walls.

Sergeant Perez was in the room.

"Kowalski?"

"Sergeant. We meet again." They shook hands.

"Your friend?"

"This is Falco. He's my consultant."

"OK, Falco," he said as he extended his hand in greeting. I took it.

Kowalski asked, "Where's the body?"

"Bedroom. Back."

He pointed at a door to a hallway and led us to the threshold.

"This is where I butt out. I don't need to see it again," Perez said.

We walked through it, turned left, walked to the back, and into the last room.

There she was. Her face a mask of blood and exposed flesh. Her hair matted in blood. Her ribs bruised from savage blows. And the knife wounds. She had been stabbed multiple times. Once in the abdomen, once through each breast. Her face was slashed and the killer had plunged a knife into her torso about fifteen times. Clearly angry overkill.

"What do you want from me?" I asked.

"We've come upon these killings over the years. They seem to come in spurts. We had 12 in the 70s. 15 in the 90s. 6 in the early 2000s and now this. The first in a new series. I believe all the victims were killed by the same killer. But we are no closer to an identity than we were 40 years ago. I don't really care who gets the credit. I want this animal killed."

I dipped my hand into her blood and tasted it. It tasted good. My mind rushed out into the city. I came upon a bus driver. His name was Raymond Carver. He lived in the Mumford district. I saw his home and him in it. I saw him kill the prostitute and a parade of his victims rushed before my mind's eye. A total of 79 came before me. Far more than Kowalski's estimate. Each one a person with a mother and father and siblings and men who loved them and never forgot them, hoping they would return someday. 79 women with compromised dreams and tragic ends. They would never return. All at the hands of this beast: Raymond Carver. I looked at Kowalski and smiled. He nodded his head and I left.

Raymond Carver. He was black and 69 years old. He lived on Norwich Road between Oakdale Blvd. and Ridge Road.

Tonight I didn't need my car. I levitated and floated toward his neighborhood. I reached about 1500 feet, began to descend, and dropped into his backyard. I glided up to the second floor, found the outside door unlocked, and entered the house.

It was a nice home. Lovely woodwork. I floated down the stairs toward the kitchen. There were children's crayon artworks adorning the refrigerator door. A door opened. I ducked around a corner. A large black man came down the hallway and walked toward the refrigerator. He opened it, pulled out a large container of orange juice, and drank in deep. I revealed myself. His eyes opened wide. He spilled some juice on his chest.

"What the fuck?"

"Raymond."

"What are you doing in my house? How do you know my name?" he whispered.

"I know more than you could ever imagine, Raymond."

"What are you talking about?"

"The women you've destroyed. The lives you've taken. Tonight's the reckoning."

"I haven't hurt anyone. You're fucking crazy. Look at my refrigerator door. I'm a grandpa!"

"There're a lot of grandpas who've hurt people. I know you. I know your crimes."

"I've committed no crimes!"

"Really? I was just at a crime scene where a nude prostitute had been stabbed 15 times at least. Her face slashed, her breasts stabbed. That wasn't a crime?"

"I don't know what you're talking about. You have the wrong guy!"

"No, Raymond. I have the right guy. I tasted her blood and it led me to you. You're definitely the right guy."

Raymond began to get fidgety and clearly nervous. "What the fuck are you talking about? I've never killed anybody, ever."

"Never killed anybody, ever?"

"No never."

"Raymond. You're lying."

"I'm not!"

"I suppose this dialogue has become unnecessary."

"Please leave."

"In due time," I said as I reached over to him, bit the flesh out of his neck, and drank his blood down. I was incredibly sated. I severed his head and took it with me this time for the first time. I hoped to add a bit of mystery to the event. I dropped it in an alley across town. I then went home.

My phone rang. It was Kowalski.

"Falco."

"Was that good for you?" asked Kowalski.

"Yes. It was exactly what I had in mind."

4

The next day I put on my sunblock and visited the blood bank. I had a signed order from Dr. Carter of Detroit Metropolitan Hospital for 25 units of blood.

I thanked the clerk and took the product down to my Civic and drove back to my apartment.

I felt good. I had drunk my fill last night. I had dispatched a scumbag and now I had blood. A stopgap measure to sate my desires. At my core, I still needed a kill for it to be complete. But the blood kept those desires at bay.

I logged onto my email account. There was a message from a woman in Ann Arbor pleading for help with her missing husband (probably ran off with another woman).

Another email from a man asking me to find his missing wife. (probably ran off with another man). And then there was an email from Marie Sanders. It melted my heart.

Dear Falco,

I am alone. My mom went out two nights ago with her boyfriend. She never came back. I called her boyfriend. He didn't know where she was and didn't care. I called the police. They said to wait and call back in 2 days if she was still gone. They also said someone from social services will visit me.

I'm 9 years old. I love her very much. I need her. Help me. I'm afraid.

Marie Sanders

I sat there for several minutes contemplating the scenario before I responded.

Falco the Dark Angel

Marie,
I want to meet. I may not be able to help you, but I can learn your mother's fate if you help me. I will waive my normal fee.
Falco

I looked at my message, slightly disgusted at my sentimentality. Still, the girl needed help and I felt the urge to assist.

My email beeped. It was a reply from Marie.

Falco,
Please help me. I live at the intersection of Court and 7th Street in Port Huron, MI.
Marie

I'll be there in an hour.
Falco

I marched down to the parking garage and got into the Vanquish, I liked driving it to MADISON MANUFACTURING. I was going to enjoy driving it to Port Huron.

I pulled out my radar detector, put it on the dash, and pulled into the street. I punched the accelerator to the floor. The engine roared to life and accelerated with great velocity. I took the I-375, which became the I-75, took exit 53B, and got on the I-94 to Port Huron. I then opened it up. 90, 100, 110, 120, 130, 140. All the while looking for cops while passing cars with their horns blaring. I am going to help this little girl no matter what.

I reached a stretch of open road without cars in either direction and pounded the accelerator to the floor. 150, 160, 170, 180, 190, 200, 210, 220. The road was long and straight and I was exhilarated with the speed and the acceleration as the scenery flew past me at speeds I had never before experienced. I took my foot off the gas and started to coast. The sign said, Port Huron, City Limits. I exited at Lapeer Avenue and took a right. I slowed until I got to 7th Street and made a right. Four streets down was Court Street. I pulled over and parked. I had made the journey in forty minutes.

I walked down to the intersection. The home diagonally across from me had the porch light lit. The others were dark. I crossed the street twice, arrived in front of the house, and walked up to the front door. I knocked. I listened intently. I heard the soft and light feet of a child walking toward me. There was a sound of something being dragged across the floor and the sound of metal colliding with wood. I heard something metal being pulled to the side. It was the peephole in the door and I sensed an eye viewing me.

"Who is it?" a high-pitched, plaintive cry came.
"Falco."
"You came. Is it really you?"
"I drove too fast. But I liked it."
"I'd like to go too fast sometime."
"Maybe some day I'll take you for a drive."
"I'd like that."
"Is your mom home?"
"No." She started to cry.
"Would you like me to come in and help you?"
"Yes!"

The deadbolt was extracted and the door chain released. The door creaked open.

Before me was a most exquisite looking little girl. She would, of course, hate that description, being nine years old and all that. But she was so vulnerable and alone and losing her innocence that I felt my heart breaking for her.

"What's your Mother's name?"
"Martha."
"The way this usually goes is you get me a recent photograph of your Mom and a personal item. Something she wore often that might have her scent."
"Are you a bloodhound?"
I laughed. "Something like that. Bring me those things and I'll see what the next step will be."

Marie left the room and was gone for about seven minutes. I was getting a bit antsy (I swear, I suffer from ADD), and then she returned. She handed me a picture of her mother in a picture frame.

"It's from my room."

She next handed me a red scarf.

"It's her favorite."

I smiled at her. "Thank you."

She smiled back at me and sat down.

I looked at the picture and smelled the scarf. My spirit rushed out of the room, through the grid of the city until I came to Peavey and 28th St., just south of South Park, north of Electric Avenue. I saw Marie's mother. My heart sank. She was drunk and stoned. She was passed out. She was in no condition to come home to her beautiful little girl. I was angry with her.

"Marie," I said. She looked up at me with hope, the hope only a nine-year-old can hold.

"Can you help her?" she said.

"I don't know."

"She hurts herself a lot. Me too. I was hoping you could help. Can you?

I felt tears collecting in my eyes. "I'll try, darling. I'll try. No guarantees. People make bad decisions sometimes. Pride makes it hard for them to admit they made the wrong choice."

She touched my hand. "It's OK, Falco. I'm so happy you came here tonight to help me. No one else will."

"I promise I won't let you down."

I left the house and stood on the porch. I set my mind's eye on the location of Marie's Mother. I levitated to 500 feet and flew toward Peavey and 28th. I descended slowly and arrived in the front yard. I walked over and looked into the front window, through the gap in the curtains. I saw her, passed out on the couch.

I sensed someone approaching from behind and elected to wait. There was the cocking of a gun that was pressed up against the base of my skull. I froze.

"What are you doing, fucker? Peeping? Wanna see someone fuck? Cocksucker! Fucking perv!" he said as he smashed his gun into my head. I fell down to the ground. That was my way of letting him know that he had won. Problem is, it didn't hurt.

I feigned unconsciousness as he dragged me into the living room.

I looked at the unconscious woman and saw her chest was heaving. She was drawing breath. She was alive.

The man who had smashed his gun into my head and accused me of sexual improprieties was in the kitchen. I contemplated the blow to my head. His hand had delivered the blow. All of a sudden I was at his high school. He was fucking. The girl was screaming at him to stop. It was rape. I fast-forwarded to college. He offered cocaine to a girl on one condition, that she blow him. He then smashed her in the face. I fast-forwarded to the present. He had a woman on the top of a skyscraper. He angrily threw her over the edge to her death. I was seriously disliking this guy.

I slowly rose.

He turned and saw me. "What the fuck?"

"Game over."

He pulled out his gun and fired it at me. But I wasn't there anymore. I was above him and diving for his neck, which I bit into, slurping his gushing blood and snapping his wrist holding the gun, tossing it harmlessly to the right while enjoying his slow demise.

He was dead. I severed his head with my obsidian knife, took it into the backyard, and threw it into a trashcan I conveniently found there, and walked back inside.

Marie's mother was comatose. I touched her hand. Nothing.

I punched in a web search for emergency rooms. The St. Joseph Mercy at 2601 Electric Ave. was the closest. I activated the GPS app I had downloaded onto my smartphone, entered the address, and pressed start. The cool thing about it is it didn't give turn-by-turn instructions. It just displayed the destination and my proximity to it. Since I wasn't driving a car it was perfect. I picked up Marie's mother, walked into the backyard, and began to rise slowly into the night. The GPS informed me I was nearing my destination. I saw the hospital and observed a group of trees about a block south of Electric Avenue and another block west. I descended with Marie's mother in my arms amidst a group of trees and carried her toward the hospital emergency room.

I walked up to the emergency room entrance. The automatic door opened and I walked in. There were couches lining the walls interspersed with chairs. CNN was playing on the TV. There were 3 people waiting. I lay Martha on one of the couches, walked to the receptionist's area, and knocked on her frosted glass window.

"Excuse me. I saw you come in. We're a little understaffed right now. Please take a seat and someone will see to you and your friend."

"This woman needs immediate medical care. Her name is Martha Sanders. I'm leaving."

The receptionist reached for the phone and started dialing. "Excuse me, sir. You'll have to wait."

Probably dialing 911. I walked out and rushed instantly to the group of trees that had shielded my arrival. They now shielded my departure as I returned to the intersection of 7th and Court. I descended quietly, walked to Marie's door, and knocked. She came to the door and let me in.

"I have news for you."

"Yes?" she said, with pleading eyes, tears starting to form.

"I found her."

"Where is she?"

"You were right. She isn't well. I took her to the hospital, St. Joseph Mercy Hospital."

"Is she going to be OK?"

"I don't know." I brought the listing back up on my smartphone, wrote down the phone number, and handed her the piece of paper.

"Call this number. Tell them who you are, and who your mother is, and that you know she is there. They'll be able to help you."

"Falco?"

"Yes."

"Can I hug you?"

"Yes, child."

She walked toward me, trembling, and reached out to me as I kneeled to be near her. She wrapped her arms around my neck. I felt her tears streaming down her face, wetting mine. Her stifled sobs gaining power and then fully convulsing her body. I patted her on the back and kissed her forehead.

"You see? Everything is going to be OK. Call the number and let them know who you are. I need to be going now."

I rose and stepped back from her, and walked to the front door. I opened it and walked outside.

"Thank you, Falco! I love you!"

"I love you too, Marie." I had to stifle a tear of my own. I walked to my car, got in, started it up, and started to drive back to Detroit. All the while I could see Marie silhouetted in the open doorway watching me leave.

Part 5

THE GANG RESURGES

1

Frank Morgan had always been fascinated by the occult since before he could remember. He had devoured the books of H.P. Lovecraft, Dennis Wheatley, Algernon Blackwood, Rudolf Steiner, and Anton Lavey. He had always suspected there was an arcane door secret knowledge would help him open, and then walk through. He attended séance after séance seeking an authentic medium. He had taken college courses on the occult and delved into parts of the city where the occult was regarded as fact. And now he had done it. He had found and consorted with a gifted psychic who was an authentic medium that taught him how to conjure ancient spirits to seek their counsel and guidance in business and in life. The psychic bequeathed him a panel that became a window to distant events as they were happening. She taught him how to activate it with his mind. Frank had become a conjurer, and was serving a malevolent and powerful dark spirit, a spirit he had never seen, who would ask for his help from time to time.

He had witnessed the massacre at MADISON MANUFACTURING and the strange, terrifying creature that had dispatched an entire gang of dangerous criminals in a matter of moments. His gang. For now, a major source of income was gone and he would have to figure out how to get it back.

He picked up his phone and dialed Raymond Chang. It rang eight times and went to voicemail. Chang's voicemail played. "This is Raymond, Leave a message." Then the beep.

"Raymond. This is Frank Morgan. I want to talk to you about a business proposition. We have an opening at the Sikonalski group. I think you're the man for the job." He hung up and waited.

Five minutes later Morgan's cell phone rang. He looked at the caller ID. It was Chang. He answered.

"Morgan."

"This is Raymond Chang."

"First thing you're going to have to learn is to answer on my first call. When I call, it's important that I reach you."

"There are a few things that take precedence over answering my cell: bathing, taking a shit, and fucking. Otherwise, I'm there for you."

"Fair enough. Reason I called. The Sikonalski gang is no more. They're all dead. Their job is available. Interested?"

"Sure. Where's my 450K Sikonalski took from me? I want that back."

"That's mine for now. You're on probation. Now, if you decide to join me, and do the job right, 450K is chump change. I'm talking 1.5 million in a month if you deliver."

"How am I gonna build the business up if I've got no seed money?"

"I'll provide the seeds. You provide the sprouts."

2

Raymond Chang was seething inside. *That fucker Sikonalski had stolen my stash. Somebody killed him and his gang and now Morgan is offering me his job*, Chang thought. *Need to do this delicately. The punks Dell hired to take them out were worse than useless. Have to make sure Morgan never knows.* He picked up his phone and dialed up Jerry Jaworski, one of the few people who walked out of the Chattanooga Avenue massacre.

"Jerry. I need to meet with you. The fuckers who killed Marcus, Brad, and Cindy are dead and their boss wants me to take his place. Can I count on you?"

He hung up and waited. Five minutes later his phone rang.

"Sup," Chang said.

"Is this legit?" Jerry said.

"Big man down his team. We have a chance to move in and make a major score. He said $1.5 million in a month."

"What about our stash?"

"He says that's his. Same as the other fucker. He's offering three times as much in a month. I think we should do it. He's gonna fuck us up if we don't."

"You think we can really trust him?"

"Not really. But we can't afford to appear not to."

3

Frank's phone rang. He looked at the Caller ID: Dominic Dorigo, his main contact with the syndicate. He pressed answer.

"Morgan."

"Frankie! How you doin, buddy? We gotta get together soon and break open a couple a bottles of wine! "

"What do you have in mind?"

"You know. The usual. Caymus, Kosta-Brown, Marcassin, Schrader."

"Sounds tasty."

"Come over tonight. Say 7:30. We'll grill some steaks and drink some wine. You can stay in the guest room so you don't have to worry about Detroit's finest."

"Sounds great, Dominic."

"So it's set. I'll see you tonight."

"Great. There's something I want to talk about."

"Same here. See you tonight."

They hung up.

4

Stephen Richards was feeling exhilarated. He was paragliding from one of the abandoned towers of Detroit. He maneuvered through the canyons of the city, headed down to his friends and customers, and pulled up for a landing. There were a great many whoops as he glided home across the pavement.

"Fucking awesome, Steve!" Darrel exclaimed.

"Right on! Who wants to go into a tower?" he shouted.

The whoops of approval drowned out the naysayers.

"Then it's settled! We're going to explore that tower!" he declared while pointing to the horizon.

"Yeah!" the cry rose up. "Yeah! Let's kick ass!"

"As part of our tour of abandoned Detroit, we're going to explore some of the art-deco masterpieces that have inhabited the city since the 20s.

The group was touring as Abandoned Detroit Tours. They were staying in abandoned buildings around the city, trying to find the most memorable sites to be had.

"Do you see that tower over there?" Stephen cried, pointing to the Bradbury Tower.

"Yeah!" The group roared. "Let's take it."

"Yeah! Let's go!" said Stephen.

5

Frank pulled up into Dominic's driveway on Arden Park. The home had once been owned by the founder of K-Mart, but due to the urban blight that was Detroit, Dominic bought it for a song: 6 bedrooms, $125,000. An old style mansion from the 30s. In its heyday, it was worth 3.5 million dollars. Dorigo had made quite a killing.

Morgan walked to the front door and rang the bell. It sounded like chimes.

Tony Califano, Dominic's enforcer opened the door.

"Come on in, Frank. Dominic's in the kitchen."

Frank felt a little uneasy seeing Tony. It didn't necessarily mean anything, but Tony's presence meant this was going to be a serious meeting.

The big front room was sumptuously decorated. To the right were leather sofa sectionals with an enormous glass-topped leather ottoman/coffee table with end tables and chairs. To the left was an enormous dining room with a long mahogany table and chairs. The walls were filled with family photos in elaborate gold leaf frames. There were several dramatic landscape paintings. At the rear of the room was a reproduction of *Rain in an Oak Forest* by Ivan Shishkin, depicting a couple walking with an umbrella during a light rain. The painting was filled with soft light, featuring luminous highlights and deep greenery. The wall to the left was adorned by a reproduction of *The Heart of the Andes* by Frederic Edwin Church, a lovely scene of mountains and forest with a waterfall at the center, a grave marker, and snow-capped peaks in the distance.

Frank followed Tony through the door, into the kitchen and family room. Tony picked up a wine glass filled with white wine.

"Hey, Frank! Grab yourself a glass," Dominic said as he was trimming six enormous, well-marbled New York steaks. He had a big glass of red next to him.

"Hi Frank," Paula Dorigo said. "Good to see you." She was making a salad, a glass of white wine at her side. The aroma of potatoes baking in the oven was intoxicating.

"What've you got?"

"Just what you see."

There were open bottles of Marcassin Chardonnay, Pahlmeyer Chardonnay, Kosta-Browne Pinot Noir, Caymus Cabernet Sauvignon, and Schrader Cabernet Sauvignon. Frank grabbed a Riedel Burgundy glass and poured himself a modestly large pour of the Marcassin. He swirled it in his glass and put his nose into it. He detected aromas of lemon, lime, apple, pear, caramel, and buttered popcorn. He took a sip.

"Wow. That's really delicious. Deeply concentrated with a thick, viscous mouthfeel, complex flavors, and a long finish. I've heard this stuff was great. I could never find it. You always bring out the good stuff, Dominic."

"You gonna drink may as well drink great wine."

"Here, here honey," Paula said raising her glass in a toast.

Frank clinked glasses with the others, took another sip, and relaxed a bit.

The kitchen had a huge granite-topped island in the middle of the room with dual sinks in it. There were granite-topped counters on the other three walls. There was a large Wolf Range oven and stove, a stainless steel Sub Zero refrigerator freezer as well as another set of dual sinks.

The kids; Peter, Francesca, and Dino; were in the family room opposite the kitchen. They were streaming *Cow & Chicken* from the Cartoon Network on the 90-inch LCD monitor on the wall.

"Check out these steaks, Frank."

Frank walked over to the cutting board where Dominic was working. The steaks were 2 inches thick and exceptionally well-marbled.

"USDA Prime, baby," Dominic exclaimed.

"How do you prepare them?"

"I got a special rub I made. Kosher salt, smoked paprika, lemon zest, black pepper, cayenne, and thyme all mixed together. I rub both sides with it and then with crushed garlic. Douse it with red wine and olive oil. Come out back with me," Dominic Dorigo said, chinning Frank toward the sliding glass doors.

Frank followed Dominic out the back door and onto the patio. There was a large gas grill built into brick and granite. There was a wet bar, a refrigerator, and a smoker. There was a large patio table that was set with seven places.

"Here's the grill. It's hooked up to the natural gas. I can cook on it 365 days a year under the awning."

He turned on the gas and pressed ignite for each burner in turn.

"Six burners in total. I'll preheat it to 700 degrees. Throw the steaks on for two minutes a side then turn all the burners off but the two outer ones, turn them to low, and 2 more minutes: perfection.

"What did you want to talk to me about, Dominic?"

"The Sikonolski deal. Tough break for us both. Have any ideas how to replace that income?"

"Turns out the dealers Sikonalski hit could be poised to move into their shoes. This guy Sikonalski spared, Raymond Chang, has his own supply lines into Asia. He's been bringing in primo smack from suppliers in Cambodia. He's got a coke network set up too. Some of the same guys we use. Some we didn't know about."

"Good news. Let's hope these guys are smarter than Sikonalski. He was a hot head and some of the psychos he had in his crew gave crime a bad name. Made us all look bad. Still, they made us a lot of money."

"You got that right. Here's to new beginnings," Frank Morgan said, tipping his glass to Dominic. They clinked glasses and took a sip.

"This is the life, Frank. Great wine, great food, family, and friends."

by Randall Moore

Part 6

ABANDONED DETROIT TOURS

1

In the latter part of the 19th century, inventors competed with each other to create a pencil that didn't need sharpening. What resulted from these efforts was the automatic pencil. Housed inside a metal case was a pencil lead, lodged in a metal spiral, held in place by a rod with a metal stud attached. Twist the cap, the rod and stud move down. In the early twentieth century came the innovation of the colored pencil. The graphite core replaced by pigments, dyes, clay, and gum.

Phineus T. Bradbury made his fortune in automatic pencils. His triumph was creating over 70 shades of colored automatic pencils. By the early 1920s, his net worth was over 800 million dollars. He had always had a passion for architecture, felt a need to leave a legacy, and hired architects to build a tower in the heart of Detroit.

Construction began in 1924 and was completed in 1928 in the style known as Academic Classicism, touched with a bit of Beaux Art and Futurism.

Bradbury died in 1946 and the building was inherited by his sons: Hampton and Horatio. The two brothers converted the penthouse into a private nightclub they used for entertaining clients and guests. They named it the Tip-Top Club. It was quite the place. Renowned jazz and big band singers and musicians played for enrapt audiences of revelers in the exclusive venue. Some of the luminaries that played the Tip-Top Club included Billie Holiday, Louis Armstrong, Ella Fitzgerald, Frank Sinatra, Billy Strayhorn, Benny Goodman, Jimmy Dorsey, Nat King Cole, and Duke Ellington. In the 50s artists like Chet Baker, Dave Brubeck, Bill Evans, Stan Getz, and Miles Davis would grace the stage of the Tip-Top.

After the death of Horatio in 1963, Hampton sold the Bradbury Tower to the Griffis Group, a real estate management company that leaped at the opportunity of ownership of a prestigious address like the Bradbury Tower. In its heyday, the Bradbury commanded some of the highest ground rents in the city, housing doctors, lawyers, city officials, and business executives.

As the city began its steep decline in the mid-70s, tenants began to move out, rents began to decline, vacancies multiplied and fortunes were lost. The Griffis Group offered the Bradbury for sale in 1996. There were several suitors for the Bradbury Tower but no takers.

Finally, in 2003, The Hidalgo Group purchased the Bradbury Tower. They had overestimated both the fortunes of the city and the demand for the building. They experienced grave financial difficulties and were forced to shut off electricity in the building, causing most of the remaining tenants to move out. The Bradbury was done.

In 2006 the Hidalgo Group declared bankruptcy and forced the remaining tenants out. The building has been vacant ever since.

by Randall Moore

    Stephen Richards led his merry band of intrepid Abandoned Detroit Tours into the Bradbury Tower, 38 floors, 475 feet tall. The group flowed into the lobby. It was near dusk.
    The lobby was crowned by an enormous beaux art dome. Dramatic ribbed sections of stone curved up toward double circular stone reinforcements. The ribbed glass sections were filled in with frosted glass panels. Every fifth panel contained a floral element. At the top of the dome was a square with glass panels displaying a floral pattern.
    "Pretty remarkable construction. The people who walked through here in its heyday inhabited an ennobled space to marinate in. Not holy, but close. It embodies the celebration of an advanced age now gone and decaying. It awaits renewal or final destruction," Richards said.
    "Heavy, man!" said Li Chen. Li was a second-generation Chinese-American who was fully assimilated. He sounded Anglo. He was a chemistry and physics major. He was lean, handsome, and analytical. He loved the outdoors and architecture. "What do you think, Annette?"
    "Pretty amazing. This is definitely a time gone by," said Annette Franklin, a petite, pretty woman with an amazing constitution. She competed in Iron Man competitions and stayed fit by climbing mountains, lifting weights, and running.
    "I find it ironic that an architectural adornment would exist in an age that wouldn't know how to recreate it. Kind of like how the West forgot how to make concrete after the fall of the Roman Empire," said Scott Stoner, a sensitive, smart man with a devil-may-care attitude, and a sense of humor that armors him from disappointment.
    "Fucking A!" said Michael Smith, a black New Yorker who could pass for white on the phone. He was bright, energetic, and handsome with a big heart. He really liked the ladies. "What do you think, Marlene?"
    "Awe-inspiring. It's amazing to realize that there are incredible interior spaces in this city that are totally neglected to the point of destruction," said Marlene Washington, a statuesque black woman with an amazing figure. She'd been

fighting the men off since she was thirteen. "What do you think, Cal?"

"You're right. There's nothing like this in Bozeman," said Cal Purcell, native of North Dakota, now from Montana. He's an outdoorsman and avid hunter on a lark, coming to the big, dark, dangerous city.

"All I can say is this is pretty cool," said Kevin Handy, an insurance salesman and weekend bicyclist and rock-climbing enthusiast. His wife, Liz, was a fitness freak, in incredible shape, and kept up with Kevin step for step.

"I didn't expect we'd find something this interesting to look at," said Rebecca Baker, who winked at Michael. Her husband Don pretended not to notice.

"Let's go," Stephen Richards said. "There's a few more places to see before we make camp."

He led them through a door and into what appeared to be a stairwell but was not. The group walked up to the banister and looked down and then up into a remarkable octagonal observation deck that served no other purpose than to allow the occupants of each floor to look up and down the center of the building. The stairs were off to the side. They were four floors from the bottom, but possibly as many as 34 floors were above them. This opulent use of interior space was meant only to delight the eye and inflame the imagination.

"Amazing," Chen said.

"Let's go down," Stephen Richards said.

Richards led them down the stairway, Darrel Carter taking up the rear. Stephens opened up a door at the bottom and walked into a long hallway. They entered an enormous lobby and walked through carved double doors that had images of deer and ferns. They walked into a once ornate theater with sculptured molding with columns and a baroque style dome. There was a filigreed screen to the right and a ruined stage at the center with stadium seating curving around the proscenium. It was lined by a baroque cornice and with incredible latticework carved into the ceiling and the columns. The seats had long ago been removed from the theater. Only the wooden platforms remained. It looked like a cathedral of the damned, its accoutrements now decaying. Broken pieces of its ornate filigree, having rained down on the floor, covering it in dust and debris.

"Let's set up camp here," said Richards amidst the debris. "Find a good place to lay out your sleeping bags and let's get ready for dinner. Darrel?"

"Aye, aye, sir!" Darrel Carter responded enthusiastically. Darrel was Richards' second in command. He shared Stephens' passion for extreme sports and was totally into base-jumping.

He took off his loaded backpack, unpacked the camp stove and the compact propane tank, and hooked it up to the stove. He next took out a large aluminum pot and some dehydrated casseroles: twelve servings of Beef Stroganoff. He pulled out 3-liter bottles of water, poured them into the pot, and lit the burner.

The group shuffled about finding individual nests to feather. Everyone selected a spot on the wooden platforms that once housed chairs for watching whatever performance emitted from the once glorious stage. The couples set up their sleeping bags away from the singles. The single men on one of the platforms. The single women set up one level above them.

"Hey, Cal," said Marlene. "Is it true what the guys are saying about you? Are you packing?"

Cal smiled and nodded his head slightly. He reached into his fanny pack and pulled out a loaded .45. "Yeah. Old hunter's habit. Never know if you're gonna need this for a surprise encounter with a bear, or... some old boy."

Marlene smiled and pulled out a Glock 9. "Me too."

The water started boiling and Darrel stirred in the dehydrated Beef Stroganoff stirring it meticulously. It was amazing how the previously inedible concoction began to soak up water and thicken, and actually begin to smell like food. Pretty tasty food.

"Soup's on!" said Darrel. "Bring your own dish and I'll fix you up."

The group shuffled and formed an informal queue.

"Hey, Marlene. What do you say we do some exploring of our own after dinner? I've got some places I'd like to show you," Michael said.

"Sorry, Romeo. I'm sure you do, but this girl's got standards to live up to. Besides you're too short for me."

"Size doesn't matter when you're horizontal."

"The only way you're getting horizontal with me is if I knock you out."

"I knew you wanted me. You sure do know how to sweet-talk a guy!"

She smiled at him and shook her head. She'd been at this game most of her life. She wanted a man in her life, but not one like Michael. She'd had enough Michaels to last a lifetime.

They shuffled through the line, got their night's meal, retreated to their sleeping areas, and ate their dinner.

"What do you think?" Kevin asked Liz.

"About what?"

"The food, the trip. Our adventure."

"The food sucks. The trip is kind of cool. So yes. I'm glad we came. This is one lunatic idea of a vacation, but I'm fascinated by this architecture."

"Glad to hear that, honey."

Rebecca Baker dug into her re-hydrated, freeze-dried dinner, and rolled her eyes. "Next time I get to choose our vacation. I think a cruise would be a lot more fun. At least the food would be better."

"There's a bigger selection of a lot of things."

"What's that supposed to mean?"

"I saw you looking at that black guy earlier."

"What's it to you? I can look all I want."

"That's not what I'm worried about."

"Look. I admit I've had my flings. But you don't have to throw it in my face every chance you get. Your attitude is getting a little old."

"Want a drink," Don said, pulling out a fifth of Grey Goose.

"Now you're talking." She pulled out her camp cup and held it in front of Don as he filled her cup. "Now that was real thoughtful. Thank you, Don."

"It's no big deal," he said as he filled his cup. They touched cups and sipped the fiery liquid.

Stephen and Darrel had set up their own area down by the stage.

"Here we are again," said Darrel.

"It just doesn't get old. This incredible place empty. It reminds me of some of the spots Sadaam's Republican Guard vacated after we drove them out of Kuwait. Ornate mansions, trashed by savages, trying desperately to leave their mark, like a dog peeing on a fence post. 'Bout as meaningful."

"What an amazing place this must have been in its heyday. Now just a ruin. What a waste," said Darrell.

"If the city ever comes back, someone might restore it. They also might want to knock it down and build something more modern in its place."

"I hope that doesn't happen. A place this special needs to be preserved."

"I'm going to turn in now. See you in the morning."

"Roger that."

Part 7

Moloch

1

What could only be called a demon lived in the penthouse of the Bradbury Tower. It had wings and horns like a ram and a snout like a wolf. It had eyes. They glowed red, but the irises were slits, like a reptile's. It had hands and claws. Its feet had claws as well. Its skin was tough and leathery as though layer after layer of scar tissue had built up only to have pus-filled sores erupt from the surface, heal, and erupt again. After years of neglect, the skin was truly frightful. Its name was Moloch.

There were four other creatures that lived just below the penthouse level. They were all like the demon, just not as fully revealed. The least devolved was a female. She could still take human form. And she was most beautiful and alluring, with long black hair and an hourglass figure with large breasts that stood high and firm on her chest and an ass that made easy prey of the men who naturally lusted after her. Her name was Diva and when she lured men back to her lair she transformed as she had sex with them. Her fingernails lengthened and hardened into claws as did her toenails. Her teeth became sharp and long. Her eyes glowed red, and her skin became wrinkled and leathery. She usually finished them off before they did.

The second female had lost all her womanly charms many years ago and was now just a vicious, hollow creature yearning, thirsting for fresh souls to consume. Her name was Lilith. She was nearly bald now. Only thin wisps of white hair fell from her skull. Her face was filled with sores. Her breasts were hollow, shrunken, sunken bags of skin. She had begun to develop claws on her hands and feet. Her teeth were permanently sharp and angular, very canine. She would grip her prey with her claws and rip their flesh with her powerful jaws.

The first male was a bit more advanced than Diva. In his human form, he was handsome, dashing, and sophisticated. He had black hair that was a tad long that women found attractive. They were happy to go home with him to experience a night of passion, which would happen, but as the evening progressed, and the sex became more intense, he would transform into an inhuman creature, not unlike a large rat with whiskers and saw teeth. He would bite the woman who had given themselves to him in the neck, the breasts, and the vagina. He always drew flesh and blood. Like Diva, his loathsomeness was only revealed when it was too late. His name was Fyren.

The second male, and the last of the coven, was the most devolved, and closest to the Master. He had sprouted a set of horns. While smaller than the Master's, they were objects of envy from the others. His claws had begun to develop and his face elongated. Instead of wings, he had developed a layer of skin, which when he opened his arms would spread out so he could leap out the window, glide on the wind, and surprise his next victim. His name was Malvoglio.

In the penthouse, Moloch, the malevolent stirred and rose. He breathed in and faced his urges. He walked over to the picture window facing downtown Detroit, exhaled a groaning, hollow, guttural howl and felt the deep longing, the deep need gnawing inside, commanding him to feed. He looked down and saw a woman walking alone on the street. He pushed the window open and leaped out, unfurled his wings, and glided into the night air, flapping here and there, and then gliding down toward the lone woman. With his two sets of claws extended, he grabbed her, bit into her neck, and began to drain her blood while ascending powerfully and swiftly to the penthouse of the Bradbury Tower.

As he cruelly consumed the life and blood of the woman, he reached out telepathically to Diva, Fyren, Lilith, and Malvoglio, and invited them to consume the scraps of his kill. They walked up to the Demon's lair and rushed forward to rip the woman's corpse apart and suck the blood out of every morsel of flesh, slurping up every drop of blood that stained the floor.

The penthouse was an amazing interior space. In its heyday, it could be reached by a private express elevator that was operated by a key. The key that operated the elevator also opened the door in the lobby that hid it from view. Since the elevators lacked the power to function, the only way to the penthouse now was through a secret stairway that led into the bowels of the building. There was a secret door on the eighth floor that opened into the octagonal platform and the stairway down or up.

The penthouse has high ceilings with dramatic views of the city. There is an outdoor patio that had a garden, long since left to death and decay. The main room was large and had a bar in it. There was a raised platform that could comfortably seat ten musicians and a dance floor in front of it. A grand piano had been pushed off, its top missing, strings exposed, broken, and destroyed.

A large chair now sat in the center of the stage with a table to the left. Moloch sat in the chair as though upon a throne. Diva, Lilith, Fyren, and Malvoglio approached him.

"Fyren, bring me the orb," he commanded.

Fyren went behind the bar, opened a cabinet, and retrieved a large sphere about 12 inches in diameter. It had a stand. He lifted it up and brought it to Moloch and placed it on the table to his left. The stone had been fashioned from an enormous bloodstone.

Moloch placed his clawed hands over it and encanted, "il diaspro sanguigno rivulano intrusi."

The bloodstone began to emit crimson light. Its surface became animated and began to clear, as it became a window to the bowels of the building. They could see the Abandoned Detroit Tours members sleeping.

"There they are. Right below us. You should each take one for your nourishment."

Diva, Lilith, Fyren, and Malvoglio entered the secret staircase and began to make their way down the stairs.

2

Michael woke with a start and felt the urge to get up and explore. He took his flashlight and walked back through the doors to the theater down the long hallway and into the octagonal stairwell. He felt drawn up the stairs. He walked up to the fourth-floor observation deck. There are four doors. He is drawn to the third. He walks up to it, turns the handle, pulls it open, and walks inside.

Diva was sitting on a large wicker chair. Her black leather top is plunging down to her navel, revealing the inner sides of her substantial breasts. Her nipples are barely covered. Her long raven black hair reached down to her thin waist and framed her striking face. High cheekbones, voluptuous lips, black eyes, and a slightly upturned nose. Her hips wide and inviting. Michael was stunned.

"I didn't know anyone else was here."

"I like to stay here sometimes," she said, rubbing her left breast. "But it can get lonely. Maybe you'd like to stay with me tonight?"

"I'd like that. What would you like to do?"

She rose from the chair, walked over to him, put her right hand on his left breast, and gave it a squeeze. He placed his right hand on her left breast and gave it a squeeze.

"I think I know what you have in mind," she said with a gleam in her eye.

They began to kiss and writhe in each other's arms, each exploring the other's torso with their hands. He grabbed her ass with his right hand. She pushed him back and removed her top, exposing her breasts to him. She smiled.

"You got it going on, girl," Michael said appreciatively.

"We're going to get it on."

She took him by the hand and led him to a mattress near the rear window.

3

Rebecca's eyes were open. In fact, they had been open since they had supposedly turned in. She was having another bout of insomnia. She looked over at Don who was dead to the world, his chest rising and falling rhythmically, obviously deep in sleep. She got up, rummaged through their backpack, retrieved a flashlight, and walked toward the entrance to the theater. She found herself wanting to return to the staircase with the concentric octagonal landings to get another look at it. She walked down the long hallway and opened the door. Walking up the stairs to the second landing, she noticed the first door was open. She walked over and went inside.

There was a strikingly handsome man sitting on a couch. He had long black hair that reached to his breasts. It was wavy and full-bodied and had been trained off his face. His forehead was high, his eyebrows thin and his black eyes sat on each side of his long nose. His lips were full and red and pursed into a smile. His jaw was square and his chin reached a sharp point. His chest was prominent and looked muscular under his clothing. His waist was thin, the stomach flat. His legs were long and powerful looking. His eyes sparkled, full of mischief and good humor.

"To which of the Gods do I have to thank for delivering me such a ravishing creature?"

Rebecca smiled, taking in the beauty of this remarkable looking man.

"Just dumb luck I guess."

"There's nothing dumb about your beauty. What's your name?"

"Rebecca. What's yours?"

"Fyren."

"That's an unusual name. What's it mean?"

"Wicked." He said it with a mischievous, conspiratorial tone.

"I'll bet you are," she said, charmed by this man.

He said, "Why don't you come over here and let me show you."

Rebecca smiled and walked over to the couch. Fyren stood up and kissed her hand. He turned it over, placed his lips on her wrist, and moved them gradually down, kissing her palm and fingertips. Rebecca felt goosebumps on her arms. Her nipples became erect. She stepped forward, grasped his head, and kissed him full on the mouth. He lifted her off the ground effortlessly, his tongue intertwining with hers. He laid her on the couch and sat beside her.

"I didn't think there'd be anyone like you on the tour."

"There's nobody like me on any tour," he said as he swept her up in his arms, kissing her face and neck, and nestling his face between her breasts.

Michael and Diva were completely naked and fully engaged in sexual intercourse. Diva was on top and in complete control. Michael had never been so hard and this was just what he needed on this trip. This was the most seriously out of control sexual experience of his life. But as their passion increased, he noticed subtle changes in Diva's appearance that began to become most pronounced. Tons of sweat was pouring off her skin. Her eyes seemed to grow red and he looked at her face, which had become a mask of lust and anger. Her skin had turned leathery. Her fingernails were now claws. She opened her mouth and her teeth were sharp and canine. She orgasmed while Michael came deep inside her. While they were relaxing in the afterglow of their sex, she ripped the side of his neck out and began gorging on his blood.

4

Don stirred from a dream and suddenly found his eyes open. He looked for Rebecca but her spot was empty. He looked up at where the singles were sleeping and noticed that one of them was missing. Michael, the black guy. *Great*, he thought. *My wife's off fucking some strange guy. Bitch. I should just ditch her.* Instead, he got up, rummaged through their backpack, and found his flashlight. Then he went off in search of Rebecca and, he presumed, Michael.

He left the theater and walked down the long hallway toward the stairway with the concentric octagonal landings that rose up the center of the building. He began to walk upstairs and noticed the first door on the second landing was ajar. He heard the sounds of passion emitting from the room. He walked over to the door and entered the room. Rebecca was naked and prone on the couch. Don was shocked to see her companion didn't look quite human. While he had long black hair and was repeatedly driving himself into her, he also had a long snout and rodent-like whiskers extending from his upper lips and cheeks. Then he smiled and displayed a set of elongated sharp canine teeth. Rebecca screamed as he ripped a chunk of flesh from her neck and slurped down her blood.

Don was overcome with horror and turned to flee the room and ran straight into Lilith.

Lilith was a most loathsome creature. There was no need in her for the mirage of seduction. Only the need to feed and destroy life. Her claws pierced through Don's skin and between the bones of the side of his chest and held him in a vice grip. He began to scream at a volume he didn't know he possessed. She roared as she ripped his neck open and greedily consumed his blood.

5

Scott woke up and looked around. Everyone else was deep in slumber. He was a light sleeper and had heard what sounded like a scream. Actually several screams. Blood-curdling was a term he had heard a lot. This sounded like that. It made his skin crawl, so he got up, dug out his flashlight, and walked out of the theater into the long hallway toward the staircase with the octagonal landings.

He walked through the doorway and saw an unbelievable sight. A creature that walked on two feet and had two small horns extruding from its forehead, leathery skin covered in sores with thick claws on its hands and feet. It had an elongated face that looked like it was melting. It began shuffling toward him and opened its mouth, revealing a sharp set of canine teeth. It emitted a groan and a howl. Its foul, fetid breath repulsed and sickened Scott. He turned to run, but the creature had sunk its claws into his back. Scott began to scream in utter horror, seeing his fate as Malvoglio first turned him around and then ripped his throat out, drinking from the spurting fountain of his blood.

6

"Did you hear that?" Marlene said, reaching for her Glock 9.

"Yeah," Cal said, reaching for his .45.

"Can we get a head count?" Stephen said.

"Looks like we're missing Michael and Scott," Annette said.

"The Bakers are gone," Kevin Handy said.

"I think we should check it out," Stephen said. "But only the people who are armed."

He pulled a loaded .45 out of his backpack. Darrel pulled one out of his. They walked up to where the singles were bunking.

"Anybody here packing?"

Marlene showed them her Glock 9, Cal his .45.

"Anybody else?"

The others shook their heads.

Stephen said, "OK. Bring your flashlights and move slow and cautious. I'll take point. I want you guys to cover me. If you have to shoot at anything. Make sure you miss me. I trust Darrel, but what about you two?"

"I'm a country boy. Guns are second nature for us."

"I grew up in the ghetto. Guns are pretty much second nature for me too."

"OK. Follow my lead and don't shoot unless it's life or death."

With Stephen in the lead, they made their way slowly down the hallway. The door was open and they could see Scott's corpse, in a pool of blood, a chunk of his neck missing.

"Shit. Nothing like this ever happened on any of our other tours," Darrel said.

They moved forward into the first landing and looked up. They saw four sets of what looked like glowing red eyes staring at them from the eighth landing. Then suddenly they were gone. There was a click and a sound of something sliding. It stopped. There was shuffling and then sliding again and then another click.

"Let's move upstairs," Stephen said.

They slowly made their way upstairs. Stephen in front, the other three training their guns into the darkness and made their way up to the second landing where Don's corpse lay just outside the first door to the left, his neck also missing a chunk, blood all around.

Marlene suppressed a sob, feeling a bit sick to her stomach. Cal touched her shoulder.

"It's OK. I feel it too."

She looked at Cal. Tears welled up in her eyes and a couple rolled down her cheek.

Cal said, "One time I was in the high country in Montana hunting deer. Pine forests, alpine lakes. Just beautiful country. Came across a mama bear and her cubs. The mama was foaming at the mouth. It had clear gone crazy and it was eating her cubs as they were trying to climb up to her nipples to feed. It was rabid. I puked as it continued to eat its babies. I took out my pistol and shot it in the head. Emptied my gun into it. There were only two cubs left. I picked them up and took them back to my camp where I fed them. I had to make some kind of harness to keep them from running away. I took them back to my pickup in the morning and drove them to an animal rescue place where they took over their care. I never found out what happened to them. I just assumed they were raised to maturity and released in the wild. Worst thing I ever saw in nature until this."

She touched Cal's arm. "Thank you."

"Shit!" Darrel cried out. "There's another one in here!"

They walked into the room and saw Rebecca Baker's naked corpse, a huge chunk of neck missing, and blood all over the place.

"You know we're going to have to get the fuck out of here. It's not safe to stay the night," Stephen said. Let's get back to the others and prepare to break camp."

"What about Michael?" Darrel said.

"I don't want to risk anybody else's life looking for Michael. We need to get the hell out of here. ASAP."

They looked at each other and started back down the stairway toward the bottom. Guns were raised and pointed at the unknown above.

They worked their way back to the theater.

Darrel said, "OK guys. Gather up your gear. We're leaving. This has been an unmitigated fucking disaster. Three of our people are dead. One is missing, presumed dead. My primary responsibility is to the survivors."

Everybody hurriedly packed up their gear and backpacks and left the theater, down the hallway to the stairwell where they made their way up to the fourth landing. As the others exited into the lobby, Darrel noticed a partially open door, pushed it all the way open, and saw Michael's naked corpse, his neck ripped open and blood on the bed and floor.

Marlene and Cal came up last. As Marlene began to make her way to the door to the lobby, a red-eyed beast with horns, claws, and sharp teeth landed on the floor between Marlene and Cal.

"Get out, Marlene!" Cal said as he emptied his gun into the head and torso of the monster. He ejected and slapped another magazine into his gun as Marlene whirled and fired off round after round into the beast.

"Come on, Cal! Move it!" she yelled at him. Cal ran past the beast and joined Marlene, but not before it slashed his right arm with its claws. Cal and Marlene continued to fire at the creature. It leapt up several floors and disappeared from view. They heard it land on one of the landings above them. They rushed through the door to the lobby and slammed the door behind them. Cal grabbed a bench and placed it in front of the door. He got another bench and placed it in front of the first.

"What the hell was that?" Stephen said

Cal said, "I don't want to wait around and find out. Let's get the hell out of this place. Marlene?"

"Fucking A."

Cal and Marlene ran to the exit, into the street, and disappeared down the boulevard.

When the rest exited the building, Stephen took out his cell phone and dialed 911.

"I want to report a murder. Actually, three murders."

Darrel showed Stephen four fingers.

"Four murders."

"Where are you calling from?" said the 911 dispatcher.

"Don't you guys have GPS tracking my phone right now?"

"Yes."

"Well, I'm right here. I'm not leaving. Send some officers over right away."

Five minutes later five black and whites pulled up.

An officer got out of the first car and walked over to the group.

"Who called this in?"

"I did."

"Who am I talking to?"

"Stephen Richards. And you?"

"Sergeant Franklin Perez. What's going on here?"

"I run a company called Abandoned Detroit Tours. We take groups into some of the architectural treasures that are falling apart in this city. We give them a last taste of the glory that once was Detroit."

"Sounds like a damn fool idea to me. Run into some gangbangers?"

"I wish. We could have handled some punks. This is worse. A lot worse."

"Maybe you should show us."

The other officers started putting up crime scene tape as Richards and Carter led Sergeant Perez into the lobby. They moved the benches Cal had placed in front of the door to the stairwell and opened the door.

"Better be careful. A couple of my customers were shooting at something in there," Stephen said. Perez and Richard pulled their guns out and walked into the stairwell. Carter joined them.

"Over here, officer," Carter said, leading Perez into the third door. They saw Michael's naked corpse, neck torn open, blood everywhere.

"Shit. They all like that?"

"Pretty much so. There're two on the floor two levels below us and one at the bottom."

They accompanied Perez down to the second landing where he saw Don Baker's corpse, and into the room that contained Rebecca Baker's naked body.

They then led Perez down to the first floor where they viewed Scott Stoner's corpse.

"Well. It's as you say. All of them killed similarly. Thanks for reporting this. We're going to want to have more extensive interviews with you and your people."

"Whatever we can do to help, officer. I'm devastated," Richards said.

"Let's get back up top."

They walked up and out into the lobby, and outdoors.

"The two who ran off. What were they shooting at?"

"I don't know, but they fired off a lot of rounds."

Perez addressed the other officers.

"We got a hot scene. Seal it off with tape. Don't touch a thing. Put a call into CSI and get them to send an emergency team down here. Also, put a call in for some detectives to come down here and begin an investigation. I've got to admit, I usually have a handle on these kinds of cases. This one I haven't got a clue."

Everyone moved off to take care of their duties. Perez pulled out his cell phone and dialed Kowalski.

He picked up after three rings.

"Kowalski. Sergeant Perez. I'm at a crime scene that looks like it fits in with some of the weird shit you're working on. I'm at the Bradbury Tower. Four stiffs with their necks ripped out."

"Jesus. Can't these fuckers take a day off?"

"In Detroit? Never!"

Kowalski hung up and stared pensively into space. He picked up his phone and dialed Falco.

Falco picked up after the fifth ring. "Yeah, Kowalski. What's up?"

"I've got a case that may require your expertise."

"What is it?"

"We've got four stiffs at the Bradbury Tower who've had their necks ripped out. I'm going to assume they're missing a substantial amount of blood."

"Am I a suspect?"

"No. You behead your victims. These heads are attached to their bodies."

"Sounds like I'd better bring a knife."

"Whatever you think is best."

"I'll meet you there in twenty minutes."

I opened the refrigerator, pulled out a bag of blood, poured a big glass, and slurped it down. It tasted good and nourishing. I pulled out Victor's obsidian knife and placed it into the sheath I carried on my back. I then put my black trench coat on over my leather jacket, let myself out of my apartment, and walked down to the parking garage where I got into my Civic and drove out to meet Kowalski.

When I got there Kowalski was talking with Perez. Perez eyed me as I came up on them.

"This guy again. You sure you know what you're doing Kowalski?"

"Sergeant Perez," I said offering my hand to him. "I only try to humbly help. I have the utmost respect for the difficulties and challenges of your job."

He took my hand, sighed, and we shook.

"Well, if Kowalski thinks you can help, I'll just have to go with his judgment."

"Thanks for your vote of confidence, Sergeant. I'll do my best."

"Take us to the stiffs," Kowalski said.

"Follow me, gentlemen."

Perez led us into the lobby and I marveled at the incredible domed ceiling overhead as we walked into a stairway with an amazing octagonal interior space. Perez led us into the third door on the floor, and we saw the body of a naked black man on a mattress, his neck ripped open and blood on the floor.

"Show us the others," I said.

Perez led us down to the second landing and the body of a man lying on the floor, his neck ripped open. He then took us into the first door on the left where he found the body of a naked woman with her neck ripped open.

Then he took us down to the first floor where we saw the last corpse: a man with his neck ripped open.

"Thank you, Sergeant Perez. I'll take over from here," Kowalski said. "You're dismissed."

Perez left us by walking up the stairway and exiting into the lobby.

"You know what I have to do?"

"I know, Falco," Kowalski said with a knowing glance.

I reached behind my neck and pulled the obsidian knife out of its sheath and beheaded the man on the floor. I then went up to the second floor, beheaded the man on the landing, and then the woman on the first floor to the left. I then headed up to the fourth floor and beheaded the man on the third floor to the left.

"It was necessary," I said. "There are too many monsters in Detroit already. We can't afford four more."

"Kind of screws up our crime scene. I'll have to have a chat with Perez. Do you think you can do what you've done before?"

"Why not?" I said as I dipped my hand into the blood of the man on the fourth floor. I tasted it. It tasted good. I started to project into the city and ran into a crimson wall. I pushed forward. The wall pushed back. I could see nothing.

I rushed down to the second floor and tried the same with each body. The result was the same. I was blocked by a crimson wall and saw nothing.

I ran down to the first floor and tasted that victim's blood. Again, my psychic powers were thwarted. It was as though my radar was jammed. I saw nothing.

"My powers are useless here. I see nothing. It's as though a greater power has superseded my powers. It's jamming my radar!"

"Any ideas?"

"Just one. There's a woman I need to see."

7

I got in my Civic and headed over to 666 Gehenna Street in search of Mama Midnight. It had been ten years since we met. She told me how to find Julie. She confirmed what I was to become. She told me she had ways of hurting me if I came back to see her. I was coming back but I had no bad intentions for her. I needed to ask for her help. I parked my car across the street about three doors down with a good view of the front door, waited, and thought. There was a sign to the left of her front door advertising PSYCHIC READINGS.

I hadn't tried to contact her for ten years. I mean, her threat was pretty potent and she seemed like the kind of person to come through on a promise. I dialed Kowalski.

He picked up on the fourth ring.

"Kowalski."

"It's me. I was wondering if you could run a reverse phone book check for me and get me a number?"

"What's the address?"

"666 Gehenna Street."

"OK. Let me call you back with the number."

"Thanks."

Five minutes later the phone rang. It was Kowalski. I answered.

"Yes?"

"The number's 779-2442."

I ended the call and dialed the number. She picked up after the seventh ring.

"Hello," she said in her sing-songy Caribbean accent.

"Mama Midnight, I need your help in something."

"Few peoples calls me by that name. How you know me?"

"Ten years ago you gave me some valuable advice. You helped me help someone very special to me."

"Tell me."

"I was bitten by vampires ten years ago. You told me I would change. You were right. I did change. I am a creature of the night now. You told me how I could find my girlfriend and because of you I saved her life and killed the coven while I changed."

"I told you I got ways to hurt you if you come back. You comin back?"

"That's why I'm calling."

"Go on."

"I learned to channel my bloodlust. I don't know why no one ever thought of it before. I suppose the hunger is so overwhelming that the need to feed supersedes any other thought. I have fed exclusively on criminals, killers, child killers, rapists, thieves, mobsters, pimps. Just one scumbag after another. Maybe you've read about my work in the paper? Headless body found drained of blood? Film at eleven? I may be a bloodsucker, but there's no need to make any more of us."

"So you telling me you be a good vampire."

"I'm still a monster. I've just discovered a way to be of service to society."

"I have noticed your crimes over the years. When I learn about the killed, I think it sounds like justice."

"I was found out by a policeman. He's asked my help in solving unsolvable crimes. I find them and they never hurt anyone again."

"So what do you think I can do for you?"

"You taught me I had innate psychic powers, which I have developed over the years. I have a business where I find lost people. But mostly I find kidnappers and murderers. They're my next meal. If I save a kidnapped person I demand and get a handsome reward. It's been very lucrative. I like to think of it as combining business with compulsion.

"Yesterday I was called to help at a crime scene that was obviously committed by vampires. Normally when I come to a fresh crime scene I merely taste the blood of the victim and my second sight leads me to the perpetrator where I have visions of the crime and crimes committed by the perpetrator. You know, I don't feel remorse about consuming these monsters.

"Anyway. There were four murdered. Throats ripped out, blood drained. I dipped my fingers in the blood on the floor and felt my spirit rush out toward the location of the monster that perpetrated this crime and rushed into a crimson wall that pushed back on me, breaking the spell, and I found myself falling back to my place. This repeated three times with the subsequent victims."

"I remember you. You done good for a demon. I remember the night of the Blood Moon. A house burned down. Five decapitated corpses burned. I knew was you. I thought you consume your girl. I never knew one of you could do like you."

"Julie's alive because of you."

"No, child. She's alive because of you."

"I need your help. I am blind in this."

"The ones you kill before. I knew of them. Victor was the most powerful. The others useless. You now face greater power. You take Victor's bloodstone?"

"Yes."

"Keep it with you always. It has powers it can channel for you."

"I have it."

"Good. The ones you seek have much more power than Victor. You may not be able to stand up to them."

"Can you help me?"

"Give me a day and call me back. I have something for you then."

"Thank you."

"Goodbye."

She hung up. I felt lost and uncertain of what to do next. I drove back to my place, parked my car, and went upstairs.

8

Julie was waiting for me outside my room.

She said, "I didn't know where else to go."

"You should go home to Dan and your girls."

"But I need to see you."

"Here I am. Happy?"

"Don't mock me."

"Sorry. But I took a great interest in ensuring your happiness. I guess I'm feeling a little unappreciated right now."

"Rick, Rick," she stepped forward and placed her hand on my right cheek and neck. "I've wanted to caress you and hold you for years. Don't deny me."

"You have a family now. This won't end well."

"Please!"

I remember how I'd been putty in her hands before. How I'd caved into her every desire and we were led into a nightmare that continued to this day. I grabbed her wrists and pulled them down to her sides.

"No!" I said forcefully. "This is wrong! You need to go back to your family!"

She looked at me, tears streaming down her cheeks.

"I'll leave now, Rick. But we're not finished."

She turned and walked down to the elevator. It opened and she rode it down out of my life.

I opened my door and secured my lair. I walked into the bathroom and looked into the mirror. Tears were streaming down my cheeks as well. I hadn't realized how much she had affected me, how much I was still in love with her, how much I wanted her, wanted to be with her. But it could never be.

9

Julie dialed Dan Stone. "Honey?"

"Julie?"

"Can you come and get me?"

"Right away. I've been so worried. The girls too. What's been going on?"

"I'll tell you when you get here."

"OK."

She thought of Rick. He was her one great passion. She knew it now. So long without him. Dan was wonderful to her and the girls. Even more than that. He was their father. But what she had experienced with Rick awakened the desire she felt at the base of her soul. "I'm a horrible woman!" She thought of leaving Dan for Rick. Dan was so attentive and considerate. Yet she felt passion for Rick. Self-loathing rose in her breast as she vowed to find a way to reconciliation between her passions and her reality.

She threw herself onto the bed and began sobbing intensely into her pillow.

10

I dialed Mama Midnight. She picked up after the third ring.
"Hello."
"It's me. You remember?"
"I remember."
"What do you have for me?"
"You come up against some bad, bad power. You up against two close to Victor's power and three greater. You need potions I gots, and you need God's love, which I know you ain't got."
"How do I break through their psychic barrier?"
"Come to my home."
"You sure? Last time I saw you, you said you had something bad for me."
"That's right, demon. Try anything, you find out."
"I won't try anything."
"Good. Come."

I hung up and left for the parking garage where I got in my Civic, powered it up, and drove out of the parking deck in the direction of 666 Gehenna Street.

I found a place on her street, parked, and walked up the walkway to her door. I lifted the enormous knocker and knocked three times. I heard the shuffling of feet. The door cracked open, held by the chain, and was confronted by the old, wise eye of an elderly black woman. I took off my shades.

"Better," she said as she slid the chain off the bolt, opened the door wide, and let me in.

"In case you be getting any ideas, I still have the means to hurt you."

"Thanks, Mama. You're safe with me."

"OK. First things first. You've found the most powerful coven in the Northeast. The leader, ancient. Maybe 4,000 years. The others are also formidable. One is 800 years. Another is 600 years. The two babes are 200 and 300 years each. Victor was 700 years and you defeated him, but you did so in the company of infants. They blocked you because they have a more powerful bloodstone than yours. They be living in the tower the murdered were found. You don't have to use your powers to see that. You just have to find their lair and kill them. Providing they don't destroy you first."

"You mentioned some potions that could help me."

"I only have a little bit. First I have a preparation for you. I ground up the bones of saints, mixed in a little holy water and wormwood, and stirred in a bit of hydrochloric acid, all wrapped up in a pretty little package with a bow. Throw it at them. It will break on contact and cause agonizing pain. I made twenty of them."

"Good."

"I've also prepared deadly herbs laced with an accelerant. Mandrake, Belladonna, and Henbane mixed with gunpowder and gasoline. Light the fuse and toss it. It will explode on contact and the deadly herbs will be infused beneath the skin. This will hurt them greatly and distract them. You have twenty of these.

"Finally, I want you to see what you are up against," she said, leading me to a sitting room off the side of the living room. I sat down. She pulled a drawer open, pulled out a dull flat pewter panel, and set it on an easel.

"Focus your mind on the panel and you will see."

I reached out with my mind into the panel as she said I should and I was amazed at what happened.

It was as though a light lit up from inside it. I now saw the inside of the room the evil dwelt in and the visage of each of them. I was horrified. Not just by their ugliness and evil, but by the knowledge that some people thought there was no such thing as evil.

I saw them all and knew their names. Diva, Fyren, Lilith, Malvoglio, and Moloch. The five monsters that ruled the Bradbury Tower. I now knew who they were. I knew they must die.

"Here. Take this panel. See them. Defeat them."

11

I went back to my apartment, opened the door, and secured it. I placed the pewter panel next to my computer and looked into it. I found that when I focused my mind on it, it began to glow from within and I could see the interior of the penthouse. There was a stage with a chair and a table, a dance floor in front of the stage, and a bar in the rear of the room. It looked like it had been a nightclub at one time. Probably a private playground for the rich and privileged.

As nothing was happening I used my mind to turn off the window into the penthouse, got up and walked over to the refrigerator, opened it up, took out a bag of blood, and poured a tall glass. It felt wonderful going down. Refreshed, I took out my cell phone and dialed Kowalski. He answered on the sixth ring.

"Kowalski."

"Falco here."

"Well, did you find out anything?"

"I did. Turns out there are five very dangerous creatures like me living in the Bradbury Tower. They killed those people. They will continue to kill until they are stopped."

"Can you stop them?"

"I don't know. They are all much older and more experienced than me. If I go after them it's kill or be killed. Either I destroy them, or they destroy me."

"Is there any way I could help?"

"I don't know. Probably not. I did get some potions from the psychic who helped me find them. They may have the capacity to hurt them, but I don't know how powerful they are. The only way to know is to engage them and that's risking it all."

"I appreciate what you've done for us so far and what you've done in the past. I'd like to help. There are some other officers who'd like to help too."

"The level of Evil I may face is beyond your ability to withstand."

"Doesn't matter who's first through the door. It's good to know there's somebody behind you who's got your back. I've got your back, Falco."

"Maybe these potions can help keep you safe. I'll have your back too."

Even though I possessed the potential for immortality, I knew that death awaits even the undead. I mean, Victor was gone by my hand. I could be gone as well. Frankly, it wouldn't be that bad a thing. A relief, actually. These urges. This desire. This foul compulsion would be over at last.

Still, if I died at the hands of these monsters, the living would face a curse I couldn't allow to continue. Therefore, I was determined to destroy them or be destroyed.

12

I decided it was time to visit the Bradbury Tower. I entered the stairwell of my building and walked up to the roof. The door was bolted. I unlatched it, walked onto the roof, levitated up 250 feet, and drifted toward the Bradbury Building.

When I reached the tower I circled it, looking for signs of life. Seeing none I descended and landed noiselessly on the patio. I thought I heard shuffling from inside the penthouse and levitated up about 250 feet further, hopefully unobserved.

One of the windows of the penthouse opened from a hinge and out leapt a creature with horns. With wings unfurled it soared through the canyons of the city. It suddenly swooped on a lone figure, a man, grasped it with its claws, and began to feed. It flapped its wings and reached up to the penthouse and through the open window.

It reentered the penthouse, gorged itself on the victim, and tossed it aside. It sat down on a chair on the stage and waited.

Falco the Dark Angel

Four figures made their way up from the floors below and fed on the scraps of the demon's victim. One of them walked behind the bar, opened a cupboard, brought out an orb, and placed it on the table next to the demon. It was an enormous bloodstone! It began to glow with a throbbing crimson light. Mama Midnight was right. My ring was minuscule in comparison.

Suddenly I sensed a consciousness attempting to penetrate my mind. I flew two miles away and landed on top of a skyscraper. I wondered if I'd been compromised. I then felt the consciousness attempting to penetrate my mind again in an effort to force its will on me.

I heard a rush of wind behind me and turned to see a creature approaching with its arms open with skin stretched from its elbows to its hips, gliding on the wind. It had horns and claws and was rushing down on me with its jaws open and claws extended. I sidestepped it and flew up to a steeple atop the building across the street.

I heard the flapping of enormous wings approaching me from above. I looked up and saw the demon rushing down at me with its claws extended and jaws open, saliva dripping from his razor-sharp teeth. I leapt off the building and flew down the street and made a left turn, taking refuge in the sheltered entryway of an abandoned office building. I'd been compromised.

I stood in the dark and waited. I saw the first creature hurtling toward me from my left and I heard the wings of the second as they prepared to converge on me. I suddenly leaped into the air to the top of the skyscraper across the street and flew twenty blocks away, taking sharp left and right turns. I stopped and listened intently. Hearing nothing, I leaped into the air, flew at an incredible rate of speed away, and dropped softly onto the roof of my building. I stood there silently for several minutes, listening and scanning the sky for movement. Hearing nothing and seeing nothing, I opened the door to the roof, bolted it behind me, and made my way inside and down to my apartment level. I entered my apartment and sealed it up.

I went into my tomb and rested.

13

In the morning I decided to visit Julie and Dan in Bay City and walked down to the garage. I looked at the Civic and the Vanquish. *What the hell?* I thought. *Might be the last time I drive it.* I unlocked the Vanquish, powered it up, and headed to the exit.

I made my way to the 75N and set my sights on Bay City and Julie.

The Sun was out in full force. Fortunately, I had my sunblock on, my fedora and sunglasses, and long sleeves. I parked the car and walked up to the door. It was about 1 pm. I knocked.

I heard a rush of little feet running toward the door. I heard the latch turn and the door opened a smidgen. A most delightful little girl looked at me with a smile on her face.

"What's your name?" I asked.

"Susan."

"Is your Mom and Dad home?"

"Yes." She said as she ran off into the interior of the house yelling, "Mom and Dad. There's a man here to see you!"

Dan and then Julie reached the vestibule.

Julie almost blurted, "Ri... Falco!"

"Are you really Falco?" Dan said. "I've wanted to thank you!"

I smiled and let his warmth enter me.

"Thank you, Dan. I was wondering if I could have a few minutes alone with Julie?"

"Of course."

"We should go to the backyard," Julie said.

"Alright."

We walked out the back door and strolled into the garden.

"Why did you come?"

"I face a challenge. I may not survive. I wanted to see you one last time. If that's what it is. I have something to tell you."

"What?"

"That I've always loved you. That I've always watched over you. I made sure that you ended up with Dan. I've always tried to make sure that your happiness would be secured."

She reached out and touched my face with her right hand.

"I now know that I've always loved you, Rick. I know things have changed, that we may never, ever be together. I don't know what you're capable of, but I love you and want you forever. Can I kiss you?"

I thought about it. What the hell? "Yes."

We embraced, our lips met. Her mouth opened as did mine. Our tongues entwined. I lowered my hands from her shoulders to her hips and pulled back from her.

"It would have been great if it had been you and me."

"It still could be."

"How?"

"I don't know. There has to be a way."

We walked back into the house.

"Nice to meet you, Dan," I said offering my hand to him.

He took it and we shook, I turned and left their home, got into the Vanquish, and powered it up down the 75S, back toward Detroit.

"What was that all about? I saw you kiss. Are you in love with him?" Dan said.

"Darling. You don't know what you saw," she said guiltily. "It was nothing."

"It didn't look like nothing."

Moloch looked into the bloodstone orb and laughed with a deep baritone.

"I think we may have found something this interloper may care about. Fyren and Diva? I want you to go to Bay City and bring this family to us."

I pulled into the garage and parked the Vanquish, got out, locked it, walked into the building, and up to my tomb.

14

Frank Morgan got up in the morning, showered, dressed, and went downstairs to the kitchen. Dominic was making espresso.

"Like a cup?"

"Definitely. How about a double shot?"

"Coming right up."

He fired up his dual boiler semi-automatic espresso machine and brewed Frank a double.

Frank took a sip.

"You sure know how to live, Dominic." He tipped his cup to Dorigo and drank it up.

"I'm going to have to run, Dominic. Fabulous dinner. Incredible wine. Give Paula my best."

Frank walked out the front door, got into his car, and drove to his place. When he got there his panel was glowing crimson. It was the dark spirit he served sometimes. He picked up the panel and opened his mind to the energy. He saw himself driving a limousine to the Bradbury Tower around the back at 8 pm, park and wait for riders who would come out to him. He agreed to the request in his mind and the panel faded to its natural color. He picked up the phone and called up one of Dorigo's limousine services, Dream Limo.

"Dream Limo," the voice of a cheerful young woman chirped.

"Let me talk to Gianni."

"Hold on. I'll connect you."

There were three rings. He picked up.

"Gianni."

"Gianni. It's Frank Morgan. I need to borrow a black Lincoln Town Car. The one that seats six passengers."

"I'll have it gassed and ready for you, Frank."

"Good. I'll be over this evening."

At 7 pm Frank drove over to Dream Limo, parked, went to the garage, and approached one of the attendants.

"I'm Frank Morgan."

"Yes, Mr. Morgan. We've been waiting for you. Right this way."

The attendant led Frank into the garage and pointed his limo out to him.

"This is the one. Black with blackout windows. Very private. Let me pull it up front for you. If you've never driven one before, handling them can take some getting used to. But it's a great vehicle."

Frank went up to the front and waited as the attendant pulled the limo out of its space and drove to the front. He showed Frank how the remote worked on the keys and traded places with him.

"Have a great time," he wished Frank.

"Thanks."

He put it into gear and drove over to the Bradbury Tower, pulled around back, and waited.

Within a few minutes, a door opened, and out walked two people. The first was a spectacularly beautiful woman wearing what looked like leather. She had long black hair and an hourglass figure. The other was a barrel-chested man with a slender waist and long, wavy black hair. He looked powerfully built and athletic. Morgan rolled down his window. Fyren came up to him and handed him a slip of paper with an address: 13657 N. Monroe St., Bay City, Michigan.

"We'll ride in back. We're bringing back four passengers."

Frank released the door locks to the back doors. Fyren and Diva got in.

Frank pulled away from the curb and headed to the 75N.

"Can you lock the doors so they can't be opened from the inside?" Fyren asked.

"Sure. Windows too."

"Good. When we pick up our passengers disable the doors and windows. We don't want anybody going anywhere else but here."

Where are we taking them?"

"Right back here."

"Very good."

Frank pulled onto the 75N and drove toward Bay City.

It was nearly 10:15 pm when the limo slowly drove up to 13657 N. Monroe St. Fyren and Diva got out.

"Wait here. This shouldn't take long," Fyren said.

Fyren and Diva walked across the street toward the Stone's house.

Julie was sitting at her computer working on her blog, answering posts, and compiling the latest information on the arts from around the globe.

Fyren and Diva floated over the Stone's backyard fence. They both concentrated and sent their minds toward Julie's and beckoned her to open the back door and come into the backyard.

Julie began to feel light-headed and suddenly had the urge to get up and go out into the backyard into the night air. She rose and walked to the back door, opened it, and walked out.

"Good girl," Fyren said, grabbing her to his chest, placing his hand over her mouth. "You know what to do, Diva."

Diva smiled, nodded her head, and entered the house. She looked toward Julie's room and saw that it adjoined another. *Probably the bedroom with the husband in it.* She turned left, and went down the hallway with two doors, opened the door to the left, and walked in. She saw Susan sleeping in her bed. She walked over and picked her up. Susan stirred and woke up.

"Who are you?"

"I'm a friend of your mother. Your mother wants me to bring you and your sister to her."

"I don't know who you are. My mother says not to talk to strangers."

"Now be a good girl and be quiet."

She carried her across the hall into Lucy's room, picked her up, and carried both girls out into the hallway when Lucy woke up and started crying.

Dan woke with a start and rushed out of his bedroom and saw Diva holding his girls.

"Who are you? What are you doing to my children?" he demanded.

Dan heard a sound to his left and saw Fyren holding Julie with his hand over her mouth, muffling her protestations. Dan rushed toward Fyren and threw a punch at his head. Fyren caught it with his hand and pulled him sharply toward him, head-butting Dan severely. Dan dropped. He looked at Fyren and then at Julie.

Fyren said, "Now let's be cordial. We're all going to take a little trip together. We have a car outside. I promise you'll be comfortable." Fyren flashed a dashing grin.

"What do you want from us?" Dan said, confused and frightened.

"You'll find out in due time," Fyren said.

"Let's get moving," Diva commanded.

They walked out the front door and down the street toward the limo.

"Our chariot awaits," Fyren said flamboyantly as he opened the limo's back door and pushed Julie in.

"Your turn," he said to Dan, who got in. Diva got in carrying the two girls. Fyren got in last, closed the door, and said to Frank, "Let's go."

Frank disabled the door and window locks, pulled the limo away from the curb, and headed back to Detroit.

They arrived back at the Bradbury Tower. Fyren and Diva exited the limo and escorted the Stones out. They returned through the door they came out of to get to the limo. Frank drove the limo back to Dream Limo, handed the keys to the attendant, got into his car, and drove home.

by Randall Moore

Part 8
THE RECKONING

1

I looked at the panel Mama Midnight gave me and focused my mind on it. It began to glow and then reveal the interior of the Bradbury Tower penthouse. I felt heartsick when I saw what it revealed. Julie, Dan, Susan, and Lucy brought through the stairwell before Moloch.

I called Kowalski.

"Lieutenant. I want you to know that I'm going in. The Bradbury Tower."

"Why the urgency?"

"They have Julie and her family."

"Give me an hour to see what I can raise on my end to help. I can't promise anything. At the least, I'll be there."

"Hour max. Then I'm going in."

Kowalski thought of the best justice-minded cops he knew and called them one by one. They were Perez, Johnson, and Rodriguez. He asked them to meet him at his home. They were there within fifteen minutes.

"Thanks for coming on such short notice. I didn't know who else to call, but you were it. You can back out at any time. No shame. Seems I've discovered who's been capping all the scumbags in my jurisdiction for the last 10 years. Thing is, I like the guy. He didn't mean to do it, but he's been doing our job. Not just our job, but from the cop up to the DA to the executioner, he's been doing our job. Worst of the worst. They're all dead once they meet him.

"So you got this vigilante…"

"I wouldn't say that exactly."

"What would you say?"

"Look. This guy's done a couple of hundred years of police work in the past few years. He's going up against some major bad guys who have been taking out citizens of our city. They've taken a family hostage. I promised I'd have his back. This is completely off the books. This is personal. I want to know if you have my back?"

"You put it that way, Kowalski, I'll have your back at the gates of hell," Rafer Johnson said.

"You might not be far off from the truth."

"You can count me in," Rodriguez said.

"Me too!" Perez said.

"OK. Get body armor, helmets, and whatever heavy artillery you've got. Shotguns, automatic weapons. Something tells me we're going to need it all.

Kowalski called Falco. He picked up on the second ring.

What's going on Lieutenant?"

"I've got three guys. I make four. We're ready to follow you into the Bradbury Tower."

2

Lucy and Susan were crying hysterically. Dan was shaking in fear. Julie looked at Moloch with disgust and revulsion. It was all starting again. When would it end? Fyren and Diva stood behind them.

Moloch looked them over with his glowing red eyes with the reptilian slits and said, "I had you brought here in hopes that your friend would come to help you. He will not be able to save you. We will make it quick when the time comes. You live because he still lives. When he dies, you die."

"What are you?" Julie demanded.

"Some would call me a demon," he said with a chuckle and a snort through his snout. "I've been called as much over the ages. The truth is I am very old and experienced in the petty weakness of men. I feed on your kind."

"You're a monster!"

"Yes. I am. I am more monstrous and powerful than you can ever imagine. Before the night is through you may yet witness my power and glory."

"Let our children go!" Dan exclaimed.

"They will be the first I will consume. And then we will consume you.

"Fyren and Diva!" he barked. "Take them to the bedroom in the rear and secure the door."

Fyren and Diva stepped forward. Dan and Julie turned and looked at them.

"No!" Dan shouted as he recoiled from them.

"Take us instead!" Julie shouted. "Let them go!"

"I've heard it all before," Moloch said, sounding bored. "You will all die for our nourishment."

"Please! No!"

Moloch began to cackle, first quietly, then louder, booming his voice into the room.

"Don't make this difficult," Fyren said. "Follow me. I think you'll find the accommodations comfortable."

"Alright," Dan said with a defeated look on his face, motioned for Julie to take charge of the girls, and followed Fyren to their quarters, Diva taking up the rear. They walked up a set of stairs and into a hallway. Fyren led them to the door at the end of the hallway, opened it, and directed them inside. There were two beds, several chairs, and tables. There was a single window. It was their sole source of light.

Fyren said, "Oh, the window? Just in case you're wondering, it doesn't open. If you did manage to smash it and climb through, you would experience a sheer drop of 35 stories to the concrete below. Not a pretty way to go, but quite effective."

Fyren closed the door and latched it from the outside and he and Diva returned to the main room and Moloch.

"They're secured, Master."

"Yes. I know."

Moloch reached out to Lilith and Malvoglio telepathically and beckoned them up to the penthouse level. They came up.

"Thank you, my children. I thought it would be best to shield our guests from your loathsomeness. My own appearance has caused quite a few humans to die of fright. To have them see all of us together could have had a most regrettable effect on them. We want the interloper to engage us in combat and then we will destroy him."

"Yes, Master," they both intoned.

3

I had asked Kowalski and his fellow officers to meet me in the alley below Billy Barkey's former apartment. Before departing I donned my shoulder harness with the dual spring-loaded swords and put on the sheath that held my obsidian knife and slipped it in. I next took my two .45s and placed them into the holsters at my sides. I then packed my daypack with eight loaded clips for the .45s, Mama Midnight's concoctions and a box of strike anywhere matches. I put the pewter tablet in as well. I then slipped on my bloodstone ring. I thought back to my battle with Victor and remembered the gas bombs I made that fateful night. I decided we were going to need some of those for this battle. I opened a drawer near my tomb that contained old linen and sheets. I gathered it all up and walked down to the parking garage, got into my Civic, and drove out into the night.

I headed first to a liquor store where I purchased a 20-pack of Coors Light in the bottle and a package of half-gallon re-sealable plastic bags. Tossing those in the back, I pulled into a gas station and asked for a 5-gallon container of gas. I gave the attendant a $100 bill as a deposit. He filled the container and I left knowing he hoped I wouldn't return and he would be $100 richer.

I then drove over to the alley, parked my car, and waited for Kowalski and his boys.

About five minutes later they drove up in two slickbacks, got out of their cars, and walked into the alley. I got out of my car and walked over to them.

"Hey, Falco," Kowalski said.

"Lieutenant Kowalski," I said, offering my hand in respect. "Who are your friends?"

"Sergeant Franklin Perez you know. May I introduce Detectives Rafer Johnson and Tony Rodriguez to you?"

We nodded in recognition of each other.

"Can you give us some intel, Falco?" Kowalski said.

I reached into my daypack and pulled out the pewter tablet.

"I figure the way this will make the most sense to you is if you see what we face."

My mind activated the tablet and it began to glow and then reveal the interior of the Bradbury Tower's penthouse. They could all see Moloch, Malvoglio, Lilith, Fyren, and Diva regarding each other."

"What the hell is that?" Perez exclaimed.

"They're monsters, not unlike me."

"But the woman and the man. She's really hot. He looks normal enough," Rodriguez said.

"Don't be fooled by their appearance. On the inside they are just like the others," I said, pointing at Moloch, Lilith, and Malvoglio. "You've never faced an enemy like these."

"What makes them special?" Johnson said.

"You don't believe they exist."

They all looked intently at Falco.

"Explain," Johnson said.

"These are creatures of the night. They have all been alive for a very long time. They are difficult to kill and have had a lot of experience defeating men who have tried to kill them. I am one of them, but I have chosen to follow a different path."

"You've got to be bullshitting us, man," Perez said, shaking his head.

"Really?" I said before I levitated one hundred feet into the air and drifted down, landing softly on the pavement before them. "Seen anyone do that lately?"

"How did you do that?" Perez asked.

"It doesn't matter how I did it. It's just that I can. And the creatures in the Bradbury Tower can also do things you will think are unbelievable. You have to believe what I tell you. Your survival depends on it. Otherwise, they will overwhelm you and destroy you."

"Why are you doing this, Falco?" Kowalski asked.

"They've kidnapped a family that is dear to my heart: Julie's family. I believe this is their way to force me to confront them so they can destroy me. When I die they will kill them. I must try to defeat them so they may live."

"How can we help?" Rodriguez asked.

"I'm not sure if you can, but I was moved by Lieutenant Kowalski's offer to help. I have a few items that might help you."

I dropped my daypack to the ground and pulled out the bags that contained Mama Midnight's potions.

"OK. It's not much, but it may help. I've got twenty of these. You toss it hard at one of those motherfuckers and it breaks on their body. Should cause them some pain and distraction. Should back them off. There's five each," I said distributing them to the men.

"The next one is a little trickier. It's got a fuse that you light. The business end is mixed with gunpowder and gasoline that will explode on contact and infuse deadly herbs under their skin. There's five each of these." I said, distributing them.

"Come with me," I said, motioning them back to my Civic. I popped the trunk and brought out the 20-pack, the re-sealable plastic bags, linen and sheets, and the gasoline.

"I'm alive today because I defeated one of these motherfuckers ten years ago. I made gas bombs and that made the difference. You gotta cut their heads off, though. Otherwise, they might come back at you when you least expect it and kill you."

We set about dumping out the contents of 20 beers, filling the bottles back up with gasoline, shredding the linen and sheets into strips, stuffing them into the mouth of the bottles. We then sealed each one up in a re-closable plastic bag. Then we packed the bombs into the empty 20-pack carton and put it in the Civic's trunk. Then I distributed the matches to them.

"OK. That's five bombs each. If you can take out just one of those fuckers, it'll be a tremendous help. Do any of you have a sword?"

They looked at each other. Their heads shook.

"Shit. We're cops in the 21st century," Perez said. "What the hell we need swords for?"

"Like I said. You might think you killed one of them, but the only way you know they're dead for sure is if you behead them. That's the way it works."

"How the fuck we supposed to get shit like that?" Perez said.

I activated my spring-loaded swords. They shot out into my palms.

"Fucking A!" Johnson exclaimed. "That's some badass shit!"

I released the trigger and they retracted into their harness.

"Reach out to me with your mind if you have one of them compromised. If I can come, I will, and I will end them."

"I've got an axe at home!" Perez said.

"Good. Bring it. Everybody bring something that can separate a head from a body," Kowalski said.

They each rushed off to their homes to arm themselves as well as protect themselves with Kevlar and bulletproof vests. Perez got his axe. Johnson found a hacksaw. Kowalski a pruning saw. Rodriguez a drywall saw.

We all drove to the predetermined spot 2 blocks from the Bradbury Tower.

After looking over what they'd armed themselves with, I smiled in approval of their latest weapons.

Each man also had a sidearm or two. Kowalski had a double-barreled shotgun and a .45 and a .38. Johnson had a fully auto M-16 as well as a Glock 9. Rodriguez had a Street Sweeper shotgun and two .45s. Perez had a MAC-10, a .45 as well as an RPG.

"Where the fuck did you pick that up?" Rodriguez asked Perez.

"Gun buyback program. Some banger's mom sold the RPG back to the city for $200. City never got it. Thought I might need it for a rainy day. I think it's raining."

"How many shells you got for that thing," Johnson asked.

"Four."

"Hope you can hit something with it," Rodriguez said. "How 'bout that MAC-10?"

"From the other night at MADISON MANUFACTURING. Never know when you're going to need superior firepower."

I said, "OK. I'm glad you all have some badass shit. Let's focus on the gas bombs. Each of you should carry two or three. We'll split the rest into two groups and leave them in two different spots in the building, so if you have to retreat you'll have a weapon waiting for you to deploy. Besides, we don't want those fuckers blowing them up. It's just like what your dad told you in baseball. It only takes one. Make sure it counts."

I opened my trunk and each officer took two gas bombs and placed them in their jacket pockets.

"What are you gonna do?" Rodriguez said.

"I think I'll go see what they're up to."

"Before you go," Kowalski said. "I thought we should review this floor plan." He produced a bunch of printouts and placed them on the trunk of the car nearest us.

"This is the Bradbury Tower's floor plan. Notice there's no clear path to the penthouse. There's a secret elevator that leads there. There is also a hidden stairway on the eighth floor in the center of the building. As there's no power to the building, the elevator doesn't work. So the stairway is the only way. I'm not sure how to access it, but for sure the entrance is on the eighth floor."

"Then let's go into the building and find it," I said.

We walked through the doors into the lobby that was crowned by the enormous Beaux Art dome. The men were awed by the now-extinct culture that had once built this city.

Kowalski pointed ahead. "There's the door to the central stairwell. Let's drop half the bombs to the right of the door and the other half to the left."

They divided the remaining twelve bombs and placed them as Kowalski suggested.

We walked through the door into the incomprehensible interior space, open to the top and open to the bottom, an octagonal series of landings with the stairwell off to the side.

I said, "OK. We're on the fourth landing. The secret door to the penthouse stairway should be up four flights."

We walked up to the eighth landing and paused, stumped.

"You said it was secret. Seems to be a pretty good description," Johnson said.

"Spread out. Tap on the walls. Push on them," Kowalski said.

"Wait a minute," I said. "Let's use logic and find out what doesn't belong here."

"What do you mean?" Kowalski said.

"Look over there," I said, pointing at the first door. "That wall is part of the room. See how it's repeated six times? Only six walls can be a part of a room. Then we have the stairway and this extra wall. It doesn't seem to be part of either a room or the stairwell."

"Yeah! You're right!" Rodriguez said, moving toward the wall I'd pointed out. He started tapping on it and pushing as well.

"Stand aside," I said. He backed off. I had noticed a slight erosion in a two-inch length of moulding at the top of the wall. I reached up and depressed it. It gave and there was a click. The wall was released and I was able to slide it open to the left.

We walked in and found ourselves at the base of a flight of stairs that led up to the top.

"Nice work, Falco!" Kowalski said.

"Just getting started."

Everyone checked their weapons, potions, and bombs. We looked at each other. Everyone nodded OK.

"Wait here," I said.

I levitated up the center, passing each floor slowly, looking for entrances until I arrived at the top and saw there was only a thin door to the penthouse. I floated back down to them.

"When you reach the top, concentrate your mind and think of me. If you encounter resistance, think of me as well. I will hear you. Let's go."

Where are you going?"

"To see what we face."

4

I walked out into the lobby, through the doors to the outside, and levitated upward toward the tower, circling it in the darkness, sensing what it must hold.

I alighted on the outdoor patio and walked toward the door to the interior, peering into the windows, and waited for the signal from the officers.

The nightclub was empty. I knew Julie, Dan, Susan, and Lucy were in there, but their abductors were not apparent. I decided to circle the tower again. On the sheer side of the tower, I noticed a window that had no fire escape. I drew close to it and peered in. I saw Julie, Dan, Susan, and Lucy huddled together, trembling. I floated above the tower, not wanting them to notice my presence or draw attention to myself when I sensed Kowalski tell me that they were in position.

I floated back down to the patio and psychically pushed my thoughts into Kowalski's mind, telling him it was time to go into the penthouse. I flew through and smashed the plate glass windows that stretched from floor to ceiling in the penthouse, sending shards of glass flying in all directions, catching and reflecting the light from the skyscrapers and moon as they settled to the floor. Kowalski and his crew smashed the door open and rushed in, guns at the ready.

No resistance. While a relief, it brought no comfort. I felt as though I was a mouse being toyed with by a cat.

I said, "Let's find them and take them out of here."

We moved carefully up the steps in the back of the room into the hallway that led to the back. I sensed that Julie and her family were behind the door at the end of the hallway. I tried to open it. It was locked.

"Julie! Are you in there?"

"Yes! We're in here!"

I gripped the locked doorknob and felt the anger and determination course through my veins. With a sudden movement, I forced it forward, ripping through the doorjamb, splinters flying, the door opening in my hand. Julie, Susan, and Lucy rushed to and embraced me. Dan rose with a hollow look on his face and walked toward us.

"Nothing's been settled yet. We're going to try to get you out, but they're going to try to stop us. Let's go!"

I led them into the hallway and down into the nightclub. Kowalski, Perez, Johnson, and Rodriguez were standing sentry, brandishing their weapons.

"Let's move toward the stairwell."

We moved cautiously toward the stairwell when an unholy howl sucked the oxygen out of our hearts as Lilith burst through the door to the stairwell.

There was an enormous flapping of wings. Moloch landed on the patio and strode into the nightclub.

"So you think you can just take them away that easily?" He boomed, laughing heartily, sending a chill through us all.

He faced the policemen. "Do you really think you can hurt me with your weapons?"

He lurched forward suddenly, causing the cops to snap their weapons to attention.

Moloch burst out into howling, mocking laughter.

Perez reached into his pocket, pulled out one of Mama Midnight's poppers, and tossed it at Moloch with all his might. It burst on Moloch's chest and the monster screamed in pain. Moloch fell back to the ground, clutching his chest where the popper burst on him.

Moloch snapped his head toward Perez and angrily demanded, "Where did you get that?"

"You don't need to know," I said and flew at him with my obsidian knife drawn and thrust it at his neck. He was too quick, though, and flew to the top of the room. Lilith rushed at us from behind, slashing at Rodriguez and Perez with her claws. I flew down swinging the knife at her, she retreated to a back corner, hissing and growling at us.

Moloch boomed out, "Malvoglio! Come and feed on the unbelievers!"

There was a rush of air in the room as a creature as loathsome as has ever been seen entered through the smashed patio windows, its red eyes and baby horns rising. Its claws and fearsome teeth exposed. It drooled in anticipation of biting through our flesh.

Returning the obsidian knife to its sheath, I leapt up and launched my swords into my hands, and slashed at the monster. Malvoglio dodged to my left and blocked my slash. I bounced off him, leapt at Moloch, and buried my blade into his shoulder. He knocked me to the floor. I stood and faced him.

Moloch had a shocked and pained look on his face. And then he cracked a smile.

"Perhaps you'd like to join me? I may have an opening soon."

"Don't think so. What did Moses say to Pharaoh? Let My People Go!"

"You're not in a position to challenge me!"

"I just did!"

Perez lit one of his gas bombs and tossed it at Lilith, who rushed into the stairwell, and down as the gas exploded harmlessly on the stairs, igniting them.

Johnson and Rodriguez each lit the fuse of the preparation laced with deadly herbs, gunpowder, and gasoline, and tossed them at Malvoglio and Moloch. They exploded on them and they shrieked in agony. Malvoglio rushed out the door and Moloch flew through the broken windows.

We quickly ushered the Stones into the stairwell and down, while smothering the fire, all the while as I put my eyes on Moloch and Malvoglio, watching to see if they dared follow us.

We worked our way down the stairs, through the flames, step by step. We slowly got down to the eighth floor and exited through the secret door into the octagonal stairwell. After walking quickly down to the fourth level, we entered the lobby.

Off to our left was Lilith. To our right was Diva. Fyren walked through the front door and they began to converge on us in a pincer movement.

"Get some gas bombs ready!" I shouted.

There was a crash of glass from above us. The dome had been breached. Shards of glass showered down on us as Moloch broke through and began flapping his unholy wings in flight. I took off after him.

Rodriguez, Kowalski, and Johnson each lit a gas bomb while Perez loaded a grenade into his RPG.

Suddenly Fyren, Lilith, and Diva rushed at them. Perez fired a grenade at Fyren who dodged the shell, which exploded on the entryway to the lobby, blowing out most of the windows. Johnson tossed his gas bomb at Diva and scored a direct hit. She burst into flames and began to howl in anguish, but had the foresight to rush backward and roll on the ground as Johnson ran toward her with his hacksaw in one hand, and his Glock 9 in the other. Diva crashed through what was left of the glass, rushed down the street at incredible speed, and disappeared from sight.

Simultaneously, as Lilith approached, Kowalski tossed his bomb at her, exploding on her right shoulder, setting her right side on fire. He rushed at her with his tree saw, but she smashed him with the backside of her right hand, knocking him back to the wall. He pulled out his double-barreled shotgun as she approached while in flames and let her have both barrels in the upper torso. The force of the blast blew her backward. Then she fled into the darkness of the night.

While this was happening, Fyren rushed toward Perez, who was reaching for his .45, while Rodriguez aimed his Street Sweeper at Fyren and let him have two quick blasts, lifting him off his feet, dropping him to the ground. Rodriguez grabbed his gas bomb, rushed forward, and tossed it at Fyren, bursting into flames on his groin, engulfing his lower abdomen and thighs in fire. Perez grabbed his axe and rushed to Fyren, who did a back flip of 25 feet and rushed out of the building.

5

I reached Moloch and thrust one of my swords at him, but he dodged it and zoomed toward the hole in the dome he had created when he smashed through it, entering the lobby. I flew up at him to attempt to block his departure, but he swept a clawed hand at me, striking me in the face, knocking me to the ground. As he exited through the hole in the dome, I took off after him, while telepathically sending a message to Kowalski to get the men to escort the Stones outside, into vehicles and drive far, far away from here.

"Let's move the family outside into the street toward our cars and get them the hell out of here!" Kowalski said.

Perez pulled out his MAC-10 and scanned ahead for threats while Kowalski, Johnson, and Rodriguez rushed back to the Stones.

"Let's go. Falco thinks we should make a run for it. I concur."

Julie looked at Dan who returned her gaze. They each took the hand of one of their girls.

"OK. We're ready," Julie said.

Rodriguez walked behind them and lifted the Street Sweeper.

"I've got your back!"

"I've got your front!" Johnson said, taking his position in front of them leveling his M-16 to the exit.

Kowalski reloaded his double-barreled shotgun and said, "I've got point. Let's move!"

The group moved cautiously, but quickly toward the lobby's exit doors and out into the night air, all the while scanning from left, right, and center for threats. As they walked down the concrete steps in front of the Bradbury Tower, crunching broken glass down to the sidewalk, they turned left and began to make their way toward their cars.

Meanwhile, I flew toward Moloch, who had attained an incredible rate of speed and altitude, with his wings flapping. Every time I got close he would swoop down and then rise up. I was chasing, but not closing the gap.

Moloch suddenly did a steep dive toward the ground. I attempted to follow, but he was too far ahead. At the last instant, I saw him pull up and pluck a homeless bag lady off the street, and fly up toward the Book Tower ripping her to shreds, consuming her life's blood, and tossing her lifeless corpse on the top of the Book Tower. He landed next to what was left of the corpse.

I flew up above Moloch, glaring at him.

"I see you're wearing the ring," he said mockingly. "The ring you usurped from my cousin, Victor. I want it back!"

"Come and get it!" I angrily replied.

"In due time. You will soon regret having ever challenged us!"

"You won't have time to regret when I am through with you!"

Suddenly, gunfire rang out from the street below. Moloch's eyes glowed red as he chuckled and then emitted a full-throated laugh. "Looks like your friends are in trouble!"

6

Kowalski, Perez, Johnson, and Rodriguez escorted the Stones down the street toward their cars and escape to freedom. As they neared their cars, a pair of black Escalades pulled up broadside and skidded to a stop, blocking the street. Men poured out of the SUVs with guns drawn on the sheltered passenger side.

"Drop your weapons and move away from the family!" Frank Morgan commanded.

Raymond Chang, Jerry Jaworski, Franklin Mack, William Mosely, Wardell Reed, and Rick Griffith took up positions behind the twin SUVs.

"No fucking way!" Kowalski shouted back, lifting his double-barreled shotgun at them. "Back the fuck off!"

"You're outgunned officers," Morgan declared. "Drop your weapons!"

Rodriguez directed the Stones back from the scene of the confrontation, behind a large stone building sign. Perez loaded a grenade into his RPG.

"Hide behind this. It should provide some cover," Rodriguez told the Stones about the stone sign. "We're going to try to get you out of here."

Rodriguez moved back to his fellow officers, Street Sweeper at his side, a .45 drawn.

Suddenly Frank Morgan and his boys opened fire, knocking down Kowalski, Perez, and Johnson. Fortunately, they were all wearing Kevlar so the would-be wounds were just bruises.

Rodriguez opened fire at the men behind the SUVs, who took cover from the fusillade. Perez picked up his RPG and fired it at the SUVs, which were parked nose to tail. The grenade flew out at tremendous speed and exploded with incredible force at the front of one and the back of the other. Each SUV blew into the air, the gas tank of the rear vehicle exploding in flames while the engine of the front engine's gasoline ignited and creating an even larger explosion, blowing back the men seeking refuge.

I flew toward the sound of the gunfire only to witness twin fireballs as two SUVs were lifted off the ground, gunmen blown away from the explosion. I landed next to Kowalski.

"Are you alright?"

He patted his chest. "Kevlar and vest. Otherwise…"

"Let's make short work of them."

Kowalski nodded in agreement.

Kowalski, Perez, Johnson, and Rodriguez all rose and moved forward into and around the flaming carnage of the destroyed automobiles. I levitated above the scene and took it all in. Four men were on the ground, stunned, but in varying degrees of recovery. There were three fleeing. I took off after the three fleeing, flew over, and landed in front of them.

"Who the fuck are you and how did…" a man who looked to be a mix of black and Chinese began to ask, his question cut short by my grasp of his throat.

"You're not the one asking the questions here. Who are you and why are you here?" I demanded. He looked utterly terrified.

He said, "I'm Raymond Chang. I was forced by the mob to come on this job. They killed my friends and threatened to kill me unless I helped them."

"And you?" I gestured to the other two.

"Same here. I'm Jerry Jaworski. He's Rick Griffith. We're just here trying to stay alive."

"Normally I kill people like you. You're not good, but you're not completely evil yet."

Suddenly Susan and Lucy started screaming. Dan too. I left the three criminals, flew back to the source of their panic, and landed.

"My Mommy! It took her!" Susan said.

"Mommy! Mommy! Mommy!" Lucy sobbed. "I'm never going to see my Mommy again!"

I reached down and lifted her chin so she could look at my face.

"No, Lucy. If I have anything to say about it, you'll see your Mommy again."

Dan glared at me. "I don't know what you are, Falco, but if you can save Julie we'll all be more grateful than you can ever know."

"I'll do what I can."

I leapt into the night sky and flew to the Bradbury Tower where Moloch surely had Julie. My next confrontation with evil was about to begin.

―――――――――

Kowalski ushered Lucy, Susan, and Dan into his police cruiser. He got in and floored it, causing it to peel out and fishtail down the street, hopefully to safety.

"What about Mommy?" cried Susan.

"We're going to try to help your Mommy. We just want to make sure you're safe."

―――――――――

I flew around the tower several times, trying to detect Moloch. I finally landed on the patio and strode forward into the nightclub space.

―――――――――

When the explosion happened, Frank Morgan was blown back about forty feet, yet was miraculously unharmed and fully conscious. He got up, turned his back, and ran like hell as far as his legs would carry him.

He had successfully fled from the scene of carnage and defeat. His evil muse had led him into a scene of defeat. He felt used, and rightly so. He had been used merely as a decoy. He would seek another spirit in the future.

7

The wings flapped and the hideous beast flew, then suddenly swooped down to the pavement, targeting the young mother with her two children and husband nearby. Moloch scooped up the woman and flapped his wings back toward the tower. Julie screamed loud and long.

Moloch said in his deep baritone, "Hush my child. Usually, the ones I pluck are already dead as I have begun to feed upon them. You are one of the lucky few who will witness my transmutation."

Moloch successfully flew into the penthouse and alighted.

"Diva! Guard the woman! Lilith! Guard the stairway!" he commanded.

Diva took Julie by the hand, walked up the steps, and down the hallway to the room Julie was to be imprisoned in, and closed the door behind her.

Fyren said, "The invader approaches!"

"Fyren! Bring out the bloodstone!"

Fyren went behind the bar, opened the cupboard that contained the bloodstone, and took it carefully out.

"Place it on the bar!" Moloch commanded and Fyren did as ordered.

"Malvoglio! Attack the policemen!"

The loathsome beast Malvoglio jumped out the window Moloch used for his hunting forays, unfurled the skin that stretched from his elbow to his hip, caught a draft, and began gliding down the street toward the police and their captives.

Kowalski and his men were in the process of fastening flex cuffs to Mack, Mosely, and Reed when Malvoglio swooped down on them and sunk his claws deep into Mack while biting down on his neck, spitting out a huge hunk of flesh and muscle, the blood churning out of his body and into Mavoglio's greedy mouth.

"Kill it!" Kowalski commanded and Perez unloaded half a magazine from his MAC-10 into it, while Johnson fired controlled bursts of his M-16 and Rodriguez started firing his Street Sweeper.

Kowalski threw the first of Mama Midnight's preparations at Malvoglio which hit him in the face, lit one of the second, and threw it, catching the monster dead center causing him to scream and howl. Kowalski then lit a gas bomb and threw it with all his might. It smashed into Malvoglio's clavicle, engulfing him completely in flames. Kowalski unfurled his tree saw, rushed forward, and began to saw into Malvoglio's neck, cutting through sinew and muscle and bone till he reached the other side and Malvoglio's head dropped to the ground, his flaming body following suit.

Perez picked up his axe and walked toward Franklin Mack's corpse, lifted it over his head, and brought it down forcefully, cleaving the head from the body.

"What the fuck was that?" Walter Mosely cried out.

"Your lucky, fucking day!" Johnson snapped at him.

"Perez!" Kowalski barked. "Take the remaining Stones in one of the cars and drive them far away from here. Rodriguez! Take these two scumbags to jail and get the hell back here! Johnson! Let's go back to the tower and see what we can do to help."

"OK, Lieutenant!" Perez barked and walked over to Dan, Lucy, and Susan.

"You best come with me, Mr. Stone. And your children too."

"What about my wife?"

"Falco's on it. We're going to see what we can do to help. I'm going to see you to a safe place and come back here."

"Alright," Dan said. "Girls! Let's go!"

They followed Perez to his car and got in, Perez behind the wheel. He hit the switch, locking all the doors, fired up the engine, drove onto the sidewalk around the burning Escalades, and floored it, peeling down the boulevard to hoped-for safety.

Rodriguez and Johnson grabbed Mosely and Reed, shoved them into the rear of Rodriguez's car, with Rodriguez taking the wheel. He rolled down his window.

"Take care, brother. I don't think I'll be able to stand another partner."

"Shit! I already can't stand you!"

The two men laughed and then relaxed, suddenly serious and grasped hands.

"You're the best, Rafer."

"You're the man, Tony."

They released their grips and gave each other a knowing look. Rodriguez fired up the engine and took off to the nearest Police Station.

"OK, Johnson. Check your gear and let's go help Falco," Kowalski said.

They walked into the lobby of the Bradbury Tower and over to where they had left the extra gas bombs. Johnson popped a fresh 50-round clip into his M-16, checked his remaining potions from Mama Midnight, and two gas bombs.

Kowalski reloaded his double-barrel, checked his remaining potions, and picked up another gas bomb. He once again had two. They headed back to the Bradbury Tower.

8

I flew up to the tower penthouse and circled it. I could see they were inside, the crimson light from their enormous bloodstone illuminating them. I also knew that Kowalski and his men had killed Malvoglio. I was grateful that there was one less beast for me to deal with.

I flew down to the penthouse at an enormous rate of speed and stopped in mid-air in the center of the room, released the swords into my hands and began to spin like a top, faster and faster with my swords extended in a deadly twirl, cutting through whatever stood before me rushing around the room. Fyren and Lilith moved quickly and evasively, yet I got closer with each pass. I spun up toward Moloch and threatened him. He flew quickly away from my threat. At that moment Lilith saw an opening and leapt at me. I changed the gravitational center of my spin and approached her from the side, my swords slicing through her, cleaving her into eight or nine sections. I came to rest on the floor and glared at Moloch and Fyren.

Moloch glared at me, his eyes burning crimson. He encanted in his deep baritone, "Il diaspro sanguigno. Libera la tua potenza per me."

His enormous spherical bloodstone began to emit more light, crackling with crimson lightning that spread throughout the room.

"Concentrarsi sul intrusa!"

The crimson lightning emitting from the bloodstone converged on me, flowing into my body and coming out through my hands and head and eyes toward the ceiling and into space. I was trapped. I felt power being sapped from my center. I began to be lifted upward to the center of the room held up by the crimson energy. Moloch began his booming, mocking laugh again. It chilled me to my core. I began trembling in fear. I felt close to defeat. How could I have ever believed that I could outwit a 4,000-year-old demon?

"Prepare for your second and final death!" the demon declared.

Just then Kowalski and Johnson crossed the threshold into the room from the secret stairway. Kowalski saw the energy coursing from the bloodstone into my body, lifted his shotgun, and fired both barrels at the bloodstone, shattering it, the energy dissipating, leaving my body, allowing me to drop to the floor.

Moloch roared in anger and rushed at Kowalski and Johnson. Johnson threw the first potion at Moloch, catching him square in the face. Moloch fell to the ground clutching his face, roaring in agony. Johnson lifted his M-16 and emptied his clip into the demon while Kowalski pulled out his .45 and emptied his clip into Moloch as well. I leapt into action, extending my swords, coming behind Moloch, and plunged my right arm sword through his back on the right side. He moaned and howled in agony.

Fyren leapt toward me, transforming into the ugly beast he truly was with his vicious sharp teeth and rat-like appearance.

Kowalski threw Mama Midnight's first potion at his head where it burst. Clutching his head, Fyren fell to the floor. Johnson lit the fuse on the second potion and flung it, catching Fyren full on the chest as he turned to face them. Johnson slapped a fresh clip into his M-16 and started firing. Kowalski lit a gas bomb and tossed it at Fyren where it burst, engulfing him in flames. Screaming and howling in extreme anguish, Fyren fell to the ground, writhing in agony. Kowalski rushed forward, unfurled his pruning saw, and sawed Fyren's head clean off.

Moloch smashed me in the face. I fell with great force into the back bar, breaking glass and shattering wood. I rose and focused all my energy into my ring and pointed it at Moloch. There was a high-pitched whine which got lower and lower in tone and descended to the subsonic as a column of crimson energy began to extend from my hand to Moloch's abdomen. He began to scream as the energy entered him and passed through his eyes, hands, mouth, and the top of his head. I unfurled my obsidian knife and flew at him. In mid-air, I cut through his chest, reached in, pulled out his black heart, took a bite, spat it out, and looked at him.

"Not too good."

I swung the knife and cut off his head, his ancient, wicked body falling to the floor.

I floated down next to the corpse. I looked over at Kowalski and Johnson.

"Thank you. I thought I was finished."

"Think nothing of it."

"We're not done yet. We have to find Julie."

We ran up the stairs and back to the room that had been Julie's prison before. The door had an obstruction blocking the opening. Probably a chair against the doorknob. I stepped forward and flung it open, the chair flying across the room. Julie was sitting on the bed, a terrified look in her eye. The window overlooking the sheer drop was smashed. Diva was gone.

I rushed over to Julie and grasped her shoulders.

"You're safe now. Your family is safe, thanks to these men," I said, gesturing toward Kowalski and Johnson, acknowledging the rest of their crew.

"Thank you, Rick!" she said throwing her arms around my neck, sobbing against my left shoulder. "It's always you! It always was you. It will always be you."

I pulled back from her.

"Lieutenant. Take her to her family. I'm spent. I need to rest."

"Sure thing, Falco. She's safe in our hands."

I walked down the hallway, and into the penthouse, through the broken windows, onto the patio, and into the night. I levitated into the sky and viewed the skyline of Detroit. There were towers with lights blazing and towers that were dark. There were lines of headlights on the interstate and isolated headlights moving through the canyons of the city. I had just been in one of the dark towers of the city and revealed its dangerous and evil secrets. We had fought an immense evil and emerged victorious. This was not the end, though. There was more evil in this world to be confronted. Though I was evil or should be, somehow I had become an agent for good. I felt a strange sense of satisfaction, realizing that I had done well, protected the innocent, and punished the evil. I wasn't finished, though. I just needed to get to bed and sleep this one off.

9

Kowalski and Johnson ushered Julie down the hidden stairway. As they neared the exit Rodriguez entered the stairway with his Street Sweeper brandished, pointing up at them.

"Hold on, Brother. We don't want to be casualties of friendly fire!" Johnson exclaimed.

"Holy fuck! It's you, buddy. I thought I was walking into a shitstorm!"

"You missed it. You got the term right though!"

Rodriguez rushed up and embraced Johnson. He had tears in his eyes.

"I told you, you were the best!!"

"You're the man!" Johnson said, tears streaming down his face.

Kowalski said, "OK, girls! Let's get the lady back to her family."

"Aye, aye, Lieutenant!"

Kowalski called Perez on his cell phone. Turns out Perez had taken Dan, Susan, and Lucy to his home. His wife made snacks for them. Perez sat on the front porch with his MAC-10 and his .45 standing guard. His wife had a .45 in her purse and went to the range with her husband often. She was a crack shot but didn't tell the Stones anything.

Kowalski, Johnson, and Rodriguez pulled up at Perez's house with Julie in tow and parked. They all got out and walked up the walkway to Perez's front door.

"It's great to see you," he said to Kowalski and the men. "And it's awesome to see you," he said to Julie. "How did it go down?"

"Falco came through," Kowalski said. "We came through for Falco. One of them got away, though. The most dangerous ones are dead. I think we're all safe now."

Perez got up and opened the front door.

"I've got someone here you probably want to see."

Julie stepped through the front door. Lucy and Susan burst forward from their seats as though they were shot from a cannon, tears streaming down their cheeks, embracing their mother and weeping.

"Mommy! I thought I'd never see you again," said Lucy.

"Me too!" cried Susan.

"Me too!" said Dan who had joined the hug fest, tears streaming down his cheeks. "I thought I'd lost you forever. I guess we owe Falco and these men a debt of gratitude we can never repay."

"Oh, Dan! Thank you for your love and understanding. I love all of you so very much!"

They wept and embraced in the relief and pure joy of survival and restoration. They were a family once again.

"Excuse me?" Kowalski addressed them. "Perhaps we can get you to a hotel?"

"Forget it, Lieutenant," Perez said. "They're staying here with us tonight. Come by in the morning when you figure out how to get them back home."

Kowalski smiled. "OK, Perez. It's a good play. Rest well, everybody. You're in good hands with Sergeant Perez."

Kowalski, Johnson, and Rodriguez turned and walked out of the house, down the walkway to their car, got in, and drove away.

10

I lay in the cocoon of my tomb and reflected on the challenges of recent days. Julie and her family were safe. Four monsters were destroyed. One escaped. Slumber seemed just beyond my grasp, even though I was exhausted. I depressed the button that opened my tomb. It opened and I got out and walked through my apartment. I walked over to my computer, opened my email, and read through the requests for Falco's help. There were mothers looking for sons and daughters who had run away, men looking for wives who had run away. All that and more. There was an email from Kowalski. I opened it.

Falco. It was an honor to have your back tonight. I like to think we helped. I know we couldn't have done it without you.
Kowalski

I stifled back a tear and wrote a reply.

Kowalski,
I couldn't have done it without you.
Falco

I rose in the late afternoon, refreshed myself, and dressed. After a tall glass of blood, I felt ready to face the world. I applied a generous coating of sunblock, put on my fedora and sunglasses, and drove my Civic down to Gehenna Street, parked and walked down to 666, raised the knocker, and knocked three times.

I heard the shuffling from inside as she worked her way toward the door which creaked open, stopped by the chain. Her eye peered out at me.

"Mama. I came by to thank you. We couldn't have defeated them without you. Your potions made a critical difference for us."

"You're a curious one. You one of them, but not one of them. Who's we?"

"I've got some cops on my side. We've joined forces. Moloch is dead."

"Oh! Praise be to the Almighty. You might be a devil, but you's an angel! That's what you are. You're the dark angel! God's Avenger from Hell!"

by Randall Moore

Part 9
EPILOGUE

1

The music was pumping in the club. The subwoofer was pounding the low frequencies relentlessly into the room. Everybody was sweating on the dance floor, writhing and undulating to the rhythms, simulating sex, and some even beginning to start to have sex with each other.

Phillip Edwards couldn't believe his luck. He was dancing with the most beautiful woman he had ever seen. She had an amazing figure. She wore a black leather top that plunged down to her navel revealing the inner sides of her substantial breasts, her nipples barely covered. Her long raven black hair reached down to her slender waist and framed her striking face. High cheekbones, voluptuous lips, black eyes, and a slightly upturned nose. Her hips wide and inviting. She seemed totally into him.

"Come here often?" he shouted.
"First time!"
"Want to get a drink?"
"Sure!"

They retreated from the dance floor and found an empty table in the bar.

A waitress approached their table.

"What can I get you?"

"I'll have a beer, Corona," he said.

"And you?" she gestured to the woman.

"I'll have a Bloody Mary."

"OK. I'll get your drinks."

The waitress left. The woman looked at him wantonly and seductively.

"Doing anything later?" she asked.

"Maybe. How about you?"

"I was thinking we could get together."

"Your place or mine?"

"Yours, actually. I'm between places."

"Sounds good. My place then. My name's Phillip," he said shaking her hand.

"Mine's Diva."

2

Frank Morgan slithered back into his apartment, shell-shocked and bloodied but still alone. He picked up his tablet and projected his mind into it at the dark force that drew him into tonight's debacle. Nothing returned. Something terrible had happened, yet he had been spared. He resolved to conjure another spirit. One that would serve him. He would never again slavishly serve another dark spirit other than his own. He would regroup and find a resurgence.

Raymond Chang, Jerry Jaworski, and Rick Griffith saw Malvoglio tear their friend Franklin Mack apart after Falco left them. They'd run and run and gotten back to their house. Safe at last from the carnage they'd witnessed, they were glad to have escaped. Fearfully, they locked all the doors and windows and got stoned. They slept fitfully, barely drifting off in sleep, haunted by the frightful events of the evening.

In the morning, Raymond dialed Morgan who picked up on the second ring.

"Morgan."

"Raymond here. That was a seriously fucked up situation you got us into last night. Did you see what happened to Mack?"

"No. I was long gone."

"Are you serious, motherfucker? He had his neck ripped out by some animal! And you weren't there! Unfuckingbelievable!"

"Fortune smiles on me. Remember I'm an attorney and can help in ways you have no clue about. It's better for all that I be in the shadows."

"We got a couple of our boys in the slammer. Mosely and Reed. Can you get them out? Can you do something useful? I mean, you want us to make you a ton of money. We, I mean you need these dudes to make your fucking money!"

"I read you, Raymond."

"You better be doing more than reading me, Morgan. Don't ever ask me to go on a fucked up job like last night again. You almost got us all killed!"

"Loud and clear. Loud and clear."

Morgan hung up and waited in the shadows. He dialed up Dorigo.

"Dominic."

"Hey, Dominic. Frank Morgan here."

"What's going on Frankie? You like dinner the other night?"

"Killer meal. The wine was exceptional as was your hospitality."

"What can I do for you?"

"The new crew I moved into place. Two of them are in jail. I'm going to need some help bailing them out."

"Done."

"The cops who busted them were not on an official detail. It had to be some kind of vigilante action."

"You sure you can prove it?"

"No. But I might be able to push them."

"OK. Let me know how much dough you need to get them out when you find out."

"Done."

"Bye."

3

I got an email from my real estate guy. He sent me several choices of places in the city to choose from as well as several isolated country estates. I examined them all with interest. I instructed him to move forward with the purchase and renovation of two of the spots in the city and one of the country estates.

    I poured a tall glass of blood and slowly sipped it. It was restorative and satisfying. I thought of all that had transpired over the last ten years. There had been a great deal of change and suffering. Julie and Dan were safe. Lucy and Susan were safe. There was no threat on the horizon. Still, at my core, I felt hollow and alone. I didn't know if my kind could ever feel fulfillment of any kind. I suspected not. But I still hoped that somewhere, somehow I could find the love of a woman or some kind of companionship that could end this loneliness and calm the savage beast that rules my heart.

    Link to the next book in the series:
https://www.amazon.com/High-Fortress-Falco-Book-ebook/dp/B00PNRYTAM/

    If you enjoyed this book, please consider posting a review and rating on Amazon. Even if it's only a few words, I would be grateful. — *Randall Moore*

by Randall Moore

Other books in this series in order are:
    THE HIGH FORTRESS
    THE ROOF OF THE WORLD
    THE 13th BOOK
    THE MIRRORED ROOM
    UNHOLY GATHERING
    Each book contains the mix of vampires, police, criminals, demons, and magic found here.
    I have a draft for a seventh.

Other works by the author include:
    FAITHLESS HEART
    THE MASTERS OF TIME AND SPACE
    THE NOBLE HEART
    THE BROTHERS TREMAINE
    THE MERCHANT, THE JANISSARY AND THE CORSAIR
    WELLES LANG'S MAGIC BOX
    AMERICAN JIHAD
    NOMAD NURSE
    COLTON LANG

Coming from the author:
    BOISE ECLIPSE
    A TASTE OF DEATH
    INTO THE VORTEX
    A WORLD WITHOUT MEN
    TRANS-AGENT
    MOUNTAIN HIGH RIVER WIDE
    THE LIBERTY COUNTY VANISHINGS
    CHINAMAN'S CHANCE
    THE GRAND MASTER
    THE LAND OF LAYO-LA
    SKY ANGEL

Falco the Dark Angel

by Randall Moore

The author lives with his wife in Saugus, California. Fiction has become the mainstay of his current existence, yet he enjoys art, books, movies, cooking, wine, baseball, travel and the life of the imagination. If one were to listen to a bit of advice from him it would be seek the truth in all things and by all means to be kind and good to all those you encounter.

Fiction reveals emotional truth. Documentary and history demands of us to make the connection that fiction provides and once having made the connection to experience the lives thus lived. Good tidings to you all.

Visit the author's website: www.randallmoorefiction.com

Printed in Dunstable, United Kingdom